WHO'S THE DADDY

CRESCENT COVE BOOK 3

TARYN QUINN

Who's the Daddy
© 2018 Taryn Quinn
Rainbow Rage Publishing

Cover by LateNite Designs
Photograph by Shutterstock

ISBN: 978-1-940346-60-1
First print edition: October 2019

ONE

I FACED THE CHAOS IN FRONT OF ME AND PROPPED MY HANDS ON MY
hips.

What had I done?

Oh, right. I had declared to the universe that I deserved the perfect
new home. And somehow I'd gotten one.

Well, I'd gotten *this.*

I'd driven up Main Street in Crescent Cove with Oblivion playing
on satellite radio and my hair blowing in the breeze, determination
oozing from my pores. Every building with a "for rent" sign was out
of my price range. I didn't have a roommate, and a lot of the places
had views of Crescent Lake, which drove up their asking prices.

Also, I was still paying the last month's rent on my other
apartment. Because, sure, a kindergarten teacher could totally pay
rent on two places at once. That was completely feasible.

I could've asked my parents for help. A short-term loan. Money
for a lobotomy. Whichever. But I wasn't going to do that, because I'd
rather be tight for a bit than lean on my already plenty generous
parents.

My little sister, Rylee, was the one who needed loans and
emotional support and all that jazz. I was the responsible older

daughter who tried to hide her moments of irresponsibility and didn't have that many to start with.

Socially awkward might have been the title of my theme song. But the reality of my world wasn't nearly so zany.

I taught little kids. After school, I tutored students in advanced reading and two days a week, led the school's newly created "music is fun" program. Once a month, my parents, Rylee, and I met at Spaghetti Warehouse for our standing date of—wait for it—spaghetti and meatballs.

That pretty much summed up my version of excitement, unless I was feeling particularly frisky and made myself come twice via whatever naughty fantasy was currently turning my crank. Often involving Tom Hardy. Most of the time, I was too worn out from school to self-service once, never mind twice.

And dating? Yeah. Please drive through.

Minus the impromptu hookup I'd had a few weeks ago with my ex after his granny's funeral. The next morning, I'd awakened to a text brushoff.

And after I'd rocked his world in the sack.

Pfft.

I had dated sporadically after Tommy had broken up with me the first time, citing "different life directions" and "unclear goals as a couple."

Okay, then.

So this whole being impetuous and finding-a-new-place-or-bust plan of mine was so outside my sphere, I was practically dizzy.

But my life needed some shaking up. As did I.

I stopped in many places that day post-Tommy breakup part deux, and the next few that followed. Until I happened to be making oh, my fiftieth trip down Main Street and noticed the square building being renovated between the auto shop and the florist. That seemed like a convenient spot. Auto repairs and overpriced sunshine in a vase were both things I needed in my life, especially since I had no one to buy me flowers and my SUV had been on its last legs forever.

The only thing that could've made the building better was closer proximity to The Spinning Wheel, but I probably didn't need to mix dubious decisions with fifty proof. At least not until I was moved in and could walk home.

And also probably not until Christmas break. Principal Gentry would not be amused by my need for spirits of the liquid kind, rather than being filled by the Holy Ghost.

Prayers and blind optimism and possibly a healthy dose of stupidity had led me to this place. I'd signed the lease and gone back to my home in Turnbull to pack up the rest of my things—not that there was much, thank goodness, because it would've been relocated into storage—and wait for moving day.

That day was now here. One new life, coming right up.

First, I should probably unpack. And dust. And try not to laugh hysterically until I cried.

Swallowing hard, I let my gaze wander my infinitesimal space. That echoing sound in my head was the universe chuckling at me now, I was sure.

You wanted a place near school? Ta da. Enjoy.

It wasn't as if the apartment was bad per se. Yes, it was small. Optimistically, the listing had called it a one-bedroom. So what if the closet in my place in Turnbull was almost as big? I wasn't one of those women with mountains of shoes or a ton of clothes. I actually had a few sensible basics that I paired with some of the more eclectic pieces in my wardrobe.

See, practical. That was me.

Perhaps that was why Tommy had dumped me twice. What I considered being a freak in bed might be Tommy's version of ho-hum.

God, now I was getting depressed over something other than my choice in living spaces. Hell, choice? I'd had no options if I wanted to live in town and not put it off any longer.

Now I was here. And I was going to make the best of it.

I moved to the gigantic window, the best-selling feature of the apartment—okay, the *only* selling feature of the apartment—and smiled at the view. The building was at an angle across from the lake, and from up here, I could see the brightly colored sailboats merrily bobbing along the water. There was one of my students from last year, Sara Wilkes, running along with her puppy's leash in one hand and a kite in the other on the grassy area near the gazebo. Her mother stood nearby, chatting with a few other women about her age. Her friends.

That was what I needed. A bunch of girlfriends. I had some in Turnbull, mostly teachers at my former school and a few women I'd known in high school, but no one especially close.

I didn't have a best friend. Well, I'd sort of started calling Sage my best friend in my head, but I didn't tell her that because it was probably creepy. We hadn't known each other all that long and she already had a best friend. But she was definitely the closest pal I'd had in…well, ever.

Yet another reason I'd wanted to move into the town proper. Along with a new view to wake up to every day, I wanted to find a peer group. But not in those words. That was teacher speak.

I was looking for a bunch of bad-ass bitches who didn't think I was a weirdo for feeling sorry for my ex and sleeping with him instead of just, I don't know, sharing a pizza and commiseration over his grandmother. Instead I'd shared my nether regions and…

Sigh. My stomach was growling. I shouldn't have thought of pizza. The diner was just down the block, and maybe Sage was working—

Duh, she so was not. She didn't work Saturdays anymore, not since she had a smoking hot husband and a little one to get ready for.

Two things I would probably never have.

Pizza, however? *That* I could make happen.

I sat down bare-legged on the still sawdust-y floor and grabbed my purse to dig out my phone. I swiped it on and blinked at the flurry of texts from Ally, Sage's real best friend. She was super nice and seemed to have her hands full with her baby boy and a little girl who'd been in the other kindergarten last year. We didn't know each other that well, but we'd hung out a bit recently after Sage had introduced us.

We'd also chatted at the dinner after Sage and Oliver's Vegas wedding. As much as we could anyway, considering the night had been fun chaos mixed with some Sage-sized pandemonium.

Still, Ally and I were only acquaintances at best. Perhaps that would change.

Already smiling, I read her texts.

Hey there, hope it's ok I'm texting you. I got your number from Sage. Well, she didn't give it to me. I stole it.

My smile turned into a frown. Hmm. Okay. My interest was piqued.

I'm planning Sage's surprise baby shower. She has no idea I'm doing it. I'm actually tormenting her a little, making her think I just haven't thought of it. Is that mean?

Seemed a little mean to me, but hey, Ally had figured out how to have a best friend and I was just in the newbie stages, so what did I know?

I kept reading.

I want it to be a total surprise for her. Something special. She so deserves it. But her fretting about details while I'm trying to make it awesome is stressful. Performance anxiety & all that.

I nodded even though Ally wasn't in the room. I so understood.

Also, this might've been the longest series of texts I'd ever been involved in, and I hadn't even responded yet. Hell, I didn't even know where I fit in.

But now Alex is sick. You remember my son? Laurie is too. Plus, dear God, I think Seth is also. I have to reserve the space this wk. The place I had in mind is booked & I tried a couple other spots but everything is reserved. Poor planning on my part, I know.

I winced in sympathy. Aww, poor Ally. She had way too much on her plate.

Unlike me. Other than work, which did keep me pretty busy, my plate had room for a full course and then some.

Pity party for one. Table in the back.

Rolling my eyes at myself, I continued reading.

Now I'm sneezing too & I have a fever. That's probably why I'm sending you these crazy texts. But can you help? Pretty please? I'll owe you forever. I know Sage thinks of you as another bestie.

My eyes filmed over. It was probably just part of buttering me up, but that was so sweet. I was already onboard with whatever she needed. She didn't even have to throw the best friend cherry on top.

If you can help, I'll send over my lists so far & maybe you can take over? I'll jump back in and help in whatever way you need. I'm sure we'll be better in a few days so I can think again. But dear Lord, man flu is the worst. You're single, right? So lucky. Talk later. TYSM!

I frowned. So lucky? Well, that was a matter of perspective. Though I didn't envy her dealing with man flu, whatever that was.

I could practically hear Sage's bubbly voice in my head.

That's when a man is near death from the slightest sniffle. And if Seth has the man flu, then Oliver will get it too, and if he gets me sick after getting me pregnant, he's going down.

She might change some of the phrasing around, but I had the gist. Sage could make me smile even when she wasn't in the room.

That was what I wanted to be like too. Fun and spontaneous and wild, and not just when it came to big talk. Up for anything. Ready to grab the bull by the horns and ride that steer all the way home.

I would start with taking charge of Sage's shower. At least until Ally could take over again.

Planning was something I was good at. Even better now that I'd started working on planner layouts with Sage. We'd hit the craft store and now my boring school schedules were prettied up with paper tape and cute stickers and fun borders. Even my Type A nature appreciated a little embellishment of my lists.

I tugged my leather planner and one of my colorful pens out of my bag and flipped open to a fresh sheet, writing the details I knew so far at the top. Time. Date. Important info.

Right now, I had none, other than the shower was for Sage Evans-Hamilton and she was having a girl. A very spoiled little girl already, and she hadn't even been born yet. I expected Sage to tell me Oliver had purchased the baby a pony any day now.

I wasn't jealous.

Not even a little.

The fact that I'd chosen a green pen was just coincidence.

I grabbed my phone and sent Ally a quick reply.

Sure thing. I'd love to help! Just send me what you have so far, incl the guest list & where Sage is registered. I'll get right on it. Thanks for thinking of me. Hope you & the fam feel better soon!

Ally's texts saying thanks were profuse and plentiful. She promised to send over her list within the hour, which gave me plenty of time to order that pizza and get started on unpacking.

The day was looking up already.

My whole life was. A girl couldn't be down for long when pepperoni was in her future.

And I had a project.

I freaking loved projects. And getting to buy more school supplies for said project. Hey, I'd become a teacher for a reason, and it wasn't just because I loved little kids. I also had a pen and notebook fetish. Not the only fetishes I had, though I couldn't safely explore most of them.

And Tommy thought sex with me was just "nice"? Ha. Here I'd been holding back.

Whatever. He didn't deserve me.

So said Gloria Gaynor as I put on one of my favorite feminist anthems—I had a whole playlist of them, in fact—and doubled down to do some serious unpacking.

Along with a little booty dancing in between.

Sure enough, as I was digging through my box of my grandmother's china, an email came in from Ally with an attachment. I grinned as I opened it up. Almost pizza time too. The guy on the phone had told me an hour, and it was almost sunset. Busy time on a Saturday night. But I didn't want to run down and get another load of my stuff until I finished with what I had in here and refueled.

The refueling would happen quicker than finishing unpacking. I was currently in a state of hardcore flux. Boxes were open everywhere, stuff spilling out in every direction. The few sparse pieces of furniture I had were covered with crap. Luckily, the place had been semi-furnished because my old sofa was a mess and I couldn't have afforded movers in any case.

See, I needed more friends. That was yet another reason why. I was like an island, adrift without pals to help me move and make me laugh and drink cheap wine with me while I lamented ex-sex that hadn't even led to an orgasm. At least that I could remember. So that probably meant a big fat no, it had not.

I narrowed my eyes on Ally's attachment. Hmm, had she sent over the right file? This had almost nothing on it. About as little as the new page in my planner.

Quickly, I texted Ally back, sure she'd sent me an early file instead of the updated one.

Her response?

Nope, that's the one! Sorry, I told you I was totally lame & so far behind. But I know we can get caught up. Ugh, there's the baby crying again. Did I say thank you? TY so much! Xo

I blinked and clutched my phone to my chest. Okay, no reason to panic. Sage had to be registered somewhere. At least I could add that bit of info to my checklist so I could include it on the invitations.

For a guest list that contained approximately six names, and I was new in town. I had no clue who all of Sage's friends were, but I knew they were legion. She'd lived in Crescent Cove her whole life and pretty much bonded with anyone she met for more than five minutes.

I was screwed.

So screwed.

Without the sex.

I texted Sage, determined to get a win today. I didn't like having such an empty checklist. It was unnatural.

Hey there, where are you registered? Want to get the bambina a few things but don't want to overlap with your list.

Sage replied when I was digging through the box of books I'd upended on the couch to search for my first edition Keats. I knew I'd packed it. I *had* to have packed it. My bookshelves at my old place were empty. If it wasn't there and it wasn't here...

I could not contemplate it. Simply could not.

Oh, yeah, about that. We aren't registered anywhere. It drove Oliver bonkers, which was another reason I didn't register anywhere. Dude needs to learn the meaning of spontaneity. She totally doesn't need anything, btw. But if you wanna get something cute, anything works. Thank you! *smiley face* *unicorn head* *heart* *smiley sunglasses face* *baby head*

Sighing, I shoved my way onto the couch, pretending not to feel the bruises on my heart as some of my precious books tumbled to the floor. I had bigger problems.

No registry.

No guest list.

No pizza.

I could not work under these conditions.

Oh, and best of all? I had forgotten my floor lamp, and apparently, this apartment didn't have an overhead light fixture in the living room. What the fuck? And the sunset was gorgeous outside right now, but the orange and gold light would fade soon, plunging me into the blackness that matched my bitter soul.

Bah.

But all was not lost. I snapped my fingers. I had a desk lamp somewhere. Just had to find it in my twelve-thousand boxes.

I let out a long sigh and tugged on the knot in my T-shirt that I'd tied beneath my breasts. I'd changed into an old baggy shirt with my shortest pair of shorts to unpack, figuring I wouldn't be leaving tonight. The pizza dude didn't count as company. He'd probably seen much worse when dropping off pies. And he didn't seem inclined to show in any case.

His tip was dwindling by the minute. Just like my momentary cheer.

I readjusted the top knot that barely contained my long hair and rose, rubbing my nose as it twitched. I sneezed and sneezed again, then once more for good measure. Dust. Always my enemy, even if it was fresh dust from a newly renovated place.

What was next? Locusts? The plague? Fire and damnation?

A loud buzzing sound filled the apartment and I jumped, setting off another round of sneezing. When I could breathe without my eyes watering, I frowned. It sounded like a giant oven timer, but that couldn't be right. I could see the oven over my left shoulder and it definitely was not on. One perk to living in a place I could see the whole of with just one slow pivot was there weren't any hidden corners. No surprises.

The buzzer was still ringing. Must be my doorbell. That was rather heinous.

What didja expect, Ford? A tinkle of the ivories? Be glad the pizza's here.

Or else probably the first robber in Crescent Cove's recorded history was polite enough to ring first.

I went to the door and fumbled around with the call box until it crackled to life. "Hello, pizza man." I bit my lip. That wasn't gender correct. I didn't know it was a male, though he was late, so reason stood. "I mean, pizza person. Would you like to come up or should I come down?"

"I'll come up."

Okay, very deep voice. Definitely not female. A little rumbly and irritated too.

I frowned. "How do I know you're the pizza man?"

"You have a peephole?"

Was this some kind of test? "Um, maybe?"

"See my badge? It says pizza man." He made a sound of derision. "Release the door. I don't have all night."

I didn't appreciate his attitude. "Excuse me, *you* don't have all night? You are approximately," I consulted my watch, since my phone was in the other room, "forty-five minutes late. I never eat past six-thirty."

"Oh, so very sorry, lady, but it's Saturday and the shop gets busy. Now you want this double cheese and pep and sausage or what?"

Something about the way he said *lady* had my hackles rising. And maybe my nipples a little too, because I must have heretofore unexplored masochistic tendencies. "Your tip is in serious peril right now. Also, that was only double pep and cheese. No double sausage. *Single* sausage," I enunciated carefully, not fully realizing what a juvenile male would get out of my statement until he snorted.

"Got it. Too bad Fritz didn't get it on the phone though, because this pie is covered with extra sausage. Want me to take it back and get you another one? Dinner's gonna be real late tonight then." His tone was openly mocking. "Or maybe you want me to pick it off for you?"

Barely smothering a snarl, I pressed the door release. "Come on up." I gritted my teeth, my innate manners kicking in. "*Please.*"

I'd just shove the money at him and make do with my extra sausage. It wasn't as if that was a problem I had to contend with in any other area of my life.

A knock sounded a moment later. Jeez, had he run up the stairs? Must be younger than he sounded.

I yanked open the door and frowned at the big, muscular figure looming in the shadowy hallway. This was what I got for not using the peephole. Small town or not, I knew better. At least then I would've had some warning.

Some time to prepare, since now there was no doubt my nipples were doing a double-barrel salute.

I knew this man.

Just as he knew me.

Dare cocked his head, shifting his pizza box more under his arm as he let his gaze drift over me in a slow perusal. He took long enough for me to recall every bit of my outfit, from the dangling strings hanging down my thighs from my almost obscenely short cut-offs to my bare feet to the knot under my breasts that barely hid my bra.

He was checking out all of that, and he did not seem to be finding any part of me lacking. I flushed all over, gripping the knob to keep highly inappropriate things from leapfrogging from my mouth.

Sexual innuendoes were not out of the question.

Jesus, if only I'd known I was discussing sausage with *Dare*, I would've turned down the bitchy and turned up the flirty.

His had to be stupendous. His sausage, I mean. His flirt quotient probably wasn't bad either, once he dialed down the growling.

As for me, I had to have some serviceable flirtation skills somewhere. Especially when he was eating me up with his eyes and not being shy about it.

"Fancy seeing you again, Nuts Lady," he said finally, moving forward and lightly pushing the pizza box into my stomach. "Got enough pie in this box for two?"

I swallowed over the lump in my dust dry throat. The man was a sex wizard. A master. He made pizza talk into the highest form of foreplay, and I was so there for it.

"I've got enough pie in this box for everyone." As he chuckled and my face flamed, I dropped my gaze to the design on the carton. It was an old Italian dude with a huge mustache. "It's an extra large."

"My favorite size," he said lightly.

When I didn't say anything, he lifted a brow. "Can I come in?"

I wasn't sure if he was just asking about entering my apartment or entering me, but either way, the answer was hell yes. I stepped back and waved an arm. "Don't mind the mess."

"Moving day?" He stepped over the assorted crap on the floor and glanced back, his gaze roaming over me once again. As slowly as if he had all night. "New to the neighborhood, huh?"

All at once, the reality that he worked at the auto shop next door slammed into me. And by into me, I meant in between my legs.

So much proximity with that delicious male specimen.

And I'd thought this apartment was going to suck? Not hardly.

I shut the door and gripped my pizza box for dear life. "Yes. How much do I owe you?" Not that I knew why a mechanic was delivering pizzas, but right then, I did not care.

Nor did I care that he'd never reacted quite like this to me before. I could not say the same. I'd pretty much been in heat in his presence since the first minute we'd met.

Maybe it was his big oil-stained hands or the scent of gasoline and leather that clung to him. The muscles layered upon muscles didn't hurt. Or his killer blue eyes, even now shrewdly analyzing me and possibly mentally stripping me naked.

A girl could dream.

He swept his tongue inside his lower lip. "Think we can negotiate."

TWO

DARE

THINGS WERE DEFINITELY LOOKING UP.

Or maybe that was only one part of my anatomy, but close enough.

I hadn't wanted to run out pizza to the new tenant in the Forrester building. Actually, the words "I don't want to" summed up this day in its entirety. But Pop was shorthanded at the pizza shop and Wes was having a grand time helping in the kitchen, which mostly consisted of banging pots and pans along with the occasional sneaking of pepperoni under the careful supervision of my mom.

Me, I'd been taking calls and delivering pies for the last three hours since Ellie and Connor had both gone home sick. It was a damn epidemic in town.

Kinda fit this shitty-ass day. Much as I didn't want to notice the date, every year I did. It had only been two years, so I supposed it wasn't that shocking.

Two years since Wes's mom had bailed on us. At least physically. She'd been gone mentally before that.

Most of the time, I didn't think about her. My life was too full to spend on recriminations. Katherine was a big one, if only because she'd deprived my son of his mother. The rest I didn't regret. Life was rough. Sometimes shit didn't work out. But for a kid, you tried harder.

You were supposed to fucking try.

So, yeah, after finishing at the shop, the last thing I'd wanted was to be called into service to help Pop. Nor make chitchat with everyone who opened their door to me. Curse of a small town. By the fourth time I'd explained I was helping out my dad, I was ready to light up.

And I didn't even smoke.

The one good thing was that I'd been too busy to watch the clock. Now that my shift was over, I could acknowledge it hadn't been that bad. I was just tired after putting in a long day at J&T's, and I knew my day wasn't over yet—not with a six-year-old to get washed up and into bed.

Right now, I could take this unplanned break. Dad had a closer coming in who could handle any other deliveries for the night.

I was officially free.

But I probably shouldn't stay long. Kelsey and I barely knew each other. Friends of friends and all that, and recently, we'd found ourselves at some of the same events. She always said crazy stuff and tried too hard. As pretty as she was, she didn't seem comfortable in her own skin.

If anything, I was too comfortable in mine.

I didn't date much for obvious reasons. Impressionable little kid who already didn't have a mom. Semi-bitter father who couldn't be bothered with games. I was barely thirty, but when it came to relationships, I'd felt as if I'd seen it all and didn't need a repeat.

Occasional hookups were about all I had bandwidth for. Even those were damn rare. I didn't even know how long it had been since the last one.

Another reason I had no business taking a bite out of Kelsey's pie.

But she was different tonight. Not only had she stood up for herself in our little argument, she had a wild look in her eyes. She wasn't making idle chitchat, seemingly content to stand beside me at the narrow counter in her just as narrow kitchen and shift slices onto paper plates. The entire place was in a state of disarray, and there wasn't anywhere to sit. Books were scattered on the floor. She'd barely made a dent in her unpacking.

Not that I was worried overmuch about her decorating right now.

She kept licking her lips as she checked me out, as openly as I was doing the same. Not the first time for me either. I'd been behind her at Oliver and Sage's Vegas wedding and let's just say it was a good thing she hadn't been able to see me ogling her legs in her snug blue dress.

Those mile-long legs were on full display right now. A *lot* of her was on display, to be honest. Her tied off shirt revealed a healthy amount of skin and her tits were one deep breath from spilling free. I didn't know if she was wearing a bra. If she was, it was flimsy at best. Her curves were slight, but it didn't make a damn bit of difference. She was put together just right, from the tips of her red-gold hair right down to her candy pink toenails.

Fuck, even her feet were hot.

"You okay with pillows?" she asked, finally breaking the comfortable silence. Comfortable minus the definite straining in my jeans.

"You mean in general or..."

Her smile was a revelation, lighting up her golden-brown eyes in the dwindling sunlight. There was just enough remaining that the apartment—what there was of it—had a soft pink glow. Even Kelsey. Especially Kelsey. Her cheeks were flushed, and I didn't know if it was from the exertion of getting her apartment in order, or if it was due to...this.

Whatever *this* was. A mistake, probably. I was good at making them. Except it didn't feel wrong right now to be winding gooey warm cheese around my finger and dropping it into my mouth, knowing she was watching my every move.

"I mean, to sit on while we eat. As you can see, I'm still decorating." She tugged the sofa's back cushions out from under a pile of books and papers, then tossed them on the floor next to her coffee table.

"That what you're calling this?"

She jerked a shoulder and her baggy shirt tried to slip down her shoulder. No strap. Jesus. No bra was now a certainty. She was petite and perfect enough not to need one.

Fuck me running.

"My decorator wasn't available today. Just like my movers." She hefted two boxes off the coffee table.

"Let me—"

She shook her head. "I got it." She dumped them on the couch, then rushed back into her tiny kitchen. She popped a pepperoni into her mouth and chewed, her lashes fluttering as her eyes closed. "God, that's good."

Much as I wanted to watch her eat, I was stuck on what she'd said. "What do you mean, no movers? Where did you live again?"

"Turnbull. Barely a hop, skip, and two jumps away." She transferred an extra piece of pizza to each plate and brought them around the counter into the living room and placed them on the coffee table.

Snagging the beer she'd left for me, I followed her in and sat on one of the cushions. "This can't be all your stuff. How did you get the couch up here by yourself? Family? Friends?" I swallowed the cheese now stuck in my throat. "Boyfriend?"

She snorted as she rummaged in one of the boxes. "The place was partially furnished. I'm not even sure who left that beer behind. Hope it's not poisoned."

I glanced down at the can sweating in my hand. Or maybe I was sweating. The temperature seemed to be rising by the minute. "Thanks for the heads up."

"It's probably fine. Sorry, I don't have my floor lamp. Desk lamp is somewhere." She made a delighted *a-ha* noise and waved three tiny candles and one of those long lighter things chicks always seemed to have, then set the candles on the coffee table. After lighting them, she picked her way around the boxes to sit beside me. "Oh, and no way José on the boyfriend. I'll probably end up being a lesbian."

I choked on the experimental sip of beer I'd taken, coughing as she thumped on my back.

She was kidding. I was almost positive. Even my timing couldn't suck that much.

"That hard to imagine?"

I plucked up a piece of pepperoni and held it up to her sweet mouth. For fuck's sake, she even had a freckle on the bow of her top lip. "A loss for my team."

Her cheeks pinked up and the splash of freckles across the bridge of her nose added an innocence to her that I really didn't want to think about. The candles didn't do much to light the room, but added a warm glow behind her. "I was kidding." Her voice was husky and my hunger for pizza went right out the goddamn window.

"Good." I nodded to her. This was the worst of ideas and yet, here I was. "Want this or not?"

She licked her lips and opened them. After I dropped the pepperoni inside her mouth, she closed her eyes, chewed, and swallowed. Then she winced. "Probably wrong that I had unnatural flashbacks to church."

I huffed out a laugh. I never really knew what was going to come out of this girl's mouth. It could be from hanging with Sage and Ally, but I had a feeling she'd been this way before those two tried to corrupt her.

"Are you a good Catholic girl, Kelsey?"

She opened her eyes, then took my beer and set it down beside our plates. "What would you say if I said definitely not?"

I hooked my arm around her waist and lifted her onto my lap. "I'd say hell yeah."

Her golden eyes were huge as she straddled me. She opened her mouth to say something, then her eyes popped wider and she buried her face in the crook of her elbow to sneeze. "Damn dust," she croaked, eyes watering. "Sorry. Excuse me. Fuck."

It felt good to laugh. Her weight on my groin was definitely adding a buzz to my blood.

After a minute, her hands landed on my shoulders and her perfect tits were right there for the taking. I should kiss her. It was what a gentleman would do. Then again, I wasn't one of those.

Instead, I ducked my head and nudged up the knot under her breasts with my nose and found a stretchy little piece of lace beneath her T-shirt. I groaned. No bra was correct. This flimsy thing was some kind of strapless shaper. It was damp from all her work that day, but she smelled fresh. Like grapefruits and oranges had sex. Whatever the scent was, it filled my brain and set my dick to pounding.

Of course, that could be from her wiggling against me.

I gripped her ass. "You want this over in two shakes, or for me to take a little time?" I tugged at her nipple through her shirt. "I can do either."

Her fingers slipped into my hair. "Not too much time. I'm dying here."

She was eager. I appreciated that in a woman. Maybe it'd been as long for her as it had been for me.

I dipped my hands lower to the fringe of her cutoffs along the backs of her thighs. I tugged so that the material dug into her skin a little and slid my fingers under the denim from behind. Her gasp fueled me to roll my hips under her. "You like that?"

"Yes."

After shifting her scrap of panties out of the way, I eased between her cheeks and found her wet. I groaned against the lace in front of my face and shifted her higher against me. "So wet, darlin'. For me? Or just because you need something?"

"Is both a bad answer?"

I dragged my beard across her bra and found her nipple. "Best answer. We both need something tonight." I tugged her nipple through the lace bit of fluff under her T-shirt. "I'm okay with that, are you?" I tucked my fingers into her damp heat and had to bite back a groan.

It had been awhile since I'd had a slick pussy so ready and willing without working for it. The women I'd dated lately were a helluva lot more jaded about sex.

"Yes. I just want to have a great orgasm. Is that too much to ask?" She leaned back a little. "I don't think so."

I added a second finger inside her sweet pussy and tugged harder on her nipple. "Nope."

She rolled her hips away from the rhythm I'd started. "I need you..." She ground out a frustrated sigh. "More...left."

I let her nipple go with a snap of her lace and withdrew my hand.

"No. I didn't mean..." Her huge golden eyes were bright with a fever I understood. Some schmuck probably left her without a real orgasm on the regular. There was a serviceable orgasm that did the job, and then there was the kind that made everything shake. I wanted her at earthquake status.

I wasn't sure why it was so important, but I wouldn't stop until I got it.

I hooked my arm around her waist again and flipped her onto her back on the cushion. I shoved boxes out of the way and heard the scatter of books. I needed her spread out. "Do you have a bed for this?" I asked against her belly.

"No. I, uhh...I don't have one of those yet."

I glanced up from the snap on her shorts. "What?"

She grimaced. "I sort of left my place in a hurry. The bed wasn't worth the expense of moving it. But I'll get around to ordering one. Eventually." She gave me a hopeful smile. "Do you want to wait? I..." She met my gaze, her hips moving restlessly.

"We'll make it work, darlin'." I peeled down her shorts partway and found endless gold over cream skin. Her belly was soft as a peach and the more I revealed, the hotter I got. She was bare. Absolutely bare. I sucked in a breath and caught that citrus flavor wrapped in sex. I wasn't a man of many words when it came to getting naked, but right then, I wanted to get downright worshipful.

Instead, I let my mouth do the work in a much more effective way.

I licked her tight little slit. Her shorts trapped her thighs together so I turned my head a little and sealed her pussy lips with my own. Seemed fitting our first kiss wouldn't be traditional.

I circled her tight little clit with my tongue, my fingers digging into her lightly muscled thighs. I was going to peel her open and fuck the holy shit out of her.

There was no doubt in my mind that was where this kind of night was heading. But right then, what I needed from her was a quaking thigh release. The sort a man never forgot once he'd witnessed it.

Once he'd caused it.

I dug deeper and brought my thumb up to play. When she arched up off the nubby textured cushion, I held her against me and double-checked that she wasn't trying to stop me for real.

Some women weren't into oral, but the way she flung back her head and reached for her own tits told me I was doing all right. I reached up with my free hand and flipped up her shirt and that lacy thing so I could see her breasts too.

My dick was pounding in time with my brain, but I wanted to see everything. She was so long and lean with the perfect kind of curves. Tiny nipples the same color of her pussy strained up against the golden firelight of the last rays of sun and her tiny-ass candles.

The shadows and light were just enough to drive me a little too close to insanity.

I buckled it down.

Not yet.

Not time to let go just yet.

She glanced down at me with wild, golden eyes and struggled out of her shirt and the shaper thingy. I watched, my mouth still sealed over her swollen pussy. I drank down everything she gave me. I didn't mind going down on a girl. The control of it usually got me centered so I didn't blow my wad in two seconds like some chump kid.

This one was backfiring.

My blood surged and my vision hazed as I held on against her bucking hips. She tasted fresh and salty with something...extra. Nope.

Don't think about that.

Just a fuck.

I didn't need anything other than a fuck tonight. I was just messed up because of the day.

Not that I'd even thought about what today was after Kelsey opened the door. She was the opposite of my ex in every way.

Including here where she was so incredibly responsive. So very in the moment.

Her fingers slid down to my hair and the sharp tug of pain dragged me out of my head.

Not about my past right now.

It was about her. And making her come her damn brains out so I could lose myself in her for a few short minutes before I had to get back to my responsibilities.

"Dare," she said on a half whimper.

I leaned back and dragged her shorts off the rest of the way and opened her legs wide.

She gasped and tried to move up on the limited real estate of the cushion, but this was where I wanted her. Just on the edge where I had complete access to her pussy. I dragged my beard along her ass to give her an extra tickle of sensation as I fucked her gently with my tongue and wrecked her with my fingers.

The surprised cry that came out of her made me work harder. When her thighs clamped around my head, I kept going. There she was. She shook and arched up against my mouth.

Wild.

My little wild girl.

I glanced up as she soaked my face. Her red hair had come half out of its bun and was twisted around her shoulders and head, the tips sticking to her breasts as she arched and screamed.

Unable to hold back another second, I reached down to free my strangled cock, then flipped out my wallet and cursed when cards scattered. Where the fuck was my emergency condom?

Fuck.

There it was. Thank God.

How long had it been in my damn wallet?

On a hope and prayer, I sat back on my knees and rolled it down my shaft.

She reached up for me, but I brushed her fingers away. "Nah, darlin'. I've been listening to you scream and watching you shake under my mouth too long."

Her chest and neck were flushed and her eyes glassy from a truly stupendous orgasm. That made it all worth it for me. Today, of all days, I wanted to make sure one woman was happy with my efforts.

I dragged the head of my cock through her swollen folds.

She hissed and rolled her hips so sweetly. In tune now, she was eager to get me inside her. And God, it felt good to have someone want me between their thighs. Want to touch me.

I sunk into her slowly.

She dragged in a deep breath and groaned. She pushed at my shirt and I flipped it off behind me. Her gaze went even wider. "God, you're ripped."

I looked down at my chest. Between the shop and working on my house all the damn time, I had little time for the gym, but I was young and strong. At the shop, I did all the heavy work. Chasing after my son did the rest.

She raked her nails down my abs with fascination. I grinned and licked my lips where her scent and flavor had settled deep in my beard. "Hang on, darlin'. As much as I appreciate the compliment, I need to fuck."

Her eyes widened as I slid forward and went balls deep inside her. "Fuck." The word came out harsher than I intended, but she felt so damn good. And it had been so fucking long since I'd let myself take a moment just for myself.

This kind of goddamn moment.

I dropped on top of her, caging her in as I hooked her leg around my hips.

She took the hint and wrapped herself around me. I braced myself on the hardwood floor and was very glad for the cushion beneath her because I couldn't quite rein myself in.

I slammed into her until my teeth rattled, until her back arched up, and her nails dug into my shoulders. I looked down at her to make sure I wasn't being too rough, but she was right there with me.

Fuck, yes.

I felt the tremble in her thighs just as her little pants turned to groans. I was pretty sure they turned into screams, but I couldn't be sure since my brain literally shut off as my orgasm reached up from my spine and crumpled me like my race car when it hit the wall.

Everything went silent and white as I came before the world crashed back in and the tail end of her cries dented my consciousness.

Damn.

At some point, I'd crashed into her body and flattened her into the cushion. Her thighs gripped my hips, and her nails lightly trailed over my back. I brushed my lips over her neck before I rocked back onto my knees.

She hissed out a breath as I slipped out of her.

I reached between us to pinch off the condom. "Hold on, darlin'."

"Not sure if I'm…capable."

I huffed out a laugh and rolled upright. I wasn't sure I was capable myself. I rolled off the condom and tied a knot. "Can I use your bathroom?"

She waved me off. "Yeah. There's a box in there with towels and bodywash if you want a quick shower."

"Actually, if you don't mind?"

"Nope. I'll just lie here and recover."

I grabbed a napkin from the table and took care of the condom. Yeah, I needed that shower. Hot sex was messy and there was less of a chance my son would ask a zillion questions if I didn't look like I'd just had a…workout.

I hiked up my jeans—for fuck's sake, I still had my damn boots on.

Christ, we'd been really intense. I hadn't experienced something like that in a good long while.

After a quick check to make sure she was still semi-conscious—just barely—I stood and headed into the small bathroom. I pitched the napkin in the little garbage can under the sink and washed my hands. I still smelled like her. Not in a bad way.

Hell, if I had more time, I would've gone for seconds.

I dug around in her box and found a frilly bottle of orange goop. I flipped the top and there was her scent—blood orange. Huh.

Guess that answered the citrus thing she had going on.

My dick instantly jumped at the memory. Having my head

between her legs and getting an overdose of that scent had been enough to sear it into my brain.

Certainly not enough to get all Pavlovian about it though. Jesus.

I spotted a box of condoms next to the washcloths.

Hmm. Probably should have gone for one of her condoms instead of my ancient one.

Good to know in case we decided to revisit… No.

I wasn't in the market for more than one hot evening. For all I knew, neither was she.

I sighed at the naked shower stall. She hadn't put up the shower curtain yet, so I had to take a few minutes to do that. I kicked off my boots, jeans, and boxers and tripped over the fucking box. Her bathroom was barely more than a closet.

Once I'd done a quick cleanup, I got out and swore when I saw the time. Wes was going to be a cranky asshole if I was much longer. I had him on a strict schedule—for his benefit and mine. Mostly for him though. The kid had so much energy and if he didn't get to sleep near a certain time, he got overtired and it was a long goddamn night.

I was still damp as I dragged up my jeans. When I opened the door, I got a very nice view of Kelsey picking up the wreckage of our… whatever it was.

She spun around wearing a threadbare baseball shirt with a unicorn across her chest. It skimmed her thighs and made her look about fourteen. "Oh, hi." She cleared her throat.

Great.

I didn't need to think about how young she was. She couldn't be that young.

Dear God, I hoped.

I rubbed the back of my neck. "Nice shirt."

She glanced down and crossed her arms. "I like unicorns."

I leaned down and picked up a stack of papers. "Evidently. Stickers?" God, she wasn't like nineteen or something, was she? Sage and Ally wouldn't have been hanging out with someone that much younger than they were.

At least I didn't think so.

She took them from me. "Planner stickers."

"With rainbow shit?"

"Sometimes you need to put a little sparkle on a crappy day."

I took the pile of papers from her and set them on a box. "Kelsey? Tell me you're over twenty-one."

"I'm well over twenty-one."

"Good." I slid my hand around her back, groaning when her shirt rode up and I came into contact with her glorious ass. "I had fun. You?"

She tipped her head up to meet my gaze. "That was one word for it. Hell of a christening this place got."

I grinned and couldn't resist kissing her saucy mouth. She did that gasping breathy thing then went onto her tiptoes and met me head on. Damn this girl for making me want just a little more than an afternoon.

Maybe one more.

I gripped her ass with both hands and pressed my eager cock against her belly. I drew back, taking a nip out of her lower lip. "I have to go."

She dragged her nails across my chest with a little sigh. "I have tons of unpacking to do. Hope you don't think I tip all the pizza guys like you."

I laughed. "You better fucking not." I gave her one more hard smack, then a squeeze and she yelped. "See ya, pizza girl."

"A new nickname." She laughed and tugged her shirt down. "Thanks for coming, pizza man."

I laughed and snagged my shirt off the box where she'd folded it. I gave her little apartment one more look around. "You don't have any help?"

She shrugged. "I'm used to doing stuff for myself. Don't worry about me."

I nodded. I knew how that went. "Get yourself a bed. Those cushions aren't good for your back."

"Don't I know it." She rubbed her ass. "I think I have cloth-burn on my butt."

I turned her around. Sure enough there was a bit of pink on her perfect ass. And the outline of my hand. I frowned. I hadn't hit her that hard.

She tugged her shirt down. "Dare." She spun around.

"Did I hurt you?"

She pressed a hand to my belly, twisting her fingers in my shirt. "No. Nothing hurt. Well, I mean, not the bad kind."

I fisted my hands at my sides. "I was too rough."

"No." She wrapped her much smaller hands around my fist. "Don't ruin it by getting all guy-like. I liked it. At the risk of swelling your head, I loved it. I'm just a cursed redhead. Anything shows up on my skin. Wait until you see the PMS pimples. Really." She sighed. "Lord, will I ever stop talking while I'm ahead? No. The answer is definitely no."

I fought a smile. She was damn cute. "If you're sure."

"Positive. This was the perfect eight o'clocker." She laughed.

I lowered my mouth to hers. Even knowing I'd left marks, I couldn't quite stop myself from taking her mouth in a rough kiss. When I pulled back, there was a bit of beard burn around her lips. I stroked the back of my knuckle across her cheek before opening the door. "Bye, Kels."

She pressed her cheek against the side of the door. "See ya."

"Get in there. I don't want anyone else seeing those sexy legs."

She wrinkled her nose, but her cheeks pinkened and she stepped back, shutting the door.

Cracking my knuckles, I headed down the stairs, then outside. The door didn't latch behind me and I frowned as I used the steel toe of my boot to get the lock to kick in. Not as secure as it should be. I'd have to talk to Gavin, the owner of the building, tomorrow.

I shook my head. I didn't have time to worry about someone else. I had enough to deal with. She'd be fine.

I dug out my phone and found four texts from my pop. I texted back that I ran into a friend and was on my way back to pick up Wes. And maybe a pizza of my own. I hadn't gotten to eat much of Kelsey's.

Neither had she. I hoped she was eating by now. My lips twitched.

Her usual dinnertime of six-thirty had definitely come and gone long before.

Also not my problem.

I headed down the steps to the sidewalk. Nope, I had more than enough to worry about. I didn't intend to add a crazy redhead to the list.

THREE

I NEEDED A QUART OF COFFEE AND A TROUGH OF WATER.

What had I been thinking?

I rolled over and groaned. Had I had my legs wrapped around a tree the entire night?

Nope.

Just for thirty blissful minutes. A few nights ago. I was still recovering.

Dare.

And oh my God, was I out of shape. Not just the sexy times kind of shape either. Though, hi, that was definitely a whole new workout.

What the hell had I been thinking?

Oh, right, I hadn't been. I'd been going with the flow. And that flow…yeah, I'd never experienced anything like it. I didn't even know orgasms were like that.

Sure, I'd had my own version of them. And even my ex had managed to use friction to his advantage a time or two. But nothing like *that*.

I swung my legs off the couch and whimpered. Helped that I didn't have a roommate to hear the actual old lady noises coming out of me. Sleeping on the lumpy couch the last few nights didn't help. When I'd rented out the place, I'd bounced on the couch and thought it was so springy and comfy.

Yeah.

Not when you slept on it for six hours at a clip.

I definitely had to look into a bed. There was a furniture store across from my apartment building. I'd been busy unpacking on Sunday and by the time I remembered to go over to check into it, they'd been closed. Then I ended up getting dragged over to Sage and Oliver's house for a picnic on Labor Day.

The furniture place wasn't open because hello, Labor Day. And okay, maybe I'd been avoiding my bedroom.

That had to stop.

I'd stop in on the way home from work.

Work. My first day of meetings and pre-planning for school. The kids got a few extra days before starting the new year. For teachers, it was madcap planning and endless meetings.

I shuffled into the bathroom and set the shower to scalding. I snapped the shower curtain open and paused. I hadn't had time to put that up before falling onto my face Saturday night.

Why hadn't I noticed that before? Like during the two showers I'd taken since.

Because you were exhausted and delirious and oblivious, idiot.

Dare.

No. Do not get all squishy because he put up a curtain.

There was no time in my life to get hung up on a guy just because we'd had an interlude.

Yeah, getting literally fucked into my hardwood floor like it was Dare's job? That wasn't merely an interlude.

Man. I shook the curtain. Not just the plastic, but the pretty purple flowered second layer on the double hook.

Dammit.

He wasn't supposed to be sweet. He was supposed to give me a screamer of an orgasm and nothing more.

Okay, so pizza too.

But that was it.

I flipped off my unicorn T-shirt and boxers and stepped into the small shower stall in my miniature bathroom. Sugarsnaps. It still smelled like him. Like me and him after we'd collapsed together.

It had been days. I had to be imagining I could still smell him everywhere.

He'd even put my soap and one of my fluffy poofs into the shower caddy hanging off the shower head. His washcloth still hung off the faucet. Okay, yes, I'd moved it a few times and put it back where he had because clearly, I was a sap.

No, not really. It was just because I hadn't set up my laundry corner yet.

The little unit had a stackable washer and dryer in one of the precious closets of the apartment. But if that meant I didn't have to schlep laundry up and down the stairs, I'd sacrifice a closet every single time.

And that meant I had to leave the washcloth in here.

Yeah, sure, Kelsey. Keep telling yourself that.

Was it wrong to wonder what he smelled like with a bit of me on him all day?

Stupid girl.

He'd probably gone home and showered off my girl scent right away. What guy wanted to smell like blood oranges? I was surprised I wanted to smell like it. I'd been the vanilla girl all my life.

Safe.

But Sage had dragged me into Bath and Body Works and we'd been testing out all the scents. Somehow I'd ended up with a basket full of citrus scents because of course, there had been a sale.

There was always a sale.

And I was always a sucker for it.

I squished the fresh orange foamy puff and activated all the shower gel bubbles. Between that and the steam, I felt marginally better.

I shoved Dare firmly into the back of my head as I packed up for school. It was technically September, but Crescent Cove certainly hadn't gotten the memo.

It was definitely sundress weather.

And since we didn't have to dress for the classroom yet, I took the opportunity to drag a cute summery dress out of one of the few boxes I'd opened in my bedroom.

I had tons of room in there because…no bed.

But at least I'd look cute.

The big red poppies probably should have clashed with my strawberry hair, but there was enough green and white to offset my skin and abundance of freckles. I didn't bother with much makeup since it would probably melt off my face.

I stepped into a pair of cute sandals with a blocky heel, grabbed my purse and teacher bag—aka bucket bag I could fit a small child in—and headed down the stairs. I had to use my butt to get the door to stay closed.

Guess I'd have to talk to my landlord about that one.

No time for that now.

Crescent Cove was about as safe as you could get anyway. The school was only a ten-minute drive from my new place. The brick and mortar school had gotten a fresh coat of paint on all the white wood accents. The church spire had been recently renovated as well.

I'd never thought I would work at a Catholic school, but I liked the kids and the sisters were surprisingly sweet. Mostly.

"Hey, Kelsey. So good to see you back again this year."

I smiled at Jenny Pollock. "Kindergarten for the win this year, huh?"

"Yeah. The classes have gotten smaller, but gosh, I love these kids."

I frowned. "Really? We were overrun last year."

She sighed. "Yeah. We lost a few kids to the public school across the lake."

"Oh."

I tried to ignore the twist in my belly. I had just up and moved my entire life to Crescent Cove because of this job.

We caught up with the other teachers making their way up the miniature steps made for children. We had our first meeting in the auditorium with both the principal and vice principal.

It was a very hearty sis-boom-rah kind of speech that had me smiling through the end of it. The nuns certainly took the cheery approach to most things. So different from the stern ones I remembered as a child in church.

These women were colorful and sweet. The iron will still showed through, but maybe the lack of full habits helped.

We convened on the elementary side of the labyrinth-like school. The once small rooms had been expanded thanks to various upgrades to the school property. The original small school was still the heart of the entire campus and home to the administrative offices.

We were moving up in the world though. This year, we all got iPads to use instead of computers.

Most of the curriculum was housed on a forum-style set up. The older students even got their homework through it and turned it in the same way. So many things had changed since I'd even been in college.

I sat at the back of the room while the rest of the teachers mingled. Most of them had known each other for years. Since I'd come in so late during the previous school year, I'd only had time to get to know a few of them in passing.

My phone buzzed in my sweater pocket.

Do you want to meet me at the Spinning Wheel tonight? Maybe we can figure out Sage's shower a little & I can not feel like a walking milkbag for an hour or so?

I grinned down at the text from Ally. She certainly had a way with words. I quickly texted back an affirmative and caught Jenny's eye. She waved me over, but another notification popped up.

One from Principal Gentry.

I frowned and opened it. There wasn't much to it beyond asking for a meeting tomorrow. I took a look around the room and noticed a few other teachers getting the same buzz.

The twist in my stomach settled.

Maybe it was just a regular meeting at the beginning of the year. Like a check-in.

Probably was.

"Kelsey, come on over here and meet Lois."

I jammed my phone back into my pocket and rose with a smile. Time to mingle. My least favorite thing to do. Kids were easy, a huge group of women…

Meh.

I put my game face on and straightened my shoulders. This was a piece of cake.

Three hours later, I wished I'd said no to Ally about going to the Spinning Wheel. I sighed as I dropped into the front seat of my car.

I cranked the air conditioning since it was still a healthy eighty-three degrees according to my phone. The resulting buzzing hum of hot air didn't help my situation. I snapped my phone onto the dash holder and flung my sweater into the backseat.

But I had a cute dress on and still most of my mascara on my lashes. I flipped down the visor to check out the status of said makeup. Okay, so some of it was under my eyes too, but I would not be defeated.

I was going out with one of my new friends. And an icy cold margarita sounded like a plan.

I settled into my car and headed toward the town proper. Part of me wondered if I should park in front of my building and walk down to the bar, but I'd been on my feet all day and the cute strappy shoes had looked adorable when I put them on this morning.

Now?

Yeah, they were the devil.

But they made my legs look amazing. And if I was really in trouble, I had sneakers in my trunk. I could totally do this.

I parked in front of the bar and did a quick pass of pressed powder so I didn't look like a sweaty twelve-year-old with a face full of freckles. One fortifying swipe of mascara for each eye helped pull the rest of the look together. I downed a half bottle of water and unclipped my hair.

From kindergarten teacher to single woman—easy peasy. Maybe I'd even get my flirt on a little. I was rusty as hell based on my absolute weirdo status Saturday night.

Then again, I'd still gotten laid, so there was that. But most men weren't all that discerning. And Dare had seemed to enjoy himself. At least I was pretty sure he had. He was a quiet one. Except when he whispered that sultry *darlin'* that had liquefied every corner of my girl parts. I could have orgasmed just from him saying that in my ear.

I might have, actually. I'd been damn close even before he'd put his mouth on me.

Again, not something I'd been expecting from such a...one-night stand kind of thing? Did it count as a one-night stand when it was more like twenty-seven minutes and half a piece of pizza?

Hmm.

I shook those thoughts off, grabbed my notebook with the shower notes, and headed into the bar. I squinted at the swift change from searing sun to dim, dark wood. The Spinning Wheel was a coat of paint away from a dive bar, but I liked the atmosphere.

Ally waved from the back of the room.

Evidently, she'd gotten the memo about cute sundress day too. She wore a black and white checked one with a little black sweater over it. I crossed to her and nearly wobbled on my heel as I noticed a familiar pair of shoulders at the bar.

No.

Couldn't be.

I was just seeing things.

A husky laugh floated out and a little shiver bloomed from the base of my spine.

Yeah. That was definitely Dare.

I wasn't sure I was ready to face him quite yet, so I sprinted around a group of college guys gathered around a table in front of one of the TVs.

"Hey," I said and quickly sat down across from Ally.

"Hey yourself. Wow. Look at you. Do kindergarten teachers wear stuff with so much shoulder action?"

I laughed. "I left my sweater in the car. It's hot as Hades."

"Is it? I can't even tell anymore. I'm always hot. Probably because I'm pumping calories out of me on a near constant basis." She lifted her margarita glass. "However, I pumped enough for three babies so I could have an adult beverage tonight."

I laughed. "Is that a thing?"

"Oh, just you wait. You are a slave to a gorgeous baby for at least the first few months. Hell, a year for some. I haven't decided if I'm going to go that long. Though if I'd let Alex hang off me forever, he would."

I winced. That sounded horrifying.

She waved. "It's not that bad. And tonight, I am just Ally who needs conversation with an adult. And to speak of baby things for someone else who is not me." She blinked at me. "Sorry. Babbling. Want a Peachy Rita?"

"Sounds good."

She gestured to the waitress and waved her glass. The girl smiled and nodded. Ally grabbed a menu off the little stand on our table. "I think I need something greasy too. I swear all I do is burn calories. I just want to eat and eat."

"I wish." I folded my hands over my planner notebook. "I had a few thoughts about Sage's shower. Any clue on a registry yet? She told me she doesn't have one, but it would be helpful for the guests."

Ally seemed to hide behind her glass. She took another gulp then put it down. "Yeah, I keep forgetting to ask her to pick somewhere."

"Well, she can do the registry online at most places. Though it seems to be easier and more fun to go around the store with one of those gun things that scans the item."

"Oh, yeah. I had fun doing that. Sage and I pretty much tagged the whole place."

The waitress came by with two more glasses and a basket of popcorn. "Can I get you girls anything?"

"What do you recommend?"

The girl flicked her ponytail over her shoulder. "Our cook actually makes a decent poutine if you like that kind of thing."

"Oh, gravy." Ally made gimme fingers. "Yes, that. A big one of that with extra gravy."

I nodded. "I'm game." I think I'd had it once in college, but it had been awhile.

"Keep 'em coming," Ally said to the waitress. She made a finger wave toward the bar. "I have a DD tonight. What's your name again? You're new?"

She shrugged. "Ish. I'm Michelle if you need anything."

Ally leaned in and stroked her hand down my traveler's notebook. "Now what is this lovely little thing? Sage has me forever looking at stickers and making all sorts of pretties in my little spiral planner, but nothing like this."

"Oh, Sage got me way down into the planner girl hole." I laughed. "I got this off of one of those buy, sell, trade places." I flipped open the blush pink leather journal. "I made a notebook just for Sage. I have a list area for guests, plus a few places I found where we could hold the shower. Or did you want to do it at your house? Or hers?"

"Hmm." Ally took another sip from her drink and pushed the empty glass away, dragging the new one in front of her. "We could do it at my house. We have a nice big backyard. Can barbecue and have cute little virgin versions of umbrella drinks. She loves those."

"Oh, that sounds fun." I sipped at my drink between scribbles into the little insert I'd printed out at the local stationery store. It had sections for lists, dates, and a whole project page. I added reminders for myself to look up drinks to take apart and make them safe for pregnant ladies. "I read up on some foods that you can and can't eat when you're pregnant. Wow, quite the list."

"I missed cheese the most. I swear, I ate a whole wheel of Brie by myself after Alex was born. I never even cared about it until the baby books told me I couldn't have it."

Michelle came back with our appetizer. My eyes went wide, and my tongue practically hung out. "Hello."

Michelle laughed. "Enjoy, ladies. Need another round?"

I looked down at my nearly empty margarita. When had that happened? "I guess so."

We had hashed out most of our ideas for the shower when suddenly, an adorably pregnant blond plopped down beside me and filched a smothered cheese curd.

A man held a napkin in front of her mouth. "Spit it out."

Sage sealed her mouth shut and shook her head.

"Sage." Oliver Hamilton—aka her studly husband—did not sound amused. He had the dad thing down pretty solidly.

She snatched the napkin out of his hand and did it herself. "Come on. One cheese curd won't hurt." She glanced up at Oliver and added a sizable pout.

"Do you know if it's pasteurized? For sure?"

Sage slumped. "No."

"Then no." He smiled down at her and brushed his finger along the skin behind her ear. "I'll make you a sundae before bed."

She smiled. "Okay, that's acceptable."

Oliver rolled his eyes. "Hi, ladies."

Ally slurped her margarita. "Did he really tell you to spit it out like a three-year-old?"

Sage smirked. "He knows I never spit voluntarily."

I choked down a laugh and felt salt burn my esophagus.

As if his saucy wife had never spoken, Oliver rattled change in his pocket. "I'm well versed in such thanks to Laurie. She also likes to eat things she shouldn't."

Ally blew raspberries at him. "You're not the fun uncle at all."

"I'll remind you of that when you eat the cookies we made tonight."

Ally's eyes went huge. "Oh, bonus points. Okay, you can have fun uncle status back, but only if there were chocolate chips included in said cookies."

"Butterscotch and chocolate chip actually."

Ally clasped her hands under her chin and fluttered her lashes. "Man, I might even kiss you."

"Please don't."

I snorted at Oliver's deadpan voice.

He ran an absent hand down Sage's hair. "Behave. I ordered you a basket of fries. You can have those to hold you over."

"Excellent." Sage leaned back in her chair and tipped her chin up to him. "Get me a fizzy water too, please."

He dutifully dropped a kiss on her lips. "Yes, dear." He headed back to the bar and Sage watched him the whole time.

Sage grinned. "We sound like we're eighty, but man, I love that guy. And he's got an ass made for spanking."

I coughed. Maybe Sage never spit, but I had come awfully close to spraying my drink. Different substance than she'd been talking about however.

She was such a dirty girl. And I loved her for it. "Is that so?"

Sage nodded. "Took some convincing for him to try it, but Oliver is game for most things."

I tried to picture it and just could not. The other way around— yeah, I didn't want to go there. Just the idea of that tall, proper guy with Sage over his lap...

I needed help.

How did she...

"You're trying to picture it, aren't you?"

I flushed. "I can't help it."

Sage wiggled her eyebrows. "He hated every second, but man, did I get plowed. Good thing I was already preggers. Probably would have been twice over if not."

I didn't even know what to say. And my inappropriate meter was usually on max.

"Stop torturing the poor girl with your sex stories."

Sage shredded my straw wrapper. "I can't help it. Who else am I going to tell them to? My mother has officially parked the RV in our driveway. Should have seen James's face when he rolled up and saw that."

"Your mom and dad are staying with you?"

"Yep. My life is officially over. They keep saying they're going to stay in the RV, but please. That's not going to happen. The only good part is that they're happy to take all the grandbabies for grand sleepovers." Sage peeked over her shoulder at Oliver and Seth. And my stomach bottomed out as Dare tucked a toothpick along the side of his mouth before laughing at something Seth said.

Suddenly, Dare turned and caught my eye.

I tried for a seductive smile, but based on his quirked eyebrow, I probably looked more like a freak.

My flirtation game was nonexistent.

Sigh. Nothing new there.

I turned back to Ally just as Sage tried to snake my notebook out from under my hand.

"Hey!"

Sage's fingers curled around the edges. "Whatcha got?"

"None of your business." I closed the notebook on her fingers and slid it off the table and into my bag. "School stuff."

Sage propped her head on her hand, tapping her finger against her cheek. "You didn't even start classes yet."

"No, but we have...stuff."

"Stuff, huh?" Sage made a humming sound.

I glanced at Ally. "Yeah, stuff."

"Right. She was telling me all about her teacher...stuff. Kindergarteners are hella crazy." Ally shrugged and took another sip.

I rolled my eyes. "How are you feeling?"

Sage sat back just as Michelle returned with Sage's seltzer and fries. "Good. Fat." She carefully selected a fry. "I had to put on my first official pair of maternity pants. Both exciting and annoying because I have cute toes and can barely see them these days. But you know," she rubbed her bump, "baby and..." She laughed softly, jerking her head toward Oliver at the bar. "Never thought I'd be so happy."

She was positively glowing.

I smiled and hoped I didn't look as green as I couldn't help feeling. "I'm so glad for you."

She reached for the ketchup right next to my bag. "I'd be happier if you guys told me about the baby shower you're planning though. That would make me super happy."

"Can't you settle for just regular happy, dammit? You aren't a bag of milk yet. And trying to have sex with my husband is a lesson in futility while Alex is teething." Ally held up her glass to Michelle. "More."

"Sure thing." Michelle glanced at me. "You good?"

"I'll take another." I moved my bag to the chair beside me. Evidently, I would need tequila to make it through the interrogation. "We're not planning anything."

Sage made a huge pool of ketchup in the middle of the fries. "You both suck at lying."

"No, we don't."

"You so do. It's good, I like that in a pair of besties."

My stomach flipped and I warmed from the inside out for a whole new reason. I hadn't been someone's bestie in a damn long time. And considering the new bestie designation, it seemed weird that I hadn't told her about Dare.

My gaze slid back over to the bar. The guys were shouting at the television. Well, minus Oliver, who appeared bored. Dare was cupping a beer in his long, battered fingers. I remembered all the little scar lines along his skin as he molded those fingers over my breasts.

When he'd been peeking over—

"Okay, so if you're not going to tell me about the shower, you're definitely going to tell me about this." Sage pointed at Dare. "You still crushing on Dare?"

I flushed. "No."

"The heart eyeballs say differently. You were flirting with him pretty hardcore the last time we went out as a group. He is hot. You know, in a not-Oliver kind of way."

I rolled my eyes. Yes, her husband was attractive. And by default, Ally's was as well since they were the famed Hamilton twins in this crazy, nosy town.

Not to say I didn't love that about Crescent Cove. I loved that everyone watched out for each other.

Except when the new schoolteacher had a white-hot one-night stand with the scruffalicious, grumpy town mechanic and wanted to keep it under wraps. Good luck there.

Yeah, that part of Nosy Town I could live without.

The white-hot part, however, I would be happy to relive. I was still walking a little funny, thanks to Dare's above average abilities. Or maybe just average—how the hell could I know? I'd only been with two guys in my life before him. And my goodness were they underachievers compared to Dare.

"I wasn't aware your peaches and cream complexion could go so…peach."

I snapped my gaze to Sage. "Har-har." I twisted the bottom of my glass in the bit of condensation from my rapidly melting drink.

"So you *are* crushing on him." Sage propped her chin on both hands and leaned in. "Do I get to start carving your initials into trees?"

"God, no." I took a healthy drink from my margarita and choked a little when the citrus hit the back of my throat.

"No hiding behind alcohol, woman. We only use it to infuse us with courage and tell excellent stories."

I finished the glass and slammed it down. "I had the sex with Dare."

Sage spluttered out a laugh. "*The* sex?"

I fanned myself with a stack of napkins. "Trust me, if you'd been there, you would agree that it definitely qualified as 'the' sex. Whew."

I was sweating just thinking about it.

Or that could've been due to the alcohol. Whoops.

"Although that would've been weird if you were there," I continued. "Sorry. I'm not into voyeurism or exhibitionism." I leaned close to Sage. "Is that another kinky thing you and Oliver do?"

"Are you kidding me?" Sage snorted. "If I showed anyone this preggo belly who wasn't responsible for it, I'd be up on a lewdness charge. Hello, humongous."

Ally let out a long sigh. "Dear Lord. I need more alcohol for this."

FOUR

KELSEY KEPT LOOKING OVER AT ME. WAS I SUPPOSED TO GO OVER there? Shit. What was the protocol for sleeping—well, no actual sleeping had been involved, but I also wouldn't have gone as far as calling it a dirty fuck with her.

She was too sweet for that.

Not that she'd been super sweet when she'd been in my lap giving me orders Saturday night. And man, I could still see the wide-eyed surprise when I'd dumped her on her back and went to town between her amazing thighs. I didn't mind oral. At times, it could be my second favorite thing about sex.

With her?

Yeah, there hadn't been an issue. Good thing, because she'd soaked my beard and even after a shower, there had been a hint of her on me into the next day.

She looked willowy in those buttoned up clothes she usually wore. In cutoffs and a T-shirt, she'd looked like every wet dream I'd had since I was fourteen. I'd always had a weakness for a fresh-faced girl.

And Kelsey fit that bill in a million ways.

But she was also the girl you dated and married, not banged out a lonely night with.

The waitress who had been taking care of the ladies' table came around the bar and I stood up. "Can I bring those over?"

She tilted her head at me.

I dug a crumpled five out of my pocket and dropped it on the tray.

"Suit yourself, handsome." She handed me the tray and took the bill.

Seth turned his back on the bar and propped himself on his elbows. "What's up, Kramer?"

I shrugged. "Just saving the waitress a trip."

"What a gentlemanly and almost charming thing to do. So why are you doing it?"

Seth wasn't wrong. I wasn't the type to play the charmer, but I didn't know any other reason to go over there. Seemed weird to just go over there to say hi. Like a high school dance maneuver filled with lame regrets and wince-worthy embarrassment.

Instead of explaining myself, I just walked away from the guys. Under his breath, Oliver made some remark that made Seth laugh.

I nearly turned around and handed the tray back to the waitress. This was dumb. I was being stupid.

But then Kelsey laughed at something Seth's wife had said and did that nose wrinkle thing that should've made me roll my eyes. Instead, it tightened my damn jeans.

Nope.

Turning around.

I didn't need this.

Then she gave me this sexy little smile over her shoulder. And my stride lengthened. I'd done far more stupid things in my life than flirt with a gorgeous woman.

"I believe these are for you ladies."

Ally made grabby hands. "Anything that doesn't smell like formula or boob juice is for me."

I blinked.

Sage took the tray. "Don't mind her. She doesn't get out much."

Ally took her drink and I had to tighten my grip on the tray so it wouldn't topple. I gave Sage an easy smile. "Straight bubbles are for you, I imagine?"

Sage sighed. "Yes, these heathens are drinking right in front of the pregnant lady who can't have a single drop."

Ally made a loud slurping sound. "Yep."

I set the other margarita in front of Kelsey. "Tequila, huh?"

She nudged her two empty glasses away. "Luckily, I can walk to my place from here."

A pop song that wasn't too obnoxious came on. I was more of a classic rock guy, thanks to my hours in the auto shop, and other days. Ones that were almost too far away to see clearly. Where burnt rubber and racing had filled my head and heart.

I shoved those memories to the back of my mind. Too long ago to go down that endless track.

I leaned just a touch closer to her ear. "Dance?"

She turned her head and her cheek brushed my beard. Her citrusy scent blended with a sharper one due to the margarita. She swallowed hard and those golden eyes went a little hazy.

I wasn't sure if it was because of the tequila or just that *thing* that bloomed up between us lately. Whatever the feeling was—and it was a very annoying feeling at that—I was willing to follow it for a few minutes. Just to remember what a woman smelled like again and not the eternal scent of motor oil, unwashed men, and peanut butter.

Wes was on a peanut butter kick and it was fucking killing me.

She nodded and stood up.

Christ, I wished she hadn't. I definitely shouldn't have come over.

The little straps of her flowery dress left her creamy shoulders bare. A dusting of freckles made me itch to get my lips on her again. We'd moved so fast the last time—the only time—I hadn't gotten to thoroughly explore all of her.

Fuck.

I shouldn't be exploring anything on her. I didn't have the time to get all twisted up over a woman. I could barely keep up with Wes and the doubles I was working, along with the days I would pinch hit at my pop's place.

But then she tossed her hair over her shoulder and took my hand.

Fuck, I was sunk.

She led me onto the dance floor and the song went slow and syrupy. It was an ex-boy band sort of song, but it didn't stop me from sliding my hand around her waist. My rough hands caught on the delicate fabric and I instinctively pulled away.

She reached around and held me tighter. Her long legs bumped mine as we instantly fell into a loose sway. She was a little unsteady on the ankle-breakers she was wearing, but I took the opportunity to draw her even closer.

Her slightly more-than-a-mouthful breast buzzed against my chest and I sighed when she settled her arms around my neck. There was nothing quite like a soft woman. I buried the need under the duty for my boy and my work, but God, she felt good.

"So, tell me, have you gotten a bed yet, Nuts Lady?"

"We were having such a nice dance until you ruined it by speaking."

I stiffened.

"No, don't do that." She played with my hair. "I was joking. Obviously, not well. I kinda suck at flirting."

"I've never been good at it either."

I settled her back against my chest and tried not to groan at the way my knee instinctively went between her thighs. Nothing about her fit the crude scenarios in my head. She was the sweet girl next door, not a chick in a bar looking for a good time. I had to remember that.

To accept that all I was going to get was a little more time with her scent filling my brain.

She reached back to toy with the hair at the nape of my neck. Her long fingers made little swirls against my freshly shorn hair. "You cut it."

I'd taken Wes to the barber for school, but I couldn't seem to spit out that I had a kid. It either ruined the moment or made things awkward and then also ruined the moment. "Gets hot in the shop."

Her long hair swirled around my forearm. A waterfall of silk against my rough arms and hands. Just like the rest of her.

"Yeah, I keep thinking I should chop mine off. It's so heavy."

"No." I growled it out way more intensely than I should have, but all that hair was… "Fuck no."

"Just like a guy. Always want us to have super long hair. But it's stick straight and flat half the time."

I moved my hand from the small of her waist up to the heavy tangle of gold and red strands. "All I can see is you on that floor with your hair tangled while I made you come."

She shivered and I held her tighter as the song blended into another slow one. There were people crowding in on us as the dance floor filled.

"I'm not good at this," she said quietly.

"You were just fine the other night."

She tucked her chin in where my shoulder met my neck. "That was probably a fluke."

I tugged a handful of red-gold silk so she had to look at me. "Then it was a fluke for us both. I can't promise you a fucking thing, but God, I want to be inside you again. On a fucking bed this time."

"I don't have one yet."

Well, I'd just have to fix that, now wouldn't I? My buddy at the furniture shop owed me a favor for towing his car from Rochester back home. It was time to collect.

She stumbled against me a little as she swayed. I couldn't take her home tonight anyway. One, she was far too tipsy. I wasn't a complete asshole. And two, Wes was at Sage's house playing with the kids, but he had a shopping day with my parents tomorrow.

They loved to take my kid out for school shopping. It was the only time they really spoiled him, so I'd stopped being an asshole about it. I could take care of my kid—and they knew that—but I couldn't deny the help was appreciated. Not when I had to pay off a new furnace for the sinkhole that was my house.

I locked down all the crap that lived in my head—kid, house, job— and spun her out in a quick twirl. Her surprised laugh filled my chest way more than it should. She was a little weird, and she said whatever came into her head. We didn't seem to have much in common.

Right now, it was just my dick talking. Had to be. And as much as I wanted to lose myself in Kelsey, it was time to go back to the real world.

I dragged her back in, deliberately crowding close. "Guess I'll see you around, Kels," I said against her mouth.

The urge to brand her was a little too intense for my comfort. That and I couldn't kiss her to a fucking Ariana Grande song. There were some lines I just couldn't cross.

"Kels, we gotta go."

She turned toward Ally's voice. The indecisive look on Kelsey's face made me want to tell her to say the hell with them. I'd find some way to get her in my arms for the night.

But then she was gone. And I was left standing in the middle of the dance floor with my dick throbbing and my head full of too much bullshit.

Sage nodded to me and I knew they'd get her home. I blew out my breath and dug my keys out of my jacket.

I had to get Wes in bed anyway. He'd be all sugared up after playing with Laurie.

Sometimes responsibilities were a bitch.

FIVE

I straightened my freshly ironed khaki skirt, then pushed up my sleeves of my baby blue sweater set. Principal meeting wear, I liked to call it. I usually went with a far more kid-proof outfit when actually teaching. But today was a good day to bring out the one cashmere sweater set in my wardrobe.

I wasn't gonna lie, it was mostly for armor. Who could hurt you in cashmere?

It was a delusion I was willing to live with.

I held my hand up to knock.

"Come in, Miss Ford."

I swallowed then turned the knob. You'd think I was in the principal's office as a student. I put on my sunniest smile. Principal Gentry still wore an abbreviated version of her habit. As if a suit and a nun's habit had a baby. "Good morning."

"Have a seat, Kelsey."

All right, so we were getting right down to it. I perched on the edge of my chair and folded my hands.

"We've had a few things change for the school year. Unforeseen things which have required me to juggle a few classrooms."

My stomach pitched. Oh, God. I wasn't getting sacked, was I? They just hired me on full-time.

She held up her hand. "Don't worry, I didn't invite you here to let you go."

That was me, poker face of the ages. I swallowed a hysterical laugh. "I'm glad to hear it."

"But there's been a shift in enrollment for our kindergarten class. I no longer need a second teacher as I did last year."

I gripped my fingers until I couldn't feel them anymore.

"However, I do need a first-grade teacher due to yet another change. Most of the children from kindergarten stayed on. You're the newest teacher with us, so you haven't gotten into planning your curriculum much."

So she thought. I'd planned out the first half of my year already.

"And from the information I have on you, you have training in all elementary education arenas."

"Yes, Sister."

"Good, good. That makes this much easier. Your classroom will have twenty-three students. Fifteen boys and eight girls. I think you may know one of them. Alison and Seth Hamilton's daughter, Laurie."

"Oh. Yes, I do."

"I expect that your personal relationship won't make a difference?"

"Oh, no. She's a delightful girl, but I fall in love with all my kids. Doesn't stop me from controlling the classroom when necessary."

"Good to hear. This particular class has quite a bit of energy. I know you'll do very well with the changes."

That sounded like a canned response. I wondered how many other teachers were shuffled around? But now I needed to start over with my teaching plan. First graders needed a lot more structure than the half day kindergarteners. They had to learn how to deal with an all-day class.

Nothing like tossing me into the deep end on the second full day of my first full year as a member of St. Agnes.

"You may join the assembly with the rest of the teachers for the rally. We're very glad to have you here, Kelsey. But I'm not going to lie. Catholic schools are having more issues with registration. We have to make sure our classrooms and teachers are the best in the county, if not the state."

I swallowed. No pressure.

"That includes how the people of Crescent Cove see our teachers. We must uphold outward appearances, just as much as those inside our classrooms."

I blinked. She wasn't even bothering to sugarcoat that one. As one of the handful of single women working at the school, I recognized the anvil hanging over my head.

No fuckups.

The rules were a bit antiquated and provincial, but I didn't want to try to buck the system. That wasn't me, and besides, my students were too important.

I wondered if Sister Gentry knew how many of the teachers mixed it up at socials. I hadn't been with St. Agnes long, but some of the teachers acted more like it was a college campus. Only they had the married cloak of invisibility and I so did not.

Folding my hands in my lap, I nodded. "Understood."

"I sent all the details of your classroom to your tablet. Beth has your new keys and updated security codes for the supply cabinets."

"Thank you." I stood and resisted the urge to curtsy.

Good grief, pull it together, girl.

I slipped out into the chaos that was the admin room. A few more teachers were gathered at the edges of the room and into the hallway.

I waved to one of the teachers I knew. Admittedly, I didn't know many of them besides names from the gossip circles. From the sounds of malcontent around me, I wasn't the only one who had gotten unexpectedly reassigned.

Avoiding a particularly loud group of middle school teachers left me on the fringes of the room. No way to get near Beth. Great.

"Are you Kelsey?"

I turned toward the male voice. "Yes?"

"I'm Caleb Beck. I teach second grade in the classroom across from you. Welcome, new neighbor."

"How did you—?" I shook my head. Gossip ran faster than water in this place. In the entire town. "Never mind. You probably knew before I did. Pleased to meet you." I shook his hand.

He smiled and the corners of his blue eyes crinkled. He waggled his iPad. "They sent out a roster of teachers. Unfortunately, it went out before a few people had their meetings."

I winced.

"Yeah, welcome to St. Agnes. Well, a true welcome. I know you covered for Judy when she went out on maternity. We lucked out when they hired you on."

I resisted the urge to cross my arms. "You certainly know a lot about me."

He gave me a sheepish smile. "The pretty ones are worth finding out about."

"Oh. Well, thanks." Yeah, I didn't know what to say to that one. Not to mention the principal's voice was still echoing in my ear. Talking to the resident flirt was definitely not a good idea. "I guess I'll be seeing you around."

"I hope so."

I resisted the urge to scrunch up my shoulders. I barely knew anyone in the school, but I'd heard plenty about Caleb. Enough that there was no level of desperation I could reach to believe a charmer like him.

I managed to make my way to Beth's desk and got my room assignment and details. Unsurprisingly, there was already an update happening on my tablet.

This place was no joke.

I followed the troupe of teachers down the hall to our next assembly as I scrolled through the pictures of the kids in my new class. I stopped when I came to Laurie. Her sweet smile made me instantly smile back. She was such a cute and precocious child.

A kid with a smirky grin filled my screen next and I instantly knew he was trouble. Hints of the devil lurked in his super blue eyes. And the faux hawk from his previous year's picture just might have been a further clue. Weston. Cute kid for sure. Onto the next ones. Emily and Jenny were twins.

God help me.

I tucked my tablet away when I got to the auditorium at the center of the school.

The next few hours were filled with information about updates to the curriculum from New York State. Then I was tossed into the elementary education minefield.

I went from two half day classes to one full. The only upside was that my day started a little later now. My nerves were jangling by the end of the second session of afternoon meetings.

I had to pull apart my entire teaching plan. How was I supposed to do that in twenty-four hours?

By the end of the day, I was pretty sure I'd become a pinball. This room for supplies, that one for music enrichment, this one for art class twice a week.

Kindergarten had been all in one room.

I walked into the sunshine at two in the afternoon in a daze, my tablet and notebook clutched to my chest. How the hell was I going to do this?

I didn't even remember the trip back to my apartment, which was scary as hell. Thank God, it was only a ten-minute drive. A blue truck was parked outside my door with a simple headboard made of wood sticking out the end of the flatbed. It was wrapped to the nth degree, but there was no denying the soft, golden color of pine. Or maybe it was maple.

I frowned. Was I getting a new neighbor?

There were a few apartments in the building, but I was the only tenant thus far. At least that was what I'd thought. The building was barely finished with renovations. Then again, Mr. Forrester would want to fill the other apartments. Empty rooms meant lost revenue. The lower half of the building no longer had a for rent sign on it either. Looked like there was a whole bunch of changes happening lately.

The apartment building door was propped open with a rock.

"There you are."

I peeked around the queen-sized mattress encased in plastic propped against the headboard. "Dare?"

"Yep." He hauled the mattress down and shoved it through the doorway without another word.

"Wait." I blew out a breath. He totally didn't wait. I grabbed my bag and slammed the door to my car. I raced after him and up the stairs. "What are you doing?"

"You need a bed."

"What? Well, yes, I do, but umm…" My bag twisted down my arm as I rushed to catch up.

"This seems a little extreme for sex. I mean, it was awesome, but do you buy beds for all your women?"

He muscled the mattress through my apartment door. Wait, how had he gotten in? I looked down at the keys in my hand and the wide open door. "Did you break in?"

He peeked around the mattress. "Not technically."

"Not sure there's a gray zone there, buddy." I ran up the last of the steps and pushed by him before he could get all the way into my apartment. Evidently, that didn't much matter. The frame for the bed was already set up with the box spring on top of it.

He wiped his brow and blew out a breath. "I came over to ask if you wanted to go with me to pick one out, but you weren't here."

"So you just went ahead and did it for me?" Outrage lifted my voice an octave or three. I wasn't screeching…mostly. Good lord, his arms were amazing.

No, that is not the point to this.

He'd just…taken over. Why? This was not okay.

"First of all, Beck owed me a favor."

"Beck?"

He nodded toward the window. "Furniture place across the way. And as much as I like fucking you, darlin', this wasn't contingent on me getting laid again. You needed a bed—and since it's been a few days since I've been here and you still don't have one…"

He gave me a pissy look which only made me want to stomp my

foot at him. I huffed out a growl. "I was getting to it. I just wasn't sure what size. As you can see, this place isn't the biggest." I ripped at the buttons of my sweater set. My apartment was on the top floor, and God, I was burning up.

His eyebrow quirked. "As I said, no payment is necessary."

"I'm hot." His smirk made me roll my eyes. "Not hot for you, you jerk. Just hot. It's like seventy degrees and the sun is blasting in here."

"Don't stop stripping on my account. I'll consider it a tip."

"You are incorrigible."

"So my mother tells me." He used the hem of his shirt to wipe his face and I lost my train of thought. I really hadn't had enough time to catalog all of...*that* on Saturday night.

I mean, it was still burned into my retinas, but it was more a hazy bit of insanity than anything I could pull together with any clarity. But wow, were there actually that many abdominal muscles in the human body?

I thought it was a six-pack.

That looked like way more.

He dropped his shirt and the smirk was back, dammit. I turned away from him and dumped my bag in the one free chair I had in my living room. The sound of him shoving the mattress across my floor had me rushing after him.

"Would you just wait a second?" I tripped over a pile of clothes I'd been sorting for another load of laundry. And hello, my bras were draped everywhere. I quickly snatched them off the rack and stuffed them in a box.

He flipped the mattress onto the box spring. "You want it between the windows or over there?"

I pushed my hair out of my face. "I don't know. It's so big. It takes up the whole freaking room."

"I picked out a headboard you could clip lights to. My...I've seen it done before."

My what? Girlfriend? Sister? Friend?

Not important. He couldn't have a girlfriend, not if he'd bounced on me. He didn't seem like that kind of guy. Otherwise, it was none of my business.

I glanced over at him. "That's a good idea. Especially with how small the room is." I twirled around and moved another box on top of the first box and shoved them both to the other side of the room. "Yeah, between the windows."

He shoved it over then crossed to me. "You look good." He rubbed one of my rapidly wilting curls between his fingers before flicking it over my shoulder. "Be right back with the headboard."

When he was gone, I spun around and winced at the pile of underwear I hadn't seen before. I popped those into one of the boxes and caught sight of my face in the mirror I'd used for makeup. Look good? Was he blind?

I grabbed my cutoffs and a T-shirt and quickly shucked my school clothes. I was buttoning my shorts just as he walked into my room. His blue eyes went hot and my freaking nipples went on high alert. And here I'd thought the scumbag clothes would bring down the awareness building between us.

Nope.

Maybe it was just the wide bed dominating the room.

He lowered the huge headboard to the floor and left again, this time coming back with a tool set. He dropped it on the bed and flipped it open, taking out a utility knife. He stripped the thing in seconds.

I was trying not to imagine how quickly he could slice off my clothes. No need to go there. He'd done an admirable job a few days ago. Goodness, I didn't need to think about that with the stupid bed right there.

He lifted the headboard and moved to the windows. His freaking arms were bulging. He didn't look like he was particularly huge, but there was no denying all the ropey muscles under his simple Ford T-shirt.

"Can you hand me the drill?" He poked his head up from behind the headboard. "And the long screws."

Drill.

Jeez. *Get a grip, Kelsey.*

I unhooked the large, very professional drill from the big yellow case and brought it over to him. I wasn't sure on the size of the bit— and the only reason I knew the term was from watching HGTV. I took the trio with me and rounded the bed and headboard into the small space he'd made for himself.

He was laying across the floor and his T-shirt had peeked up again. More eight-pack action for my viewing pleasure. He held his hand out and I put the drill in his hand, then opened the bits for him. He gave me a half smile and took one then the screw from me before he crammed himself under the bed to attach it to the frame.

It only took three minutes, but I was suddenly very glad he'd done the work for me. Three minutes for him would have been more like thirty with many swear words and broken nails for me.

"You really didn't have to do this." I stroked my hand down the simple lines of the headboard. I probably wouldn't have picked something like this, but it worked in the space so well. I probably would have gone for something huge and tufted that wouldn't work at all.

But I'd never been able to have a nice bed. I usually received hand-me-downs from my family and bought at consignment sales. I didn't mind repainting crap furniture to make it pretty, but the new was pretty awesome.

"As I said, Beck owed me a favor."

"But this favor could have been a pretty amazing bed for you."

"I have one." He sat up and gathered his tools. "You needed it."

"But this is like a thousand-dollar set."

"Two."

My eyes went wide. "Dare."

"It was a big favor. Besides, he makes this stuff. He charges too much."

"He made this?"

"Yeah. Runs the furniture shop but most of it is his stuff." He shrugged. "Local boy done good, right?"

I sagged onto the bed. "It's too much."

59

I nearly asked if he was trying to Christian Grey me before sense kicked in. Dare was no megalomaniac bazillionaire.

He did have a caviar-level penis though, if such a thing existed.

"You appreciate it, right?"

"Of course I do." Just as swiftly, I stood up. "Thank you so much." I looped my arms around his neck for a quick hug.

He didn't seem to know quite what to do with his arms. Then he awkwardly patted my back. "It's fine. Besides, I'm not being completely altruistic, Nuts Lady."

"Is that so, Pizza Guy?"

He huffed out something between a grunt and a laugh. "You're fucking gorgeous."

I stepped back from him and the backs of my knees bumped into the bed. "You're just saying that because there's a big ole bed behind me."

"I don't say shit I don't mean."

"Yeah?"

"Yeah. Besides, you know you're gorgeous. I'm not the first guy to say it."

"Who says?"

He tunneled his fingers into my hair and gathered the strands at the base of my neck. Probably sweaty strands, but what was a little perspiration between friends? "There can't be that many stupid men on this planet."

"Wrong answer. But no one says it like you do."

SIX

I wished I hadn't said that. His eyes went wary and I wanted to chew off my damn tongue. "I just mean all rough and gruff." I swallowed down a hysterical laugh. "Sometimes a girl likes it rough."

"Is that so?" His fingers twisted my hair a little tighter.

I trailed my finger down the center of his chest to the hem of his shirt and snuck under it to flick open the button of his jeans. "My job just got really complicated and I want to forget about it for an hour. Think you might be interested in—"

"Yeah. I'm fucking interested." He interrupted what was going to be a saucy little question and closed his mouth over mine.

Thank God. I didn't want to screw this up by inserting my foot in my mouth again. I was perfectly happy with his tongue instead. Good thing, because holy mercy, was it talented.

And he did not waste time. Did I mention thank God? Because I really didn't want to think right now. My brain was still spinning with the quick change in my entire teaching plan.

He tugged my hair. "With me, darlin'. Or we don't do this."

"I'm here." I snapped back into the moment and focused on his icy blue eyes. "I'm sorry. Please make me forget about today." I could see the indecisiveness living in his frown lines. I reached up and brushed my finger down through the furrow. "None of this." I boldly arrowed my touch down into his beard and tugged lightly.

It was short and very neat. I didn't have to worry about something nesting in there like some men. So blond and dense with a touch of golden streaks just like his hair.

Like the outside wanted to give him a little shine.

Except he worked in a dark car shop, didn't he? How did he get all those tan lines and streaky bits?

His other hand coasted down my ass and gripped tightly. "Stop getting all thinky or I'll have to find a way to empty that mind of yours."

"Oh, yeah?" I pushed up his shirt and went for his nipple. His chest was smooth and muscled. Where his face was dense with hair, his chest was hairless. Except for the line leading into the snap of his jeans.

No, that was definitely not smooth.

I didn't know quite what I was doing. My ex had expected things, and I knew to do them, but it felt different with Dare. I wanted to touch and taste. I nipped at the side of his pectoral muscle and started to slide lower.

Instead of allowing me to go for the blow job I'd been intending— what man didn't like that?—he cupped my face and dragged my mouth back up to his. The kiss was wild and dirty. There was no hiding from what he wanted.

And I so didn't want to hide.

Reckless abandon ahoy.

He pushed at his jeans and the heavy thud of his work boots nearly clipped my toes. I lost my footing and bashed into him. Instead of annoyance, he used the momentum to spin me around to face the bed.

He curled his forearm around my waist as he pushed down my cutoffs. "Don't need these." He lifted me and dumped me on the naked mattress.

I shot a look over my shoulder. "Dare."

He reached behind his neck and grabbed his T-shirt, dragging it over his head. "Yeah? You wanted to be distracted, right?" He kicked my legs apart. "I aim to provide."

I collapsed onto my chest and struggled onto my elbows only to have him haul me up and move me higher on the bed.

"I need a little room, darlin'." He lowered his mouth to the dip right above my butt.

I wiggled, suddenly nervous and uncomfortable. My butt was not my finest asset. A strangled giggle broke free. Asset indeed.

He pushed my shirt up with his nose. "Find this funny?"

"You probably wouldn't."

He tucked his hand under my belly and down between my thighs. "I prefer screams to laughter."

I hissed out a breath that ended in a laugh. Something very hard, and very insistent dug into my thigh as he shoved my shirt higher. I definitely didn't find that funny. Nope. Just wanted more of it. And not poking me there.

I shifted restlessly under his touch, trying to urge him higher. Suddenly, all the sunlight in my room was gone as my shirt got tangled in my hair as he tried to get it off me. I arched to help and he flipped the cups of my lacy bra up. His rough fingers abraded my skin and made my nipple tighten. "Holy crap, right there."

He tugged harder. "Weren't kidding with the rough. My hands aren't for pretty skin like yours."

I couldn't see him, but his words were doing a very effective job. I put my head down and tried to get myself free. Dare decided to go for my panties instead. He inched back down my body and pulled them down as his mouth followed the trail.

I crashed into the mattress, my head going fuzzy with disorientation just as he licked from my clit to...oh, God. He wouldn't. I shrieked a little as he buried his face deeper.

I managed to get my shirt off and greedily inhaled oxygen. I didn't think I could get any wetter than I had last weekend, but he definitely proved me wrong. The man was dirty and raw. He held me open when I'd have pushed him away. I'd never let anyone go for there. Hell, I had barely done doggie-style in the past. I was far too self-conscious about my flat ass compared to the rest of me.

Not that I was overly curvy anywhere, but…

"Guh," I muffled a moan as he licked and stroked and used his fingers to stretch me everywhere.

"I love eating your pussy. Fuck, it's like sunshine and honey with whatever that orange stuff is." He mumbled against my center as he filled me up with two fingers…maybe more. I couldn't tell anymore. All I could do was push back on him.

My brain was blissfully empty as I chased whatever it was between us. This place where sex and lust got all fuzzy and fizzy at the same time. My skin burned as he spread me wider. My nipples ached as I rubbed myself against the mattress. I couldn't seem to find a way to ask for something more.

For the first time in my life, my words didn't work. They were stuck between panting words of praise and unintelligible grunts as he teased me.

Finally, his name exploded from my lips as I bucked against his fingers. He stopped and suddenly, he was gone. I dropped my head onto the mattress. What the fuck?

Then I shrieked as he was back, pushing me toward the top of the mattress where the headboard was. He lifted me just enough and straddled my thighs.

What the hell? I darted a glance over my shoulder. His cock was hard and proud, jutting from his golden skin. God, that was so wrong. He was stupidly beautiful in such a rough, man's man kind of way. His forearms were tightly muscled, dusted in golden hair, but it was his hand I couldn't stop staring at.

He was dragging a condom down the length, his gaze on my ass. I shook at the thought of him coming for something more than my lady garden. He dragged his hand down over my cheeks. "Don't worry, Kels. I wouldn't ever ask for more than what you want to give." He inched closer and slid two fingers deep into me. "This is all I want right now."

Somehow *now* sounded more like a prequel than final.

I shook my head. I couldn't think about that. This was just for fun. To empty my brain for a little bit. I couldn't think about a round three. Round two was already messing with my head, making me want more.

Then he turned his hand and his thumb brushed against the other, more forbidden part of me. The one that made everything tighten. He lowered his mouth to my back as he stroked me deeper and brushed his thumb over the sensitive puckered skin. I was so wet that everything was slick and easy to probe.

Breath shuddered out of my chest and all I could do was push back on him. Instinct warred with embarrassment. Curiosity overrode it all as pleasure consumed me and the whole room hazed.

"Fuck, yeah. That's it. You're so ready for me."

I was?

I mean, okay, maybe kinda, but not really. Curiosity was one thing, but there was— "Oh, wow."

Dare pulled his fingers from me and then I was all filled up. There was nothing but his cock filling me, spreading me out until there was no room for any other thoughts. He covered me, his fingers lacing with mine as we lurched forward until we reached the top of the bed.

He braced himself over me and our mouths crashed into another hot, dirty kiss. Teeth and lips and that glorious beard teased my chin before he went for my neck.

He powered into me again and again until the headboard slammed against the wall.

That deposit was toast.

I didn't even care.

I reached behind me with one arm and we crashed forward, but then he was even deeper. And I didn't have any words or thoughts.

There was nothing but his shaft filling me, the head of his oh so talented cock slamming into something deep inside that I'd only read about in books. He bore down on me, and the sounds I made…

I was sure I'd be embarrassed later, but right now? I screamed his name as my whole body shook. He rose up behind me and his fingers bit into my waist as he thrust into me again and again.

A million different words tumbled out of my mouth. As if all the ones I'd lost earlier came careening out. In the end, the only one that mattered was, "yes."

So many ways to say yes, finally. As I literally came my brains out. I wasn't aware it was a thing. At least not until now.

His groan behind me before he finally let me go was the whipped cream on my sex sundae. I landed face first on the mattress sometime between that and a sweet kiss between my shoulder blades.

At least, I thought that was what it was. Maybe it was just him losing his balance after coming.

I wasn't sure I cared.

Post-sex bliss was a concept I didn't have much experience with. It was hard to think around.

He dragged his chin between my shoulder and neck. "You can stop saying thank you now."

"What?"

"You kept saying thank you. If I wasn't already coming, it might have distracted me." He huffed out a laugh and nipped at my jaw. "But you're welcome." Then he slid off of me and I covered my face with my hand.

Well, that was perfect. I'd gone from Nuts Lady to Thank You Girl.

Never a boring moment between us.

I flopped onto my back and stared at the ceiling. My bra was still on and the bed had moved out a good foot from where we'd started with it. All in all, I'd call that a spectacular nooner. Or was it a tryst if it was after three and before dinner? Hmm.

Dare cleared his throat and I sat up.

He leaned against the doorjamb of my bedroom. Whoa, how had he gotten so far away so fast?

"Not that it's not incredibly tempting to go for another round, but I have to go back to work for a few hours before I…" His gaze flicked down to my legs and the very naked rest of me. He crossed his arms and fisted his hands under his biceps.

Why was that so delicious? I'd never been the kind of woman to go for the jock or gym guys. Not that I thought Dare was necessarily into that either, but he was in shape somehow.

I didn't know much about him. Did I want to?

I kind of liked this physical, no strings thing we had going.

Overthinking again, Kelsey.

I glanced around the room and spotted my cutoffs next to his foot. Very nice white socked foot. That surprised me a little. The clean part, no, but that they were so white. Or maybe they were fresh out of the package like half of mine? Hmm.

He followed my gaze and bent down to get my shorts. "Looking for these?" He dangled them from his finger.

"Yes." I reached out for them, but kept myself crunched forward on the bed. Not the most attractive angle. I was going to need to clean the stupid mattress because we had definitely defiled it.

Not sure Febreze was going to cut it.

He arched a brow at me with a half grin. "Are you hiding yourself from me? I was all up in that a few minutes ago."

"That was different."

He laughed and tossed the shorts at me. "You're something, Nuts Lady. Or do I get to go with Thank You Lady now?"

I narrowed my eyes at him as I quickly stepped into the shorts and tugged them up sans underwear. God, I needed a shower. What was the booty call protocol? Kick him out? Offer him a beer? Then again, they were mystery beers. But they were sealed and they didn't seem to bother him the other day.

I blew out a breath and snatched a T-shirt off the pile of laundry on a box. "How about Kelsey," I said after I pulled on the shirt.

"Is that your name?"

I rolled my eyes and pushed him out the door with a laugh. "Think you're a funny guy."

"Not usually. You bring it out in me."

My belly went to mush and I shook my head at myself.

Nope. Do not be charmed by your two-day-stand.

That wasn't how it worked. I didn't think so anyway.

"Is this how I get treated after bringing you a bed and putting it together for you?"

"Well, we christened it too. Don't forget that."

"Oh, I won't," he said over his shoulder.

I blushed. "It really was too generous of you. I'll pay you back."

He shook his head. "You needed it."

I wasn't used to anyone doing anything for me. Of course my folks had done what they could to help out when I'd impulsively moved to Crescent Cove, but they were on a fixed income.

And I was my own woman, dammit.

"I could have gotten one." On credit.

"Now you don't need to. Just talk up Beck to whoever sees it and likes it." He frowned as he opened the front door to my apartment. "Not that I mean you should immediately show someone the bed."

I was single and could show my bed to whomever I liked. But the idea of anyone else doing with me what we'd just done was really hard to picture. And I wasn't sure I'd get the image of Dare kneeling over me with that impressive bit of hardware out of my head anytime soon.

"You're blushing again."

"Curse of my Scottish blood."

"Not Irish?"

I shook my head. "Well, maybe. Who knows? The Scottish and the Irish often have very mixed bloodlines."

"Is that right?"

I nibbled on my lower lip. "Sorry. Lots of useless trivia in my brain."

"It's cute."

"Cute?" I didn't want to be cute. Five minutes ago, I was a ball of exploding orgasms.

He leaned down and nipped my lower lip. "See ya around, Thank You Girl." Then he was gone.

I closed the door and thunked my forehead against the wood. From hot to girl next door in less than ten minutes. That had to be a land speed record.

Not that I had time to think about that. I had a first-grade game plan to come up with.

Even if part of me wanted to chase after Dare and prove him wrong.

SEVEN

September seemed to go by in a blink. It took me a few weeks to get the hang of building a new curriculum. Kindergarten was my favorite grade, but I'd done a lot of my undergrad work in middle school. Finding the right balance for children who were going to school all day for the first time was…exhausting.

Actually, everything seemed exhausting.

"Miss Kelsey?"

I looked up from my lesson planner screen that I'd been zoning out on. "Yes, Weston."

The little boy wrinkled his nose, twisting his fingers into the hem of his polo shirt. "I hafta go to the bathroom."

I resisted the urge to wince. The nervous twitch could've been caused by a number of things. Until the screech that came from the back of the room. I examined his fingers closer and saw the purple color staining the material.

Laurie Hamilton stood up at the back of the room and spun around. "Gurt. He put gurt on me!"

I stood up. "Weston."

"I didn't. I swear."

I sighed. "Then why is your hand all sticky?"

He dragged the palm of his hand down his khakis. "No, see." He held up his hand. It was still outlined with GoGurt, the favored snack time choice for many of the students.

"First of all, it's not snack time for another…" I looked up at the clock.

"Hour," Wes said glumly.

Well, at least he was listening when we went over how to tell the hands on the clock. "Exactly. And I don't know about you, but I like to actually eat my yogurt."

"I do too. But she did it."

Laurie ran up the center aisle, still screeching. "My princess hair!"

"All right, hang on."

But Laurie would not be calmed. Waterworks sprang from her huge blue eyes and her face went red and blotchy. In between each hiccuping sob, a random word came out. *Dress, pony, magical.* I wasn't sure how they fit together until she spun around and her long blond hair was matted with yogurt.

The dancing tail of ribbons in her hair ended in stars and were now smeared with grape GoGurt.

Perfect.

I glanced over at Weston. "Did you do this?"

He fisted his hands at his sides. "No."

"He did," Laurie screeched.

"Okay, honey. We'll fix it, but you have to calm down." I took her hand and brought her over to my desk where I had my emergency repair kit. Baby wipes, Tide Pen, prewrapped cheap brush. I was ready for anything. Another compartment had things for a more bloody event.

I took my kit and led Laurie to the classroom sink. "Weston, you too."

"No!" Laurie cried out again.

Patience. I had it. I'd been trained to find it and bake it into the marrow of my bones, but it was Friday. And my patience quota had died out when we'd made handprint leaves for the tree yesterday.

With paint.

I was officially frustrated. At least I still had plenty of soap at the small sink we had in the classroom. "I have to clean you both up. Wes, please wash your hands first."

"I gotta go to the bathroom, Miss Kelsey."

"Do you really have to go? Or just so you won't get into trouble?"

He started dancing from side to side and I sighed. "Go."

Wes took off at a run.

"Take the hall pass," I called out.

I sagged a little at the smear of yogurt he left behind on my desk. Where had that come from?

"Miss Kelsey!" Laurie stomped.

"Miss Hamilton, you did not just stomp your foot at me."

"But my hair." Huge tears rolled down her face.

"We'll fix it."

"How?"

I shook my pink bag. "I have magic in this bag, but we'll start with washing your hands too."

She sighed dramatically and turned to the sink made for the crew of six and seven-year-olds that I had to wrangle daily. I winced at the glops of yogurt dripping down her hair and on the back of her uniform.

I started with paper towels for the worst of it and unclipped her pretty barrette. I'd wash that by hand. The ribbons were in a rainbow of colors with stars at the ends of each.

Princess wear in the extreme.

Knowing her mother as I did, they'd probably made it, for goodness sakes. "We'll get most of it out and I'll put your hair in a braid until you can get home and wash it. How's that sound?"

Laurie hiccuped out a breath. "Okay."

"Can you tell me what happened?"

"He put it in my hair on purpose!"

"Miss Hamilton…"

"He wasn't s'posed to eat his snack yet. I told him. But he did not listen. And then there was slime in my hair!"

"Okay, okay. It'll be fine. Nothing a little shampoo and the washer can't fix. I promise."

"Mama is going to be so sad. We just made the pretty princess clip."

"I have it on good authority that your mom will be just fine. We're going to fix it. I happen to be a professional washer of princess items."

"You are?"

"I sure am."

I glanced over at the class. Most were still busy with their worksheets, but there was a good handful of them craning their necks to see us. Especially the class snoop, Olivia.

"Miss Prince, are you done with your worksheet?" I called out.

"Yes, Miss Kelsey."

Of course she was. Smart little stinker was always done first. "Then maybe you can help someone else quietly?"

I was taking my sanity into my hands by offering her up to the class at large, but I needed at least five more minutes. I got most of the stickiness out of Laurie's hair and quickly plaited it into a braid that would hide the worst of the mess.

I attacked her uniform with water, Tide pen, and the hand dryer in the room. By the time I was done, Laurie was laughing. I took her hand and brought her back into the main classroom.

Wes was peeking in from the hallway.

I patted Laurie's shoulder and told her to go back to her desk.

"You may all take out your snacks." Everyone lifted the little hinged tops to their desks and took out their one snack item that was allowed out of their lunch bags.

It was much easier to keep them focused when they had a quick break. And it cut my day into thirds. Also very helpful.

Wes finally reentered the classroom and I quickly ushered him back out into the hall. "Can you tell me what happened, Mr. Kramer?"

"No."

I crouched down in front of him to look him in the eye. "Why not?"

"Because you won't care anyway. It's just stupid."

"Of course I do."

"No you don't. Just what princess Laurie says."

"You can tell me."

"It don't matter. Can I just go back inside?"

"Wes, you can tell me."

Instead of answering, he just put an even more mutinous look on his face.

"I thought you and Laurie were friends."

"Used to be. Not anymore. She likes Jeffrey better. Whatever." He brushed by me and into the room.

"Weston."

My warning tone didn't seem to deter him. He just walked faster into the room.

Sighing, I stood up. Parent-teacher night was tonight. Just in time.

I touched the splatter on the doorjamb. "Dammit," I muttered.

More yogurt. Perfect.

"Did you say a swears, Miss Kelsey?"

I slammed my molars together as Olivia stepped in front of me. Of course it had to be this one who overheard me. "Weren't you supposed to be eating your snack?"

"I have to wash my hands first, Miss Kelsey. I don't want a sick tummy like Jessica yesterday."

"No, you're right." Three of the kids had been out with the stomach flu this week. I'd used it as a germ lesson and a lot of the kids were taking it to heart. "All right then. Off you go."

It was going to be a very long afternoon. I followed Olivia to the sink to wash my own hands and glanced over at the room as a whole. My kids—because yes, even after only a few weeks they were my kids—were eating quietly. There were a few snickers as Weston took his seat.

He simply folded his arms and stared downward.

Laurie stood next to Jeffrey as she played with the tail of her braid. She kept tossing pissed looks at Wes. Not that he looked up at all. He kept frowning at his desk until his brows snapped down over his blue eyes.

I blinked.

I'd seen that look before. But where?

"Miss Kelsey?" I turned my attention to Olivia and assisted her with pulling off a clean paper towel.

The niggling faded into helping three of the kids with their juice boxes. Making sure they were all still eating, I glanced around the room one more time and moved to my desk to check the roster of parents.

Not only was I too tired to think, I also had my first parent-teacher night to contend with. I'd taken over the last kindergarten class, so I hadn't had to worry about doing that before. It was a whole new experience in a Catholic school. The first half of them were coming in tonight, the other half on Monday.

I sat down and sucked in a grateful breath at the moment of quiet. I snuck my phone out of my desk and shot a quick text to Ally about bringing a change of clothes for Laurie. Helped to be friends with her mother. I also skimmed for more details on the baby shower for Sage.

A knock on my door had me shoving my phone away. Luckily, it was just Caleb, the teacher from across the hall, in the skinny window and not one of the sisters.

I quickly scanned the room and headed for the door.

"Ohhh." Came from the back of the room as Laurie, Olivia, and Jemma noticed who it was.

I shot a look over my shoulder and the girls laughed and went back to their conversation.

"Hi, Caleb. What's up?"

"Just checking in. I was in the boys room and noticed a little…waterfall."

I blew out a breath. "Thanks for letting me know. Had a little GoGurt malfunction."

"Happens all the time." He leaned into the jamb and I had to take a step back. "Ready for tonight?"

I gave him a small smile. "As I'll ever be."

"Just remember the parents are usually freaking out before they come in. Massage the moms."

I arched a brow. I just bet he massaged a few of the mothers. "Thanks for the tip."

"I just like to be helpful."

With getting women out of their panties. "I really appreciate it. First parent-teacher conference in a new school." I stifled the urge to babble and engage with him. I was naturally friendly, but giving this guy an inch meant entering Flirt City, and I was trying desperately not to get on the Caleb Harem radar. I didn't need any trouble with the principal, nor was I interested.

He rubbed a hand over his biceps. "We should go out after. Trade horror stories and meltdowns."

My stomach twisted. I had to physically swallow down a wash of acid. "I think by the end of it, I'll be ready for my couch and some wine and that's about it."

"I'm happy to help out there."

I just bet he was. "Thanks for letting me know about the bathrooms."

"Right." Caleb grinned and winked. "Anytime."

I moved to close the door and the acid bubbled up again. And it so wasn't going down. This time, it wasn't because of unwanted attention. "Caleb, can you..." I pushed past him into the hall and pointed toward the door to my classroom, then made a dash for the ladies' room.

"Oh, crap."

I heard Caleb's voice and I so wished it was crap. Other end, alas.

I barely made it down the hall to the bathroom, and into the stall before I heaved over the bowl. The entire room fuzzed and I tried not to think too closely about being face to face with a public toilet—*ugh* —which only made me toss my cookies all the more.

Thankfully, I was blessedly alone in the bathroom. It was bad enough to be in this state, let alone for someone else to hear it. The wash of sweat on my neck faded and the room evened out.

I sagged against the cool metal wall of the stall. I so didn't need to get this stupid stomach flu the kids were passing around. Sage's baby shower was this weekend.

After staggering to my feet, I made a bee-line for the sink. I rinsed my mouth and washed up, then ran the cool water over my wrists until I stopped shaking. I flattened my hand over my middle, wondering if that was the last of it.

I really didn't want to have to call down to the office for someone to cover for me. And I had half a dozen parents coming to see me tonight.

That was just lovely. Luckily, I kept a travel toothbrush and toothpaste in my huge bag. Being a teacher, I'd learned to be prepared for anything. I only had twenty-three little humans to take care of. No big thing.

I headed back down the hall. Caleb was passing back and forth between my classroom and his own. He spotted me and frowned. "You okay?"

"No amount of Purell was going to stop me from getting the stupid stomach thing going around evidently."

"Nope. Not when they are always putting their grubby little hands on you."

"Grubby?"

"You know what I mean."

I did. Caleb was one of those guys who thought teaching was the in-between time between vacations. I'd figured that out a week into the school year. I'd had an inkling already from his reputation, but it was obvious considering how he treated his students.

I wasn't entirely sure he knew all the names of the kids in his class without a name tag.

"Do you want me to call in the relief sub?"

"No. I don't need to bother Adrienne yet. I'll just sip water and find some animal crackers in the cabinet."

"You sure?"

"Definitely. I've had the real flu and this isn't it. Could be by tomorrow, but for now, I'm good."

"This place is one big petri dish, man. Well, holler if you need help." He was already heading toward his room when he said it.

Obviously, he meant every word.

Not.

If he wasn't getting his tongue down my throat, he wasn't interested. And he sure as hell wasn't interested in me right now. Maybe I needed to keep the stomach flu as a backup to make him steer clear of me. It was a thought.

I made it through the rest of the day by sheer force of will. The kids were happy to have a day of crafts. Even the pile of Play-Doh scraps I had to clean up afterward was worth the relatively low-stress afternoon.

We used molds of numbers and did some easy addition and subtraction so the day wasn't a total loss. By the time the bell rang, I was ready to crawl under the desk, but at least I hadn't had to run for the bathroom again.

As the kids filed out, I collapsed into one of the little chairs and put my head down on the desk. The nausea was gone, but I could literally have blinked out.

I wasn't entirely sure I hadn't when I heard Ally's voice from the doorway. "Hey, you okay?"

"Yeah, just one of those days." I got to my feet a little unsteadily. I braced myself on the back of the little chair and cursed my height. The kid-sized proportions made it feel like I had to lean down to the floor.

Ally rushed forward. "Hey."

"Don't get too close. Afraid I may be next on the hit parade for that stomach flu."

Ally took three huge steps back.

I laughed. "Yeah, no need to have that go around your house again."

"No, thank you."

"I'm glad you're here anyway."

"Yeah, what happened with Laurie?"

"Not sure what's up. As far as I was aware, she and Weston Kramer were good friends."

"Ahh." Ally winced. "Don't tell Seth, but Laurie is a bit of a femme fatale."

I laughed. "Is that so?"

"Yeah. She's been talking about—"

"Jeffrey?"

"Yes." Ally sighed. "We aren't even in high school yet. How am I going to survive this?"

"Well, I'm not entirely convinced it was on purpose, but Wes got one of those tubes of GoGurt all over the back of her uniform and her hair. And that pretty bow." I moved to my desk. "I managed to get it clean, but you might want to swish it in some watered down detergent and hang it up to dry."

"Look at you." Ally took the ribbons. "She found one on Pinterest and it was like thirty dollars. We made this one for five."

"Impressive mama."

She shrugged. "Hello, Michaels' coupons."

I laughed. "Don't I know it. Now we need those same coupons on Etsy."

We both laughed. We shared the planner obsession that was rocking the internet. We'd even had a few planner nights when we could squeeze it in until school had gotten into full-swing and my life had suddenly become a series of tests to prep for and programs for the kids.

Not to mention the never-ending meetings the academy seemed to have. I should be happy the principal was so hands-on, but it was exhausting.

"Well, I'll save you a trip for parent-teacher night if you want. Unless Seth wants a face-to-face."

"No, he's good. And I don't really want to burst his 'my daughter isn't dating until she's thirty' bubble."

"Well, she certainly has a lot of friends. But she's bright and she's done very well on the handful of tests we've had so far. Her reading comprehension is already above-average. So just keep doing what you're doing. It's obviously working."

Ally made a little gesture with her hand as if she was wicking away moisture. "That's good to hear."

"You knew she was doing well. She's in a happy home and can't stop talking about you and Seth. Well, in between being Queen Bee in here."

Ally rolled her eyes. "Not shocking. She's Queen Bee at home too."

"These are the meetings I love. Unfortunately, I have a few bad news ones to give tonight. Most of the kids here are amazing though. I can't complain in the least. Even if I'm used to kindergarteners."

"I know. I hope everything's okay there. About ten of the kids in Laurie's kindergarten class went to the public school."

I certainly hoped everything was okay. I didn't want to go anywhere. I liked my apartment, and had even bought a cactus. And I hadn't killed it. Then again, it had only been a month.

Just give me time.

"So far, so good. It's been an adjustment, but I love my kids."

"Well, Laurie loves you too. All she talks about is school and boys." Ally sighed. "Boys. God, save me."

"We've got a few nuns here that can help there."

"If Seth had his way, she'd be in the convent already."

We both laughed and Ally checked her phone. "Well, that's Ruth in the car, making sure I'm not dead."

"Go ahead. Unless you have any questions, Laurie's a joy as far as I'm concerned. I'll talk to Weston's dad and we'll get it sorted."

"What about Wes?" The deep baritone made a shiver race right up my spine and explode in my brain. I *knew* that voice.

Far too well.

EIGHT

I JAMMED MY HANDS INTO THE POCKETS OF MY FRESHLY PRESSED DARK jeans. I never freaking ironed. It felt like my whole body was starched right now. But the worst part was hearing the woman I couldn't get out of my head say my kid's name.

Did I know Kelsey was a freaking teacher?

I'd been so busy working doubles to pay for the central air and heating unit I'd had to buy for my house that I hadn't really had time to ask Wes more than a passing question about school. Not that my kid did much more than grunt at me about the subject. He was more interested in playing football with his cousins and an unrelenting obsession with Voltron. How that came back, I had no idea.

All I knew was that it was on a constant loop in my house. In fact, Netflix stopped asking if I was still watching. Okay, maybe that was a bit of an exaggeration, but even I knew the dialogue at this point.

And now this crazy redhead who had invaded my brain with her outrageous mouth and stupidly perfect body was responsible for molding my kid. That sounded about as wrong as something that might've come out of Kelsey's mouth, but holy fuck.

I stepped into the room and resisted the urge to tuck in the white button down shirt I'd put on instead of the dingy uniform I lived in at the shop. Parent-teacher night always put me in a mood. The nuns were forever looking at me as if I was less than because there was no wife at home.

I mean, there was my mom to help out, but Wes's mom had been out of the picture for a third of his life. And for the nuns, a single dad practically equated with "do we need to call social services on you?"

I took care of my kid, for fuck's sake.

I cleared my throat. "Is there a problem?"

"Dare." Her huge golden eyes were more than a little startled. She gave me a quick once over and I was glad for the shirttails hiding the bulge in my fucking jeans. It didn't matter that I was pissed at her, my dick was ready to play.

"Ohhh." Ally looked between us then she pressed her lips together and stifled a laugh. She hid it well enough behind a cough, but she definitely knew we'd hooked up. Women loved to fucking talk.

It wasn't like I was hiding the fact that I'd spent time with Kelsey on more than one occasion, but it wasn't anyone's business if we'd hooked up. At all.

"Laurie's fine. Don't worry about it." Ally patted my arm as she passed me. "They're just in a little fight."

"Over what?" I didn't want to ask. I didn't want to discuss any of this, but I knew I had to.

Kelsey licked her lips as she twisted her fingers together. "I tried to talk to Weston about—"

"Wes."

Her brow furrowed. "Yes, Wes."

I wasn't going to let her put him in a troublemaker box. He was a good kid with a shit ton of energy. I tried not to think about his teacher last year who tried to convince me to put him on Ritalin or some shit because he didn't pay attention. He didn't pay attention because he was bored, and that was it.

I bunched my fists in my pockets and stared her down.

Ally glanced at the door. "Do you want me to stay or—"

Kelsey sighed. "It's okay, Ally. I have this."

"No, I want her here to figure it out between us," I said, well-aware my voice sounded defensive. But if there was an issue, I wanted it settled now.

Kelsey smoothed her palm over the side of her leg. "It was a silly little misunderstanding. I tried to talk to Wes about it, but he wouldn't talk to me. I'm not exactly sure on the particulars other than the fact that yogurt ended up down the back of Laurie's hair and uniform."

"Yogurt?" I was dumbfounded. I'd figured he'd thrown Play-Doh at Laurie or something. "He loves that shit—stuff. He'd never waste it. I can't get him to stop eating it, for God's sake."

"I have a feeling it was an accident, but he was very embarrassed and angry. I can't help him if he won't tell me what's wrong. And if it was an accident, we could have fixed it much easier."

"Yeah, well, he's prideful."

"Shocking," Kelsey muttered.

Ally let out a bawdy laugh. "Sounds about right. And Laurie overreacted, I'm sure. It got in her hair and that girl loves her hair." She waved it off. "Again, it's no big deal. She'll forget all about it by tomorrow."

Kelsey nodded at Ally. "Thanks for understanding. And coming in."

"Feel better. I'll see you Sunday unless you're not feeling up to it."

Kelsey twisted her long hair into a tumbling mass of silk over her shoulder. "I feel much better."

I frowned. What did that mean?

As soon as Ally left, Kelsey trained those golden eyes on me. "You're early, Dare. In fact, I was expecting someone named…" She moved to her desk and flipped open an iPad.

"Charles."

"Right, Charles Kramer. I definitely didn't put two and two together. Actually, I'm not completely sure I knew your last name. We sort of didn't…"

"Talk?"

Her cheeks flushed. "No, not much." She wore black dress pants and some sort of coppery sweater that made her hair look like the pale edges of fire. She was goddamn beautiful and almost untouchable in her teacher gear.

I wanted to muss her up.

I wanted to run out the damn door.

This was not cool at all.

Especially since it was obvious she had more to say about Wes and I had a feeling not all of it was good.

She waved her hand. "Have a seat, Mr. Kramer."

"Really? That's where we're going with this?"

She huffed out a breath. "What do you want me to call you? Pizza Guy?" Her cheeks got even redder.

My eyebrow rose. "Not sure you want me to call you Thank You Girl."

She moved behind her desk and sat down. "How about we just go with Kelsey and Dare, hmm?"

That prim and proper voice was so at odds with the woman I'd originally met at the bar and again at her apartment. I was used to the girl who would blurt out anything. She definitely was like Sage in that regard. But this woman? The buttoned-up elementary school teacher?

Yeah, no, that didn't compute.

I glanced down at the miniature desk she wanted me to sit at and gave her a bland look before using the desk as a chair. No way was I folding my six-foot-two self into that chair. Fuck, no.

"I'm early because I have to go back to work. I hope that's all right with you."

"Certainly." She folded her hands. "Wes is a great kid. I don't have any real issues to go over with you—" She broke off as I stood. "Where are you going?"

"Then I'll tell him to be more careful and we're good here, right?"

"No. Not quite."

I fisted my hands at my sides. "Then what?"

She got up from her desk and came around to lean on the edge. "Mr.—" At my almost growl, she cut herself off. "Dare…" She scrubbed her palms over her pants. "This is awkward."

"Because we've been naked? Or because you don't want to tell me my kid has a problem?"

"Well, I certainly see where Wes gets his defensiveness. And that's what I want to talk to you about, but only if we can have a conversation like adults."

I crowded her against the desk, boxing her in with a hand on each side of her hips. "You were adult enough to take me into your body a few weeks ago."

Her pupils blew wide and her fingers clutched the edge of her desk beside mine. "We're not talking about that."

"Then stop trying to talk to me like I'm a fucking stranger."

Her gaze kept bouncing from my mouth to my eyes to my neck and back again. She licked her lips. "I'm your son's teacher."

"And I'm annoyingly hot for teacher evidently."

"You did not just quote Van Halen to me."

"I might kiss you just because you know the reference." I leaned into her. "I might kiss you just because."

"Is this guy bothering you, Kelsey?"

I resisted the urge to snarl at the interruption. I was already hard as hell and her sharp orange scent was making me crazy. As it was, I'd gone to look for blood oranges in the produce department just to see if that was indeed the smell I couldn't stop thinking about. That had been the name on the bottle in her bathroom, but an artificial scent might not compare to the real thing.

It was damn close.

But it wasn't Kelsey.

And my brain was definitely not engaged right now. Unless you counted the primal lizard part that wanted to rip out the douchetwat's throat for interrupting us.

Kelsey pushed me back and shifted toward the guy in the doorway. I still hadn't looked away from her, since she was my entire focus.

"Caleb, um, no. Of course not." She smoothed her hair away from her face.

What the hell was that about? I finally dragged my attention from her to the doorway. Straight-laced teacher type. Was she actually worried about this dude seeing us together?

I straightened. I was good enough to hook up with, but not to be seen with. I'd been there before. Nice girls only liked the gutter when their ankles were up toward the ceiling.

Or…

I huffed out a half laugh. Or *this* was her kind of guy, not me. "Sorry. Didn't realize I was poaching."

"You were what?" She elbowed me in the ribs. "No one is poaching on anyone and we're at school, for Pete's sake. Neither of you should be saying the things you do here."

I folded my arms and crowded into her again. "Saying things like what?"

"Are you serious right now? Are you going to pee around me or something?" She pushed me back a step, then glanced at the douchenozzle. "Never mind. This is ridiculous."

I finally recognized the guy hovering in the hallway now that I had my head in the game and not ready to dive between her fucking thighs. Beck's little brother was a teacher here. And douche still applied. He thought his marathon boy and gym rat muscles made him a man.

More than a few women had fallen for his brand of charm.

Personally, I wanted to use his head as a soccer ball whenever he was around me and his brother. Which wasn't often. He was too worried about the closest single woman in a five-mile radius.

"Dare." Caleb hovered at the threshold of her classroom. "I didn't realize you were friends."

I was pretty sure the fucknut wanted to choke on that word.

Kelsey sighed. "I'm fine, Caleb. Thanks for checking on me. Dare and I were just…talking."

Without thinking, my hand coasted along her lower back.

She looked up at me again with eyebrows climbing for her damn hairline. I dropped my hand.

Caleb puffed up his chest, but he didn't come any closer. "If you're sure."

"She's sure," I said darkly. Besides, what was this kid going to do? I could break him with my pinky.

"I can speak for myself, thank you." She gave me a sharp look, then Caleb a tight smile. "I can handle myself. He's harmless."

I gave her a serious dose of side eye. I'd show her how harmless I was as soon as we were alone. She stomped on my foot and winced for her trouble. I had steel-toe boots for a reason.

"All right. I'm right across the hall if you need me." He melted out into the dark.

"Caleb?"

He rushed back in. "Yes?"

"Close the door for me?"

I resisted the urge to smile big. Instead, I left my face stony. Caleb was afraid of me on a good day. Today was not a good day.

Caleb nodded and shut the door before glaring at me through the skinny window.

Pussy.

"You don't get to do that. Just because we slept together."

"Twice. I'm entirely sure it was memorable, darlin'. You screamed my name multiple times, each time. Even said—"

"Do not say what I know you're going to say." She stabbed a finger into my chest. "I can't believe this."

"It's a small town. Did you really think we wouldn't run into each other again outside of when it's convenient for you? I work two doors down from your apartment."

"Of course not. But this makes it a little more precarious. I'm your son's teacher."

"Considering most of the teachers in this school are married, I'm sure there's some overlap all over the place."

She huffed out a breath. "That's not the point."

"What is it then? That we slept together? Or that you're ashamed about it?"

"I'm not ashamed. Well, not really. I mean, I have needs. Every woman does. That's not the point!" Her voice rose with each sentence.

I placed my hands on her shoulders and shifted her toward me again, lowering my mouth until we were a few millimeters apart. "Then what's the problem?"

"Conflict of interest is the problem." She swayed a little and her face went as white as my shirt.

"Kelsey." I grabbed her elbow.

"Oh, God." She staggered away from me and slapped a hand over her mouth.

The look on her face had me reacting. I knew it well. I had a six-year-old. I spotted a small trash bin next to her desk and handed it to her just before she spewed. "That's it. Just get it out."

"Get away from me."

I huffed out a sigh. "Not my first rodeo, darlin'." I gathered her hair back at the nape of her neck. "You all right?"

"No. I want to die."

"Didn't take you for the weak constitution type."

She held the back of her hand against her mouth. "Flu. Kids." She moaned and went for another round.

I winced and gently led her to the sink across the room. "You done?"

"I think so."

I pushed her hair back and gave her a once over. Her color was coming back. Slowly. "Go on and wash your mouth out."

"I could just die."

"You should have been in the shop when we got a batch of bad clams. This is nothing."

She ran the water and rinsed her mouth. "Can you grab my bag from the bottom right drawer of my desk?"

I frowned at her, but figured she was upright enough for me to get there and back before she pitched forward. Maybe. She hunched over the sink and rested her head against the faucet.

I opened her desk and found a purse the size of my entire torso. Jesus. It took me two tries to get it free, but then I was back beside her. "Here."

She plucked a green bag out from the bottom with barely a look.

How she knew which bag was which among the six in there, I had no idea. But the sharp scent of mint disrupted the sour aroma.

While she was brushing the sick out of her mouth, I found a trash can liner and dumped the little wastebasket into the bag and tied it off. The little plastic bin was pretty and frilly like a girl. And also had a basket weave that would never recover. Better to just put it all out of its misery.

I put the bag near the door and went back to her. "All right?"

She blew out a slow breath. "Yes. We've had three kids out with the stomach bug. It's not shocking I got it."

I leaned forward and touched my lips to her forehead. "No fever."

She blinked up at me. "No. I'm probably in the contagious phase. Which doesn't bode well for you."

I shrugged. "I rarely get sick. Motor oil in my veins."

She tied her hair back into a low tail. "I hope that's true. It's not fun in the least. At least according to the moms I've talked to."

"Maybe you should cancel the rest of the meetings tonight. Just in case. I can, uh, take you home if you want."

"Yeah, I think I'll send out an email to the other parents, but I can get home on my own."

"Are you sure?"

"I'm a big girl."

"Yeah, but I'm going back to work anyway, so I'm right there."

"Then I won't have my car."

"I can have one of the guys pick it up."

She rested a hand against my chest. "I'll be okay."

"All right. I can take a hint."

She gnawed on her lower lip. "It's not that. I hope you know that."

"Sure, whatever."

"And that's what your son does. He obviously has learned it from you."

I folded my arms.

"That too. Look, Dare. He's an amazing kid. I'm not disputing that, so don't get all…growly."

"I'm not."

"You are. But he's obviously got something going on at home, or because of this thing with Laurie. Just promise me you'll talk to him."

"I will."

"Good." She stepped back and I immediately wanted to pull her closer again.

And that was stupid. Very stupid. Obviously, she had her own reasons for not wanting to start up something with me. My own list of reasons was about as long as my arm.

The top three reasons all included my kid.

Now I had to talk to him about some girl. Seth Hamilton's kid no less. Wes was six. Just the thought of girls at his age made me want to hide under the hood of a car. Maybe I could teach Wes how to take apart an engine.

Surely that would be easier.

Fuck.

"Feel better." I backed away and crossed to the door. I snagged the trash bag as I strode out and didn't look back.

Even if a strong part of me wanted to gather Kelsey close and take care of her. That was the most dangerous part of all.

I lengthened my stride down the hall, dumping the bag in one of the janitor bins on my way out the door.

I jammed my aviators on my face and put her out of my mind.

I'd done it before. I could do it again.

One of these days, it would finally stick.

NINE

I SLEPT ON MY LUMPY COUCH. IT MADE ME WONDER IF HALF MY stomach queasiness came from the smell of the ancient fabric. Which started me down the path of cleaning my entire apartment at dawn. All eight hundred square feet of it. It didn't take long.

Just like my unpacking, though I'd stretched out that awful task as long as humanly possible.

Since I didn't have another episode—yay extra strength Febreze and baking powder trick on Pinterest—I went full tilt on the baby shower prep for Sage. At least the non-cooking things. No need to infect the world if I was sick for some reason and just not showing symptoms.

Well, except those two exceptional moments yesterday.

Someday, I'd stop cringing about it.

When I was ninety maybe.

I worked on shower prep for a bit and then passed the rest of the day on my sofa. Watching TV and surfing online seemed to be about the extent of what I had energy for.

As was driven home to me with sterling clarity when I woke up with my neck bent at an unnatural angle and my face smushed into a Febrezed cushion the next morning.

What was my damage lately? This was like a super stealth bug or something. Kept coming and going without warning. But today was the shower, and I needed to get my butt moving.

Making a fleet of paper cranes from a tutorial I found on YouTube seemed safe. I could always spray them down with Lysol. Not that they should hold germs in the oxygenated air—thank you, weird science trivia lodged in my brain. In that regard, I shouldn't be causing any problems with the women and children who would probably be in attendance.

Before I'd fallen asleep last night, I'd spent a couple hours swearing at my smart TV since the little screen of my phone wasn't enough. Apparently, I needed the videos approximately forty-two inches in size to learn how to make the paper cranes. I fell asleep dreaming of them.

I really had to stop sleeping on the sofa. Especially before nine o'clock. What was I, seven years old? It wasn't as if I didn't have a truly stupendous new bed to sleep on. But sleeping there made me think of Dare, and thinking of Dare made me think of wall-knocking sex or puke.

Right now, neither of those options did much for me. So…couch it was.

Lame. So lame.

After a shower and no other stomach episodes, I used part of the morning to finish my little project.

I started with the big ones that we'd hang from the trees in the backyard. When I only mangled fifteen of the hundred sheets of origami paper or so, I moved on to little ones that would perch on top of the cupcakes from Sugar Rush, a super cute bakery in town. Okay, possibly the only bakery.

When my hand started cramping, I switched to texting Ally to make sure everything was ready.

I got three replies and finally a photo reply with her middle finger in crystal clear focus with a half dozen tables already set up in her backyard. Okay, so I was being a little anal about the party.

But I really wanted it to go well. I liked having girlfriends. Was it so wrong to show them that?

I frowned down at the pile of paper cranes. Okay, maybe I was overdoing it a little. But then again, Sage was the one who told me stories about how many of these crazy paper animals Oliver made her.

I sniffled and wiped my hand under my nose. Why the hell were my eyes leaking? I huffed out a breath and got up to wash my hands and face and blow my nose. Maybe I was sicker than I'd thought. There was no reason for me to be getting all teary about paper cranes.

Just because I'd never had a guy in my life who cared enough about me to obsessively make little paper animals didn't mean my life was incomplete. And okay, so what if my ex-boyfriend had treated me more like an afterthought than his partner? That was on me too. I was the one willing to take scraps.

That was so over. Crescent Cove was my fresh start.

I exhaled and waved a hand near my eyes to dispel the rest of the tears then stalked over to my phone and opened my music app. I didn't have to sit here in silence and cry about dumb stuff.

Because the dumb stuff pushed me into thinking too much about a certain single dad I had no business worrying about. He hadn't even had the decency to tell me he had a child, let alone that said child was in my class.

Who got the name Dare from Charles, dammit? Not that Charles suited him. Maybe Charlie, but definitely not the name fit for a royal. A guy with *that* name would not have the kind of oral prowess that made me dream about him four weeks-plus later. Even just remembering it made my toes tingle.

And other things.

The fact that I'd never had such things happen between my legs in my life could account for some of it. Like never to the tenth power of ever. But that didn't mean I should still be thinking about him.

I couldn't even do a one-night stand properly. Okay, so it was two nights, but it wasn't even like it was a wild weekend. Two distinct moments of madness.

Three if I counted the way he pushed me up against my desk. Until memories of almost tossing my cookies in his face made me reach for my phone. Talk about ruining the moment. I didn't need to relive that particular personal movie reel.

Cranking the volume on the Matt Nathanson song, "Faster," did the trick. I shook my booty a little as I gathered the cranes carefully and put them in a huge box to take to Ally's house.

Next was the little name cards for the mason jar favors. I should have done them a week ago, but getting the reports ready for the parent-teacher meetings had consumed most of my evenings. Falling asleep before nine each night wasn't exactly helpful for getting things done either.

As I finished the tag for the last of the mason jars on my counter, they all began to rattle from the rumble of something downstairs with a heavy bass. I'd put on my cleaning playlist, but growl rock was not my preferred genre. Nor could my little speakers hit that volume. I reached over for my phone and hit pause.

Sure enough, music was pulsing through my floorboards. One person had moved into the other end of the building on my floor, but the storefront beneath me had been empty even prior to me moving in.

I stuffed my phone into the back pocket of my jeans and went to investigate. The blast of the scent of coffee when I opened my door threatened to put me on my knees.

Whoa, nelly.

I drank my morning coffee to perk up my brain, but it had never been a staple in my life beyond that. In fact, a Diet Coke was just as effective for me. I crept down the stairs to the lobby of the building. The unmistakable scent of chocolate and coffee beans hung in the air like a fog. The butt end of a truck blocked the double doors of the previously newspapered windows.

The old plate glass windows had been replaced with more ornate glass with gorgeous arches. A petite woman with the smallest paintbrush ever was slowly drawing something on the window in gold paint. Her lower half was moving to some internal beat that did not match the overhead song. A bright turquoise rag swished around like a tail from the back pocket of her overalls. It matched the Chucks she was wearing. A bright pink T-shirt and high lemon-blond ponytail finished out her ensemble. Oddly, the upper part of her was rock steady, as if it was completely separate from the bottom half of her.

A shrill whistle made me scrunch up my shoulders and stumble back a step as strapping guys wearing gray uniforms with a patch on the pocket that said GF pulled huge pallets of coffee through the main aisle and disappeared down the back hall.

In the middle of all the chaos was a girl—no, a woman. I hated it when people called me a girl. I was twenty-six-years-old, for heaven's sake. But my red hair and freckles made me look years younger. Especially when I couldn't be bothered with makeup.

But this woman had a startlingly angular face and an athletic body. She wore a black tank top and slightly faded black jeans with black and white Chucks. She was shouting over the deafening sounds of music and machines. Her inky hair was piled up on her head in a messy bun that I never could quite pull off and her face was completely devoid of makeup. Siberian Husky blue eyes suddenly pierced me where I stood.

"Hi."

"Who the fuck are you?" she asked.

My eyebrows shot up. "Upstairs neighbor," I shouted back.

She mouthed, "crap," under her breath. Only reason I knew that was the champion lip reading capabilities I had thanks to years of teaching kids. Five-year-olds were prime mumblers.

I put my hands on my hips as she walked around the boxes before finally stroking her hand along a very large black and purple commercial coffee machine adorned with...flames? Definitely not the same kind I'd seen in Starbucks. Nope, there was nothing standard about the beast of a thing. Or the way the woman petted it with a smile on her face.

The smile faded as she got closer to me. She gestured toward the door and I followed her out to the front of the building. We squeezed by the truck as she gave a parting order to a wiry guy with jet-black hair.

She turned to me. "Hey, sorry. I meant to give you a head's up about the cafe." She wiped her hand down her denim-clad thigh, then held it out. "I'm Macy Devereaux."

I glanced down at her hand, then at her eyes. They were a truly startling blue, and I'd never batted for the other team. At least not yet. I shook her hand. "I'm Kelsey Ford."

"Hope not a relation to the car people, because Fords blow." She winced. "Sorry. I keep trying to return the rude button, but it comes back like a zit every time."

I snorted. "I have a babble button. Return policy sucks."

Macy barked out a rusty laugh, as if she didn't use it very often. "We should be done around dinner time. Then things will quiet down."

I had the baby shower today, so that wasn't a big deal. Every day though? "The music?" I asked.

She nibbled the corner of her lower lip. "About that part."

I sighed. "As long as it's not to this level every day, we're cool."

"Oh, no. I need to hear my customers." She smirked and shoved a hank of bangs out of her face. "Rock music tends to get people moving when it comes to unloading so I usually crank it. That and it keeps conversation down to a minimum."

"Wonder if I can try that on six-year-olds."

It was Macy's turn for her eyebrows to shoot up. "Uh, not sure *Sesame Street* should ever be at that level."

"More like *Magic School Bus* these days."

She frowned. "I think I watched that as a kid."

I laughed. "You know how it goes these days. They steal all our cool stuff."

"Ain't that the truth. Not that I know too much about kids, but the stores are full of stuff that looks like glammed-up versions of our childhood stuff."

"No kids?" I asked.

"God, no." She shuddered. "I have two cats and call it good."

"Me neither." But the longing was there. I tried not to think about it much, but with everyone pregnant around me, I couldn't help but wonder.

Work usually stuffed it down. I was exhausted taking care of twenty-three six-year-olds. Did I really want to run after a toddler right now?

A flash of a little boy with bright blond hair and wary blue eyes ran through my head. Why Wes popped in my head, I didn't know. He was a great kid, but he wasn't the easiest to get to know. Or maybe that was because his father was equally as wary, and I couldn't stop thinking about him either.

I plastered on a smile. "Well, I'll let you get back to it. Sorry to interrupt."

Again, Macy gnawed on the corner of her bottom lip. "You like coffee?"

"Not really." I winced. "Probably shouldn't say that to the head barista in charge."

"Change that barista to bitch and we're close. Actually, that's probably even better. If I can get a non-coffee lover to dig my stuff…" She shrugged. "Well, it would be pretty rad."

"Rad?"

She shrugged. "Blame my brother. Anyway, come on in and try the new espresso I'm working on."

"I don't know. Espresso is kind of bitter."

"Not mine. And I have a nice chocolate kick to balance it. And to add to its addictive quality."

"I do like chocolate."

"Only assholes don't."

I laughed as I followed her back inside. She certainly said what she wanted to on the subject. I had a feeling she'd like Sage and Ally as well. They were also more into coffee than I was.

Macy rounded the counter to the huge L-shaped coffee bar, then stroked her hand down the purple beast of a machine. "What's your tolerance?"

I climbed on the rich toffee-colored stool. "Are we talking one to ten?"

She shrugged. "That works."

"Probably a three. I'm naturally a little high-strung."

"That doesn't shock me, Red." She dumped beans into a grinder and started fiddling with the pots lined up in front of her. "I make a proprietary blend, but have to wait for all my product to get here. I'm missing a truck. It's somewhere in Rochester."

"Oh, then it's coming today?"

"It better."

I frowned. "It's Sunday."

She grunted as she locked a large handled cup into place. "I'm aware." The machine hummed to life. Instead of the super loud hiss I was used to, the machine seemed to hum and vibrate.

When the espresso was extracted, my mouth literally watered. I couldn't remember the last time that had happened with anything other than the chocolate fountain at my cousin Zelda's wedding. The espresso was sharp and heavy, and almost warmed the air with the flavor and scent.

Macy steamed some milk and fiddled with something else then poured the chocolate and little metal cup of espresso together into a mug. Next came the milk with a flourish of foam. A pretty leaf appeared with a deft flick of her wrist before she pushed the mug in front of me.

"It's not overly hot. I don't like to scald my milk or the customers."

I looked down at the huge mug. It wasn't that deep, but nearly the size of a bowl. I cupped my hands around it and groaned. "That smells amazing."

"It tastes even better."

"I believe you." I took a sip and literally groaned. Pretty much as I had when Dare had done that thing with his tongue.

Macy used a rag to wipe down the spigot used to steam the milk. "I know my espresso is amazing, but not usually that good."

"What?" I swallowed another sip. "Oh, it really is. I'll need one of these every morning of my life."

Macy laughed. "Coffee doesn't make me blush."

"Oh." My flush deepened. That explained why I felt as if my temperature had risen a bazillion degrees. "Not sure anything has made me groan like that beyond one thing." I cleared my throat. "That's all."

"Well, I do call it the Chocolate Orgasm, so that's fitting."

The foam went down wrong and I coughed.

Macy smirked. "We like crazy names. Welcome to Brewed Awakening, Kels."

"What a great name."

"I thought so. The sign is coming this week."

"When do you open?"

"Halloween. My favorite holiday."

"That's awesome. We needed a decent coffee shop. You can get a good cup at the diner, but it's nothing fancy. Probably why I preferred Diet Coke."

"Blaspheme."

I laughed.

"Hey buddy, you mind not blocking my freaking bay?" Angry male reporting for duty.

"We're working here." The second guy said it with a rumble. "Piss off."

I sat up straight.

Macy swore and rushed around the bar. "Crap. Joey!" she yelled as she sprinted for the double doors.

I moved to follow, but went back for two more swallows to finish my coffee. I couldn't help the secondary groan when I heard the first male voice again.

"What did you say?"

I knew that pissy voice. I scrambled off the stool and followed Macy through the door.

Dare stood beside the truck. His huge shoulders seemed even more massive in the white tank top he was wearing. A grease smear slashed across his chest and shoulder, and the snug material emphasized his ridiculously attractive muscles.

Hell, *all* his parts were ridiculously attractive.

Parts I knew a little too well and yet not at all. We'd barely gotten our clothes all the way off before we were tearing at each other like two horny teens. Because I would have remembered the star-shaped pattern of freckles on the tanned skin between his shoulder and neck.

I probably would have traced it with my tongue.

Pull it together, Kels. Jeez.

Dare had his arms crossed over his chest and his hands fisted under his insanely ripped biceps. He was crowding into the wiry dark-haired man who had been unpacking the truck.

Dare was a good three inches taller than the guy who had to be Joey. Not that the scrappier dude was backing down. Dare let his arms fall to his sides, but it didn't stop the ripple of muscle. Instead, it seemed to only flex and vibrate more.

Had he always had so many freckles?

Focus.

Oh, but I am.

"Dare," I said breathlessly.

He shot those wicked blue eyes my way and my breath stalled. He frowned then refocused his attention on the guy. "I asked nicely." A little muscle fluttered in his jawline as his teeth clenched. "Twice. I need to get the car I'm working on out of the bay and test-drive it."

"And I told you we would be done soon."

"Okay, okay." Macy moved between them. "Joey, just drive around the corner and park in front instead of taking up half the street."

"We have two more pallets to get off the truck and we're done."

I stepped forward. "We're...friends." The frustration vibrating between the men zinged along my skin like a current. Or, possibly, it could just be because I was *this* close to Dare again. I didn't really want to think about it. I curled my fingers around Dare's forearm. "You could give him what? Twenty minutes?"

Joey's mouth thinned. "Fifteen."

"Even better." I tugged Dare inside the coffee shop. "You should try one of Macy's coffees."

"I don't like that shit." His jaw was still set and his brow was creased with a stubborn scowl.

"I guarantee you'll like hers."

Macy glanced between us. "Right. Well, I do straight coffee too, Mr…"

"Just Dare." He said it to Macy, but didn't stop glowering down at me.

I wasn't sure if it was wrong that my nipples were tight and pointing at him like a target or if it was just my natural status around Dare. I let him go and stuffed my hands in my pockets. "Just come in for a second."

"I should get back to the shop."

"It's Sunday."

"Yeah? Cars still need to be fixed on Sundays."

"Where's Wes?"

His eyebrow zinged up. "With my mom, Miss Ford."

I stabbed my finger into his chest. "It was just a simple question. And it's gorgeous outside, that's all."

"Yeah, well, I got bills to pay." He backed up and started for the door.

"Dare, wait." I glanced back at Macy and she waved me off with a look that said he was my problem.

And he was.

Because I couldn't stop thinking about him and yet kept jamming my foot into my stupid mouth at the same time. I huffed out a growl and hooked my arm through his to stop him. "Wait."

"I don't have time to stand around with you, Teach."

"Is this going to be a thing now?"

He stared down at me. "I don't know. You gonna judge me every three seconds about my kid?"

"No, of course not. He's a great boy. I was just worried about him and needed to tell you about it. Would you rather I ignore him?"

"No." He fisted his hands at his sides. "I ask him stuff. Make sure he's doing okay in school. He's not even seven yet, for fuck's sake. All he wants to do is play with a football or baseball. I figure that's a good thing."

"It is. And he's a well-adjusted kid. It doesn't matter that he only has one parent. He's obviously got a great family unit around him regardless of your single status. I mean, you are single right?"

"I wouldn't be hot for teacher if I wasn't, Kel. What kind of an asshole do you take me for?"

I huffed out an annoyed sigh. "Why do we always argue?"

"We don't always argue. We're pretty good at fucking too."

I swallowed and sagged against the brick of J&T's Automotive. "You can't say stuff like that."

He crowded into me, bracing his hand over my head. "Oh, yeah, why's that? Am I lying? Or are you just lying to yourself?"

"Of course not. And I—of course I liked it. You just don't need to call it that."

"Fucking?" He leaned down and the sharp scent of oil hit me followed by his usual crisp clean manly scent. The kind that made me want to bury my nose right into his neck.

His gaze dropped to my nipples. He brushed the back of his knuckle along one aching tip.

I couldn't help the moan that escaped. All he had to do was look at me and my body wasn't my own anymore. It was thrilling and unnerving at the same time.

"I'm all dirty right now, but I can appease you if you want." He nodded toward the dark garage. "Lay you out on the Camaro I've been working on all morning."

I let out a shaky breath.

"Wrap those long legs around my waist so I can bury myself deep." His voice was grumbly and low. "If you only knew how many nights I thought about it."

"Why didn't you call me?"

"So I can be your fuckboy? Nah."

I flinched. "Do you have to be so crude?"

"No. I just like to see you get angry."

"That's perverse."

He grinned against my mouth. He didn't press our lips together, just let me feel the warmth of his breath. Somehow that was even more erotic. "Kinda."

I moved in even closer. I liked kissing, but we didn't really do that. It was more of a dive in and get naked sort of scenario. And I really wanted to try out the kissing thing with him.

Angling my head, I gripped the ribbed material of his shirt and went up on my toes. I'd take the lead on this kiss if need be.

I am first grade teacher, hear me roar.

His sexy eyes fired and his lips molded to mine. Stage one kiss liftoff. Hell yes.

Score one for the flirting failure.

Then my mouth watered. But not in the good way. "Oh, God, no." I shoved him away just in time and ran for the alleyway between my building and his.

And lost my Chocolate Orgasm about three feet from him.

Again.

God, kill me.

Like an actual bolt from the blue would be nice. A bit of sizzle and only the ashes of my mortified self would be left behind.

"Oh, shit." He rushed toward me instead of away. His hand was gentle on my back even as I wanted to die.

"Go away."

"It's not the first time I've seen you like this."

I pushed at him weakly. "I know, which makes it even worse. How am I supposed to look at you now?"

"Well, I'd appreciate you brushing your teeth, but otherwise, I'm good. I have a kid, remember? I've had projectile vomit hit me in places I don't want to talk about."

"Oh, God." I heaved again and he sighed.

"All right, c'mon. Let's get you into your apartment."

"No. I mean, yes. I'll go, but you don't need to come." I sagged against the wall. I had to get ready for the shower. If I could even go to the shower now. Tears burned the back of my eyes. Dammit, I'd been fine all day.

"I don't know what kind of an asshole you think I am, but I'm not gonna leave you like this."

I closed my eyes. This so wasn't happening to me.

Suddenly, I was scooped up into Dare's arms, and then he headed toward the front entrance of my apartment building.

"Dare!"

"I like it when you say my name, but maybe keep it down so everyone isn't staring at us, huh?"

I gripped his arm as I noticed Joey giving us a look before shaking his head and going back to his unpacking.

"Got your key thing?"

I sighed. "Yes, but I can walk."

"Don't argue with me, Kel."

I tried not to shiver at the shortened version of my name. I was usually called Kelsey or Kels by most people. But the way his voice rumbled around that one syllable was just…*guh.*

I dug my keys out of my pocket and waved them over the security panel. Dare juggled me enough to open the door and took the stairs two at a time. With me. I was tall and my weight was evenly distributed, but did I mention the tall part?

I wasn't a petite little thing.

He carried me like I was nothing.

"You're not going to yak on me, are you?"

And there went the romantic part. "I'm going to try really hard not to."

When he got to my door, he set me on my feet.

"I can take it from here."

He pushed open the door without saying another word.

I sighed and followed him inside. "Honestly, I'm good."

"Yeah. You seem it. Which is why I'm still here."

And actually, I did feel a lot better. The shakes were gone and I was actually ravenous. Which just didn't make any sense at all.

I stalked across the apartment to my tiny bathroom. "I really appreciate you helping me out and I'm sorry I ruined the…moment." I just wanted my toothbrush. Maybe I could wash the taste away and my memory at the same time.

Oral B probably didn't have this scenario in their marketing repertoire.

I heard the quick pop of bone and tendon and winced as Dare cracked his knuckles outside my door. "Do you want to watch me brush my teeth too?" I rinsed my mouth out with water, then a quick shot of Listerine before I loaded up my electric toothbrush.

When he didn't answer me, I went ahead and started brushing. He'd already witnessed me in the worst situation ever, so what did it matter if he saw me foaming at the mouth too?

I did the full two minutes that was directed and then attacked my tongue to get the rest of the awful taste out of my mouth. And still, he paced outside. I finally rinsed and patted my face. My color was back and I felt fine.

Weirdest freaking stomach flu of my life.

I shut off the light and frowned when he jammed his fingers into his short hair until it spiked up.

"Honestly, I'm fine. I feel much better."

"Yeah, I bet you do."

"What's that supposed to mean?" I put my hands on my hips.

He tipped his head back. "You sure you have the stomach flu?"

"I told you it was going around in my class."

"Most people with the stomach flu are on their ass with a fever and begging to die a merciful death."

"I guess I'm just lucky."

He stopped in front of me. "Yeah, or you're pregnant."

TEN

THE WAY HER FACE WENT ASHEN MADE ME FEEL A LITTLE BETTER. NOT the paleness. I stepped forward just in case she did something crazy like pass out on me. But because obviously, she hadn't thought about her flu possibly being a nine-month affliction.

There wasn't a calculating bone in her gorgeous body.

And the way those huge doe eyes got just a bit wider told me everything I needed to know.

I gentled my voice. "Pregnant."

"No. We used…" She held her hand out. I grasped it, relieved when her fingers curled around mine. I didn't realize how much I needed it until she latched onto me.

Katherine had shot a beer bottle at my head when she'd told me she was having my baby. Helluva way to start our happily ever after. No wonder she walked away when Wes was barely more than a toddler. Amazing she'd lasted that long.

"Nothing's one hundred percent."

"No." She shook her head. "That can't be it."

"Can't it?"

She shook her head, her gaze darting all over her room without landing on me. "I wasn't sick in the morning. I…" Her words drifted off as she tried to come to terms with the idea of it. Denial was spinning her eyes like a slot machine.

No spinning lights with jackpot there.

Even as my gut spun just the same, I wanted to drag her closer. I couldn't even figure out why. The same kind of crazy emotion that bombarded me the minute she got close to me. Now it was growing. Like the tangled bougainvillea vine I'd tried to unlace from my fence at my house.

But it kept coming back.

No matter how many days I put between us, she was the vine I couldn't get off my skin, out of my senses, out of my damn brain. I laced our fingers. Maybe I didn't want to fight it anymore.

"Hey." I cupped her jaw and turned her face toward me.

She frowned and shook her head. "I wasn't sick in the morning."

I laughed. "Morning sickness is relative, darlin'. It can happen anytime. My cousin had it at ten in the evening every night for a month."

"I don't even make it to ten o'clock."

My gaze sharpened on her. "Tired all the time?"

She pulled away. "I'm a teacher. Of course I'm tired all the time." She paced away from me and back, her long fingers making fists, then releasing before she tapped her thumb along the pads of each finger.

"Counting?"

She pushed her long reddish-gold hair away from her face. "What?"

"Fingers."

She fisted her hand again. "I don't have time for this."

"Afraid it doesn't work like that."

She dug her phone out of her ass pocket.

Those damn shorts were going to be the death of me. Ancient, frayed in all the right places. The wear mark riding high on the sides where her endless legs met her hips. Christ, the dreams I had about those legs. I wanted them wrapped around my head again. She was surprisingly toned and firm and when she was lost, screaming my name, she forgot how strong she was. In my dreams, I'd happily suffocate with her taste on my tongue.

I sucked back a groan and dragged my shirt down over my work pants. She didn't need to see the proof of what planted that baby inside her. Maybe a baby. I crossed my arms over my chest. "We'll go get a test." Or seven. Needed to be sure.

"No."

My arms dropped to my sides. "What do you mean no?"

"Not now. I have Sage's baby shower in..." She swiped her hair out of her eyes again. "I have to go. I have to get ready." She paced her postage stamp-sized living room and then quickly rerouted herself to the bedroom.

I followed her, standing in the doorway. The last time I'd stood in this exact spot, she'd been splayed out on the bed recovering from what we'd done. I tried not to think about the way I'd rolled her over and slammed into her like a careless asshole.

I'd tried to keep myself in check, but Christ, she fit me in every damn way. As willowy as she was, I hadn't felt like I was fucking a skeleton. She'd cushioned me in the best ways and when she pushed back against me for more...

Fuck, she'd come so hard.

Swallowing a groan, I gripped the doorjamb and willed my dick to behave.

She started to lift her shirt. "Do you mind?"

"Nope."

"Get out."

I jammed my fists into my pockets. "We need to talk about this."

"Later." She dug through her closet before returning to her bed with a dress covered in huge red flowers. "I have over fifty people that will be descending on Ally's place in ninety minutes."

"A test takes five minutes."

"Dare." She swung around to face me. "We'll discuss it later."

Damn that teacher voice. It fucked me up all the time. I crossed to her in two strides and pulled her up against me. "You're not putting this off."

"It's just—"

"You know it's not a stomach bug."

She dug her fingers into my chest. I resisted the urge to back up and away from her. I was dirty and she was so fucking clean. Hell, I'd been working under Stu Jerico's Camaro for hours to pay for a heating and A/C unit on my house.

A baby? How the hell was I going to afford that?

And still, I couldn't resist the urge to drag her even closer. I didn't want to let her drive off and push the idea of it away.

Maybe she wouldn't want it.

The thought hadn't occurred to me before this very second and I tightened my hold on her. Instead of flinching, she tipped her head up at me defiantly. "My…" She swallowed then her short nails dug into my skin. It felt good. Raw and real. "My period is never timely. It's probably nothing."

"Then you won't mind taking a test."

"Why are you pushing so hard?"

"Why are you playing ostrich?"

She frowned. "Why do you know that?"

"What?" My brows snapped down to mirror hers. "Oh. Animal Planet. Getting off topic." She did that a lot. She wasn't exactly a scatterbrain, but she did have her own thought process, that was for damn sure.

"Dare." She sighed and dropped her head against my chest.

I arrowed my hand up and under her hair to massage the nape of her neck. Her firelight hair twisted and flowed around my skin. Her scent floated up, so clean and bright with that sharp tang of citrus that always threw me off. I dropped my chin on the top of her bent head. "Better to know," I whispered.

"After," she said again and pulled back, turning toward her bed and the garden party dress that didn't fit in my grease monkey world. I backed out of the room without another word and left her apartment.

I couldn't stop the slam of the door.

What the hell was I thinking with pushing on this? She was bright with her career ahead of her. What would she want with me? I was a good lay. A great lay when it came to Kelsey. And she fucking fit me like no other woman had. But in the end, it was just sex.

I slammed out the front door of the building. The truck had moved. Finally.

It was a damn good time to take the Camaro out for a test drive.

I climbed behind the beast of a muscle car. My fingers knew the gauges and the familiar shape of the stick shift set in my palm.

Like my racing days.

The motor growled around me, reminding me of the days before I was a dad. Before Katherine had ripped open my life with the belligerent news that she was pregnant.

The day my life changed.

After that day, I no longer looked at the endless track in front of me and saw the bumper of a car as my greatest obstacle to overtake. Speed and my periphery were no longer the only things I had to worry about.

I had someone to take care of. Two someones. But Katherine had never been happy in the crappy apartment I'd scraped together my savings to afford. My money had gone into the cars, into the fees, into the training to be the best racer on the course.

It had taken time to save money for a house. But formula and diapers, doctors' visits and prenatal classes had dented the savings train. Weston had been worth it. Even if Katherine had never quite fit me, Wes had from the moment the nurse had put him in my arms.

I downshifted into fourth and opened up the engine as I got out onto the highway. It purred and hummed for me, the growl so like the beast I'd driven all those years ago. I raced away from the dark thoughts of Katherine and all the disappointments she'd voiced nearly every day of our marriage.

Signs for a drugstore and gas station at the next exit had me downshifting and pulling off the highway. I glanced down at the gas gauge. First, I'd refill Stu's tank.

Unfortunately, the beast of a car came with a similar tank for the gas. I winced as the dollars on the pump kept clicking higher and higher. Worth it for the few minutes of freedom.

I tipped my head up to catch the apple cider scent across the street. Even the food trucks were decked out for fall. My stomach rumbled at the fried churros and hot cider being passed around to the line of people.

It was a bright fall day with the perfect crispness to the air that reminded me of orchards and fat pumpkins. Maybe I'd take Wes to Happy Acres next weekend. It was the perfect time for all of that. Let him run off some steam in the corn maze they put together in Turnbull.

But first, I had a test to buy.

I maneuvered my way over to the drugstore with only a few grumbles and swear words. There was a reason I liked my little town. This traffic and bullshit made my pressure rise. Add in the female aisle and I was twitchy as fuck. Pads, tampons, and creams. Christ. But at the end of it were the condoms.

"Thanks, condoms," I muttered.

And the all-important tests.

Four shelves of them.

"Jesus." I grabbed tests from each shelf until my arms were full. How to know which ones worked the best? I didn't want to cheap out at the worst possible time.

On the way down the back aisle, I grabbed a huge-ass water. Evidently, she'd be doing a lot of peeing.

After another dent made in my credit card, I was heading back to Crescent Cove. I could be jumping the gun, but I'd listened to my gut for most of my life. The times I hadn't, I'd ended up spinning out on the track, or marrying a woman meaner than a half-skinned snake.

I wasn't wrong about this.

Ignoring the tug this crazy woman had on me? Yeah, that was the part that was driving me insane. Not Kelsey. When I had her in my space, it felt more perfect than anything I had a right to feel. Add in the strings of a baby. They were as delicate as a spiderweb, but I felt them already.

Part of me wanted to hack at them with the same machete I used to try and kill the vines trying to take over my backyard. As I pulled into the land of babies and pink and blue balloons, I knew how useless it was to try.

I fisted the bag and strode into Ally and Seth's house. I'd been here before on the nights Seth and I had hung out, so I was used to strolling in. The door had a big welcome sign on it and directions to go into the backyard for the baby shower.

Christ, I hadn't even changed or brought the car back to the shop. I went right to her. Maybe that spiderweb idea was more of a bullseye than I'd thought.

"Fuck it," I muttered as I pushed through the door and into paper bird land.

Already my balls were shrinking. Perfect.

Women were zooming around the kitchen. Most of the party was in the backyard where I could see through the window that even more paper birds were plunked on every table and floating from the trees.

In the center of it all was Sage Hamilton with her huge smile. People kept bringing her food and trying to get her to put her feet up.

"What are you doing here?"

I turned toward the whispered fury of the woman of my dreams. Probably a few nightmares in there, but mostly hot and sweaty naked dreams. I took the huge punch bowl out of her hands. "What are you doing?"

"*Me?* This is not a Jack and Jill party."

"I don't know what that means. Where do you want this?"

She frowned at me and started doing that thing with her fingers again. Maybe it wasn't a counting thing. Nervous? About me?

Hmm. I wasn't sure if I liked that idea or not. Hell, maybe it was about the drugstore bag in my hand.

I pushed it at her and lifted my other hand to keep the large bowl of ice cream and foamy soda from tipping over.

She peeked in the bag then quickly shut it. "Oh, crap. What...I, oh my God."

"A reasonable facsimile of what got us in this situation, but I like the breathy moans you add in."

She blushed right up to the roots of her reddish-gold hair. She turned me around and aimed me toward the backyard. "Put it on that table over there." She glanced down at me. "You still don't have a shirt on."

I glanced down at my tank. "I do."

She huffed out a breath. Though it did seem a little more strangled than a moment ago.

I navigated around clusters of laughing women and deposited the punch bowl on the table. As soon as I had, Kelsey steered me back inside. "You have to go."

"Ashamed of me, Kel?"

"What? No. No boys allowed, that's all."

"Then I'll get out of your way. Just as soon as you go upstairs and take a test."

"I saw about five in there."

I reached for the bag she still carried and pulled out the large bottle of water. "I'm prepared." I frowned. "What's in the punch?"

She rolled her eyes. "Pregnant lady here. It's non-alcoholic."

I narrowed my eyes.

"Not *this* lady."

"You sure?"

She swallowed. "I've only had…maybe water? I don't know. I've been running around."

I took the cap off the water and handed it to her. "Drink."

"Thank you. Though, hi, I can hydrate myself just fine." After taking a quick sip, she took the cap from me to close the bottle.

"Gonna need more than that, darlin'. You've got some peeing to do."

"What?" Her huge brown eyes got even wider.

"Those tests aren't going to take themselves." I gently urged her forward and up the stairs.

"We are not doing this here."

"We are." I smacked her perfect ass. "Move it."

"You are incredible."

"Pretty sure you've told me a variation of that before at…intimate moments, but thank you."

She whipped around and all that glorious hair of hers twirled with her. Goddamn, she was fucking beautiful. Even if she was mad at me. The dress swished around her killer legs and I resisted the urge to lift the hem and see just what she had under there.

We got to the top of the stairs and I headed for the bedroom down the hall with her in tow.

"Dare, this isn't our house."

My chest tightened. *Our.* Helluva thing. I kept up a determined pace. "I helped Oliver retro fit a tub in Seth's master en suite. It's quiet back there."

"Still not my house or your house. We can't just—"

"Kel?"

With an exasperated huff, she looked at me. "What?"

"Shut up and go pee on these tests. Then we'll know one way or the other if we have a situation on our hands."

Her color went up again, but this time, it wasn't an embarrassed flush. I was pretty sure she was about to show me that irate side of her that made my balls tighten and my dick get so hard that I couldn't think around it. "No time for mad. You have girls downstairs, remember?"

She growled.

It was cute. Mostly.

I touched the bag. "Off you go."

"I can't just pee on command."

"Drink up, buttercup."

"I can't even believe you." She headed into the bathroom, then shoved the bag into my gut and pulled out her phone, texting madly before tossing it on the counter. "I'm only doing this so you'll leave."

"Sounds good."

She pushed her hair out of her face. "I can't believe I'm doing this in Ally's bathroom." She let out a breath. "I don't even have time to look at the instructions. We're about to do the gifts. Can't this—"

"No." I dug into the bag and started breaking open the boxes. "You open it and pee on it. Five minutes later, voila. It's simple."

"So you say."

I handed her a pile of plastic sticks. "Go."

She paused before nudging me out and closing the door to the small room housing the toilet. "I hate you."

"You're breaking my heart."

When she was gone, I sagged against the bathroom counter. Why did this woman have to make everything so freaking difficult?

Her phone started buzzing behind me. I glanced down to see it was Ally. There were many exclamation points and caps. No way I was reading that one.

"I can't pee with you out there," she shouted.

"Grow a pair, darlin'. I ain't going anywhere."

"I don't want to grow a pair." She mumbled something under her breath.

"You wouldn't be swearing at me in there."

"Maybe."

I couldn't stop the grin. She was exasperating as hell, but fuck if she wasn't adorable. And now I was just being an idiot.

Her phone vibrated and bounced. Ally was not happy evidently. I pushed the phone back to the side of the counter and paused when I saw a text from someone else.

Who the fuck was Tommy?

My gaze swung to the door and back down to the phone. I curled my fingers into my palm and tried to glance away, but I saw enough to make my blood sizzle. I could hate myself tomorrow. Hell, an hour from now. She was inside that damn bathroom taking a test to see if she was having my goddamn baby.

I picked up the phone and opened the text.

Hey babe. I'm in town. Wanna catch up? Had fun the last time I saw u. Wouldn't mind a repeat performance.

There was a goddamn winky face at the end of the text. Was this dude five? What the fucking fuck? I hit delete before I could stop myself. "Fuck," I muttered.

That was smart. Not. I curled my fingers around the phone.

Dickhead.

And this time, the sentiment wasn't entirely aimed at the guy texting Kelsey. Why had I just deleted that damn text?

Easy answer. Because she was mine, and that asshole clearly hadn't appreciated her judging from his tone.

Except she wasn't mine. At least not yet.

Just in my head.

Ally came around the corner huffing. "Where is she? I've been texting her!"

I shoved her phone behind me then gripped the counter. "Can."

"Charming." Ally glanced at me and the bag beside me with a frown. "Everything okay?"

There was a crash from the powder room and suddenly a flush and Kelsey came rushing out. "I'm sorry. Is it time?"

I frowned. "Can we have a second, Ally? She'll be right down."

"We're about to open presents, and Sage is asking for you. She knows my secretarial skills are shit. You'll write down the names correctly. She's about a second away from turning into a pumpkin if she doesn't get some cake, and it's going to take at least an hour to open all the presents. The shower isn't exactly proceeding like we intended, but whatever. As soon as she gets some cake, she'll need to lay down. Or maybe give birth."

My jaw dropped. "Like today?"

Ally laughed. "No, I'm exaggerating. She's not having contractions or anything. She's just wiped out. Me too." Ally shook back her hair and tugged at her dress. "Sage loves the garden party vibe, but I'm dying. And if I have to do small talk with one more person from town, I'm going to literally drown them in the punch bowl. So if you could save me, that would be great."

I opened my mouth, but Kelsey rushed forward. "Of course."

"We only need five minutes."

But of course, I was overruled. As always.

"It's fine." Kelsey gave me a hard look. "It can wait."

I raked my fingers through my hair. She pushed me aside to use the sink and washed her hands, then reached behind me for her phone and pocketed it. I grabbed her hand. "Seriously?"

"I did what you asked, now I have to go finish what I started. I can't help it if you couldn't wait a few hours for your answer," she said through gritted teeth.

And then she was gone.

"Fuck." I spun around and groaned at my appearance. No wonder Ally had given me some side-eye, for fuck's sake. I looked every bit the scruffy mechanic I was. All these women in their Sunday best and I was way out of place and out of their league.

I tipped back my head and counted to ten.

Hell, if I added on another ninety seconds, I could go check the tests myself if she didn't fucking care.

At least she wouldn't be running to some asshat named Tommy tonight.

Yeah, it wasn't cool I'd deleted that text. And I'd come clean about it.

Much as I didn't necessarily want to.

I stalked into the tiny closet and found the row of tests lined up on the top of the toilet tank on a double layer of toilet paper.

Only Kelsey.

I shook out my hands and exhaled a slow breath before I looked at each test.

Positive.

Pregnant.

Plus sign.

Two lines.

Pregnant.

No denying that one.

I scooped them up and stuffed them in the drugstore bag. Halfway out the door, I backtracked and washed my hands and tried to get some of the motor oil off my skin.

It was the least I could do before I went down and got my girl.

ELEVEN

"THERE YOU ARE!" SAGE BEAMED AT THE SIGHT OF ME AND ALLY hurrying across the lawn. She made it halfway out of her bow-adorned princess chair, sighed, and sagged back down. "I was going to hug you both, but too much work. So I'll just wave."

I smiled wanly and tried not to look at Sage's belly. It was far more fascinating to me than it had been just a day or two ago. Probably because I'd just peed enough for Austin Powers on a bunch of surprisingly tiny sticks.

There was no way I could be pregnant.

We'd used condoms. And we'd only had sex twice.

Two measly times.

And then there was Tommy.

Oh, God.

I clutched my stomach and stared unseeingly at the paper cranes and bright balloons and women wandering about in pastel dresses. All of a sudden, this whole scenario seemed more ominous.

Especially if the baby I could not, absolutely could not be carrying belonged to Tommy.

No. No. Oh hell no.

I'd only had sex with him after Granny Flo's funeral out of guilt.

He'd left me alone in bed the next morning with a text goodbye, and it had been a relief. Contrary to some wives' tales, ex sex was not the best sex. Or even halfway semi-good sex.

I wasn't even sure he could've planted one in me, that was how lackluster it had been.

Dare, however, could impregnate me with a damn look. And he also had prior history.

Sweet Jesus, he was a known inseminator!

"Kels, you okay?" Ally stepped in front of me and wagged her fingers in my face. "You look pale. It's not that stupid flu again, is it?" It was her turn to lose the color in her cheeks. "Oh no, you helped make the fruit babies."

Those stupid melon balls I'd fashioned into baby heads would haunt me forever. As it was, I no longer even liked cantaloupe. The smell had actually made me kind of sick.

Gee, wonder why, Pregnado.

It was like Sharknado, but worse.

"I'm fine, honestly. I'm not contagious. I don't think. Though maybe *she* is." I glanced at Sage, but luckily, Ally had already been pulled away by one of Sage's friends who was having a Scotch tape emergency.

I was beginning to wonder if pregnancy wasn't catching in this town. What were the odds that it could jump so often from one unsuspecting chick to another? Sage's baby had been unplanned. I was pretty sure Ally's had been too, though they'd intended to try because Seth wanted another kid or something. All I knew was I'd just peed enough for a buffalo and I had to freaking go again already.

Unless it was stress spraying, something was not right in my uterus.

Dear God, I needed a chair.

A drink.

A do-over.

Only one of those things could I have, and it was only because I gestured for another lady to move. Since I think she thought I had heat stroke, she quickly scuttled away and allowed me to crash into the uncomfortable wicker seat.

"Presents time," Ally called gaily and I moaned.

Not even quietly either.

Several women glanced my way and I smiled weakly in apology. Someone passed me a non-alcoholic lime chiller and I may have offered to give her my firstborn.

Totally kidding, of course.

Mostly kidding.

God, I couldn't be pregnant. I had no idea what to do with a baby. I was used to dealing with kids, but my preferred age group was already mobile. Except for the occasional stomach bug, I'd never had to help clean up a sick child. Definitely never toilet-trained or any of that.

But Dare had.

Dare wasn't a newbie.

Except what if Dare wasn't the father? Then what?

I shut my eyes as cool lime-flavored liquid slid down my parched throat. No use getting ahead of myself. Maybe those tests would come back negative and I wouldn't have to think about any of this. Not about child-rearing, or telling Principal Gentry I was unwed and knocked up, or confessing to Dare that he wasn't the only dude who'd possibly fertilized my lady bouquet.

A girl could dream.

One of the women wandered past with a tray of drinks for those who weren't imbibing from the punch bowl. I lurched from my chair to grab a pink one, nearly knocking the woman off her heels. The woman stared at me, aghast, and I waved my face with my hand. Heatstroke could be used as an excuse for all sorts of things.

"Alcoholic?" I gasped.

No, I didn't gasp. Of course not. Asked breathily.

Better.

She shook her head and continued on as I gulped down the sickeningly sweet liquid. She cast a narrow-eyed glance at me when I pitched my empty plastic cup into the garbage can about two feet to her right. Make that two empty cups.

"Whoops. Sorry."

"Kelsey, are you ready?" Ally was smiling at me, but there was no missing the pinch marks around her mouth and eyes. I was already derelicting my duties.

One best friend demotion coming up.

I hurried over to the long table weighed down with Sage's gifts. "Let's pop these suckers open," I said with all the cheer I could muster, tugging on the festive green ribbon around a huge round present.

Which then broke through its wrapper and somehow spewed rainbow foam blocks all over the grass.

Including a projectile one that landed on the lap of one of Sage's college friends seated up front—and knocked her merlot-colored drink all over her lacy white sundress.

"Oh, shit, this is wine." She jumped to her feet and a circle of her sorority sisters hustled forward to help her clean up.

"I'm so sorry. Oh, I'm so sorry!" I bent to grab the colorful foam blocks that were all over the grass, nearly tripping over several in my haste to get to Sage's wine-drenched friend.

But she was already rushing away, surrounded in a classic girl huddle, so I fell back and shoved foam blocks into their entirely inadequate mesh sack. I glanced at Ally, who was smiling in that strained way that always seemed to follow me when I was operating at full socially awkward strength.

"I'll just keep track of names and gifts in my planner," I said weakly, pulling the sides of the wrapping paper together and looping the straggly bow lamely over the top.

I looked around for my hobo bag—I'd brought it out here earlier for this purpose, I knew I had—but didn't see it anywhere. Until a pair of work boots appeared at the edge of my peripheral vision right before a tanned hand held out my familiar navy leather planner.

"Looking for this?"

"Thanks." I snatched it from Dare and nodded, not meeting his gaze. "You're a male," I reminded him out of the corner of my mouth as laughter broke out from the crowd. But it was hushed, as if they were giggling behind their hands at us.

No, at *me.* Might as well be honest in my own head. I was the one who'd ripped apart the present and now I couldn't even find my own belongings without Dare's help.

He'd helped me find a lot of things, including my uterus just long enough to plant a baby there.

Maybe.

If there'd been planting.

If it had been him.

God, it had to be him.

"Are you okay, darlin'? You looked flushed. And you're mumbling to yourself."

"I'm fine. Great actually." He pushed a chair at me and I slumped into it gratefully. This had to be a heat-related illness. I'd forgotten sunscreen today, so I'd probably be burnt to a crisp to boot.

Lovely.

"I'm ready to begin," I smiled at Ally and pretended I couldn't hear the continuing laughter.

Dare was not getting the hint.

"You sure about that?" Ally asked, raising her brow at Dare. "The other guys are in the man-cave downstairs if you want to—"

"How come he gets to be out here?" Seth's voice rang out clearly from the back stoop. "We were banished, and the newbie to the crew gets an all-access pass?"

Sage let out a giant sigh. "No. No men. Not you, Seth, not you, Dare—sorry—and definitely not my husband. Go play with yourselves or something."

This time, there was no mistaking the laughter, including from Dare and Seth. And even me, a little. Just a little though because sweet marmalade, I had an alien invading me.

Possibly.

Sage sighed heavily again. "Not like that. Filthy minds, all of you. Though you do you, boo. But I meant Xbox. Video games. Air hockey. Whatever men do when they're alone and blissfully wedded, so blissfully they have no cause to bitch." She pointed at Seth. "Right?"

Seth held up his hands palms out. "Nirvana is my natural state, as is Oliver's, I'm sure."

Dare shook his head. "Sure seems like a lot of fuss over a baby. Hope they plan on doing this for you too."

I didn't look at him. Didn't even acknowledge his existence. I was sure he was talking in the abstract. Besides, probably no one had even heard—

"Oh my God, Kelsey, are you knocked up?" Sage's voice rang out above the piercing throb in my right temple.

"Presents time!" I called out cheerfully, as if Sage had never spoken.

But no one was listening to me. Dare crossed his muscular arms and stood guard beside me as if I needed protection. He didn't say yes, didn't say anything at all. Didn't matter.

The die was cast, for the guests and for me.

Because I made the mistake of meeting his gaze for a fraction of a second and I *knew*.

He'd looked at the tests and reality was not on my side.

The non-preggo side.

Not like the universe could toss me a bone. A small celestial favor, just this one time.

Hey, the girl works in a Catholic school. New job, new life, and she's always played by the rules. This would be a spectacular screw-up at a not so good time.

I didn't even know who the father was. And that was patently ridiculous. I'd never ever slept with two men within the span of one month before—hell, within one year was a stretch—yet the first time, bam.

Twinkle, twinkle, little star with a side of baby booties, please.

Dare ran his hand down my hair and for a second, it was easier to just lean against him than to keep trying to be strong. To pretend I could handle all of this when it was clear I couldn't. He'd overstepped about five hundred boundaries by insisting I take those tests, then obviously looking at the results even before I had a chance to.

Even so, I was out of my depth and drowning. And I'd gratefully take the lifeline he was offering just by being there.

Until he opened his mouth again.

"Just saying, she's been busting her ass for you, Sage. Hope you're ready to reciprocate."

No one laughed this time.

I didn't speak. I was residing in another dimension, where my only recourse was to become mute.

Ally cleared her throat and discreetly stepped aside as Sage lurched to her feet and propped a hand on her hip. "I appreciate everything Kelsey has done. She's my bestie with Ally. They're both amazing."

At Dare's huff of breath and another stroke of my hair, I decided I needed to take the bull by the horns.

"Let's do gifts! Look at all these pretty things everyone got for Sage's little one." I grabbed the nearest item, which—shocker— happened to be the same foam block monstrosity. I let it go, but not fast enough to prevent spillage yet again.

No one cared because Sage was staring down Dare.

"You're needed inside."

He planted his feet. "Nope, I think I'm good right where I am, thanks."

The back door opened and Oliver stepped out, earning Sage's groan. "Jeez Louise, forget it. Who cares about baby shower protocol? Men and women, mingle freely! Just give me some damn cake before my water breaks."

Oliver hustled across the lawn. "Are you having contractions?"

Sage gave me a beady-eyed look as if to say *this is all your fault.* And the worst of it was, it *was* my fault.

All of it.

From the mess with the foam blocks, to not being prepared to take names, to letting Dare just run rough-shod over my reproductive organs.

"Just who do you think you are?" I demanded, turning away from Sage's flushed cheeks to glare at the object of all my frustration.

Dare and his ridiculously large dick had gotten me into this kettle.

And he was making it even worse by being all broody and hot and acting as if he was my studly bodyguard.

It was a baby shower, for God's sake. Not a crime scene.

At least not yet.

"I think I'm involved in this situation, and I'm not about to let you push me out."

I frowned. What did that mean? The way his jaw locked made me wonder if this was the first time he'd felt as if he was being shut out of a…situation, as he'd put it.

With Wes's mom maybe? I didn't know any of the story there.

Not the time, Kelsey.

Sage stepped forward, leaving a bewildered Oliver in the dust. "Situation, huh?"

Sage and Ally exchanged a look.

"Hey, guess what, everyone, change of plans. It's too hot out here for the mom-to-be." Ally shot me a loaded glance and quickly kept going. "Let's move this party inside."

"Inside where?" Came Seth's plaintive question. "You all aren't allowed in the man-cave."

Ally rushed toward the back door. "Not now, Hamilton. Ladies, follow me."

Unfortunately, she wasn't moving fast enough to prevent my mouth from detonating. Even as my lips opened, I knew I needed to shut the heck up and wait until the women dispersed.

But with one look at Dare's smug, self-satisfied expression, my panic and fear and frustration exploded.

All over Dare.

"You know what, Mr. Know It All? This baby may not even be yours!"

TWELVE

THE WORLD FUZZED OUT OF FOCUS AND I COULDN'T HEAR FOR WHAT seemed like forever. What did she just say?

I took a step back, then another. Noise came rushing in and yet it was only birds and a distant speaker pumping out music.

Pin drop moment in the flesh.

Not mine.

Not mine.

Maybe not mine.

The *maybe* part wouldn't stick. Just the idea that someone else had been inside her within enough time to plant a baby inside of her was like a seizing motor in my brain.

"Dare, I didn't—"

I held up my hand and turned to escape. No fucking way I could stand there in front of all those people and listen to her excuses. Not now.

Maybe not ever.

Not yours.

Seth stood on the back stoop, but he didn't say a word as I passed. His eyes averted to the floor.

Blindly, I swung the door open and headed through the house, then out the front door and down the stairs to the sidewalk.

Return the car. Go home.

Go home where you should have been this whole fucking time.

I didn't even remember the ride home, or backing into the bay at J&T's. It was all a haze. Hell, I didn't even know if the car had made the damn squeak that my customer had complained about.

The only thought in my fucking brain was Kelsey.

I was tangled up over a woman again, though Kelsey sometimes seemed more like a sweet younger girl in so many ways.

I'd fucked the holy hell out of her twice. But someone else had too.

And I didn't even know why that pissed me off so much. I wasn't that guy. Judgmental like the people in this goddamn town? Nope. That wasn't me. And yet, my fingers were welded to the steering wheel and I was still staring at the wall of tools sightlessly.

I pounded the dash and got out. Anger sprang out of my pores like noxious gas. I needed to get rid of this before picking up my kid.

How?

Pound it out into Kelsey.

No.

No, that definitely wasn't happening. That was why I was in trouble in the first place. My dick didn't know how to stay in my pants when I was near her. Even now, the thought of her long legs wrapped around me had me half hard.

And the baby…

The anger swelled in my head and chest. I grabbed the long crowbar and stalked to the back door of the garage and out into the back loading area where stacks of tires waited for recycling.

I swung at the largest stack of truck tires. The satisfying bounce back emptied the noise out of my head. I slammed into the stack until the reverberations in my biceps and triceps left me tingling and numb. My hand burned and my wrist sang with each blow. Sweat coated my shoulders and arms.

Finally, my hand gave way to the punishment and the crowbar clattered to the blacktop. I dropped to my knees and growled through heaving breaths until the spots dancing in my vision cleared.

The golden setting sun off the water speared down the alleyway chased by shadows and the cloying scent of burnt rubber and oil. A steadying scent. My life was connected to this garage.

Once upon a time, I'd wanted to own my own garage and pit crew, but now I liked being able to walk away each night. Sure, I had overtime coming out my ass lately, but it was because I asked for it. Because it helped me catch up when the cascade of shit came down on me from the fixer upper I'd bought when Wes was born.

He was my entire world. Even beyond Katherine and her endless unhappiness, my little boy had always been the best thing in my life.

And maybe part of me wanted more.

You could have more.

I shut my eyes against the thought and forced myself to stand. I went back inside and washed up at the large basin on the far wall of the garage. I checked my phone, swiping away the messages from Kelsey.

I couldn't go back there right now. The wild anger was too close to the fringes of my brain. Instead, I texted my mom to let her know I was on my way.

Dinner with my kid. That was what I needed to focus on, not Kelsey Ford and her huge brown eyes.

The horror in her expression when she'd shouted that the baby might not be mine was forever burned on my retinas. Horror that she had to have a man like me in her life forever? Or horror that it might not be mine?

I didn't know.

Yeah, I didn't have it in me for questions like that right now.

I grabbed my denim shirt and shrugged it on before locking up. Main Street was quiet. The whole town rolled up on Sundays by dinner time. Shops either opened for only a few hours after church or not at all. Lights were still on in the cafe, but the delivery truck wasn't taking up the entire area anymore.

I climbed into my truck. It was a quick drive to my parents' house, but the last of the sun's rays were disappearing into the brush when I drove up the gravel lane leading to the sunny yellow ranch with white shutters and trim.

My pop painted it every three years so it always looked fresh. Maybe some of the trim was a little more worn these days, but my family made do with what we had. I'd learned that from my old man.

The screen door slapped and the sound of pounding feet followed by the scrape of Sandy's toenails as she scrabbled after my son brought me back to center. Wes hopped down off the last stair and came tearing at my truck. No coat on, of course. He got that from me —forever warm. But without the sun, the October chill quickly crept into the air.

I stepped out of my truck just in time to catch Wes as he flung himself at me. He was getting a little too big to catch, but I was secretly glad he still was excited to see me. Working so much left my kid a little more sullen than I liked to admit some days.

I hoisted him up on my hip. "Hey, bud."

"Dad, wait 'til you see what I did with Grampa today. It's so cool."

"Oh, yeah?" The scent of burning leaves clung to his shirt. "Did you help in the yard today?"

"Yeah! How'd you know?"

"Good guess," I murmured and gave Sandy an absent rub along her silky ears. The Golden Retriever leaned against my thigh, pinning me against the front quarter panel of my truck. "Hey, girl." Soot clung to the fur around her eyes and mouth. "I'm guessing you guys did a little bit of leaf raking."

"Wow, you're *really* good at guessing." Wes wiggled to get down and he and Sandy ran around the house. He stopped and backtracked, peeking around the corner of the porch steps. "Come on!"

I trudged after him. Hunger was gnawing a hole in my gut, but if my kid wanted to show me the bonfire my old man was probably creating, who was I to say no?

Sure enough, Wes was running circles around the picnic table in the backyard. When he spotted me, he started jumping up and down. Jesus, the kid didn't stop until his cheek hit the pillow at night. He ran back to me, dragging me toward the wide barrels at the edge of the yard. "C'mon, I want to show you."

The snap and pop of fire licking up into the sky evened me out just a little more.

Normalcy.

Fall in Laurel was in full swing. It was the next town over from Crescent Cove, with a decidedly more country feel than the small town I lived in now. Land went back for acres, but instead of rolling grass, it was full of brush and woods. A creek ran along the back of my parents' property and a tire swing as old as I was hung from the massive oak that rained down a metric fuck-ton of leaves every year.

And from the smell of things, a lot of them were ash already.

"Pop."

"Hey, there you are. I thought you were only working a half day today?"

I shrugged and glanced over to make sure Wes wasn't too close to the hot metal bin. Eyes so much like mine were wide with little fires flickering in the pupils. Great, I'd have to add fire to my watch list for Wes. He was far too curious for his own good sometimes.

I shoved my hands into my pockets. "I need to tell you something before you hear about it at the shop tomorrow."

"That sounds ominous."

I gave him a look then glanced down at Wes. "Hey, why don't you go see if Gram will give you some cookies to take home?"

His blue eyes got even wider. "Yes! We made chocolate chips." He raced off, sneakers pounding up the porch stairs.

"Now I'm worried."

I sighed. "Yeah, today took a bit of a hard left. I'm not really sure what to do about it. I'm still thinking on a lot of it, but…" I gripped the back of my neck. "Fuck."

"Not like you to go on without spitting it straight out."

"I know. It's hard for me to say. I swore I'd never be so goddamn stupid again and here I am." I met my father's eyes. Again, so much like mine, only more weathered. They had deeper creases at the

133

corners and his hair and beard were more white than blond these days.

"Well, shit."

I winced. "That obvious?"

"Last time you came at me with that look on your face, you told me I was going to be a granddad. Before that, it was that you rolled your car on the track. Pretty sure both of them cost the same in the end."

I huffed out a laugh. "Ain't that the truth."

"Who's the girl? Please don't tell me it's Jody."

"What? God, no." I didn't think I actually had a laugh in me, but the idea that I'd hook up with the ticket girl at my father's pizza joint was laughable. "Is she even eighteen yet?"

"Why the hell do you think I asked? She's got huge hearts in her eyeballs for you, boy."

"God, really?"

He shook his head. "So, who's the girl?"

"Teacher." I cleared my throat. "Wes's teacher."

"Miss Ford?" My dad blew out a startled breath. "Wow. When did that happen?"

"You don't really want a blow by blow, do you, Pop?"

"I am partial to redheads."

I could feel my cheeks flush. Christ, my mother was a redhead. Well, she had been once upon a time. Now she was more of a salt and sand. "Let's just say it was a weak moment." More than one, but I really didn't want to get into details, for fuck's sake.

He shoved his hands deeper into his Carhartt jacket. "I raised you to be careful."

"And we were. But hell…" How the hell did I tell him it might not even be my baby? I didn't want my dad to think less of Kelsey. The whole damn town was probably talking about her already. "It's between me and another guy."

At least I was pretty sure it was just one other guy. Even the little bit I knew about Kelsey led me to think that way.

Maybe it was even the guy whose text I'd deleted. I still had to tell her I'd done that.

Shit.

Dad's eyebrows shot up into the shade of his ball cap. "Well, then."

"Yeah. I don't know the particulars. I just found out today and it's a goddamn clusterfuck. But I didn't want you to hear about it from your customers or whoever else is going to tear into her." Jesus. Just the thought of everyone talking about her had the rage bubbling in my gut again.

"This more than just a one and done thing, Dare?"

"I don't know, Pop. But if it's mine, I'll do right by her."

"I don't like the sound of that." He widened his stance and his jaw was set. "Katherine did enough damage for five women."

"I know it."

"And now you have Wes to worry about."

"Pop, I know. I don't know what the hell I'm doing yet. I gotta think on it." A fucking lot. But if that kid was mine…

Even a small chance was enough.

"And the mother?"

It was like he yanked the thought right out of my head. "I barely know her."

"Knew enough to—"

"Pop."

"What? You're the one doing the baby-making," he grumbled.

"When I know, you'll know."

"I guess that's good enough." He pulled the brim of his Yankees hat down. "I need a goddamn cookie."

"I could use a cookie myself."

"Cookies all around then. Can't wait to tell your Ma about this."

"Can I add a beer to that order?"

My dad snorted. "Maybe we should go right to the whiskey."

"Might not be a bad idea."

135

I shoved my earbud deeper into my ear to cut down on the grinding blade my boss had been using all morning. Jerome did some metal reconstruction work on the slow days in the shop, leaving me to do all the repairs.

Fourth fucking oil change in an hour. One more alignment and my day would be complete for a fucking bingo card.

Normally, the monotony didn't get to me all that much. Being a mechanic meant a lot of repetition. The days of putting together NASCAR motors—or taking apart—were past. I'd learned to live without that extra tang of sharper high velocity oil and gasoline mix that would never be a part of my life again. My little brother had taken over the reins there.

Hell, he'd passed me by about a hundred laps at this point. And most days I didn't miss it. I'd made my choices to come home and be a part of my kid's life. Being a driver or on a pit crew was an endless series of races and getting ready for them.

That wasn't the life I wanted to give Wes.

Part of the reason me and Katherine had fallen apart had been the sense of home I'd wanted for my family. It wasn't nearly exciting enough for her—especially a small town like Crescent Cove.

Unlike Kelsey.

I growled along with Godsmack's singer as I tried to loosen the rusty fucking nut on this oil pan. "Fucker," I seethed as it didn't budge. Frustration mounted as I changed out my socket wrench for a smaller size. I was at a shitty angle. When the nut stripped, my hand slipped and my knuckles scraped across a rough patch of metal on the undercarriage.

"Fuck!"

Blood gushed over my fingers and I rolled out.

"Jesus, boy. You are coloring the air neon blue. Not like you."

I blew out a breath and wrapped my rag over the cut. "Sorry, Jerome."

He shook his head. "Go walk it off. And wash that out. I ain't paying for you to go to the damn ER."

I nodded. It wouldn't be so bad except it was the third day in a row that I lost out to some car part. I already had a butterfly bandage on the same hand.

I dragged myself over to the sink and washed the blood away until it stung from soap and the pressure I put on the skin to get everything loose.

The pain felt good.

I was seriously getting fucked up about all this.

I hadn't slept in three days—at least no more than a few hours snatched in my recliner with Wes in my lap. He was just as out of sorts as I was. Nothing would soothe him. Not even online shopping for a Halloween costume and that always evened him out.

Disgusted, I dunked my head under the steady stream of water and washed away the sweat and fatigue. I just had to get through a few more hours and then I could pick up Wes and grill a few burgers. It was certainly warm enough.

As always, upstate New York had a few weeks of Indian Summer mixed in with our fall and we were right in the middle of a warm stretch. I grabbed a clean red rag from the laundry pile and slipped out of the single open bay door. I scrubbed the worst of the water out of my hair and slicked the spikes back.

I lifted my face up to the sun. I'd been under so many cars today, I didn't even realize a headache was sitting behind my eyes. Part of me wanted to ask my mom to keep Wes tonight so I could just drink until I finally passed out and slept, but it wouldn't help.

Drunk sleep never did.

"Who's the sweetest baby ever?"

My gut instantly clenched and every muscle locked in my shoulders. I knew that voice. Had been hearing it in my hazy dreams for the last few weeks since our pizza night hookup. Sometimes boner-inducing, sometimes just a soft tease.

I turned my head and everything inside me stilled. Kelsey was crouched in front of a stroller. A skirt exploding with sunflowers pooled around her. Her freckled shoulders were bare and all that golden sunset hair twisted in the breeze.

Christ, she was beautiful.

Her wide mouth split with a delighted smile did nothing to help my current situation. And seeing her with the kid…fuck.

She was pregnant.

That could be her next year, crouched in front of her own stroller. Assuming she wanted to keep my kid—the kid. Maybe not even mine.

I wasn't sure what killed me more, that it might be mine—or might not. The fact that she'd blurted out that it might be some other dude's kid was the worst part. In front of everyone. I couldn't get that moment out of my head. Was it worse to be the guy who knocked up the new teacher? Or to be the idiot who was the rebound guy?

If I wanted to, I could be off the hook. I could literally leave her to deal with it and let me know after a test or some shit. I didn't know the particulars of how paternity worked. Hell, I hadn't even thought to ask when Katherine told me she was pregnant. Add in the fact that Wes had come out looking like me down to the squinty eyes, and hell, I'd already known.

I'd loved him way before he was born.

Was I just an asshole because I was already getting the possessive vibe after a few days with Kelsey? That everything about her made me want to grab her and tell everyone she was mine?

"Fucking idiot," I muttered to myself.

Suddenly, she looked up from the baby and our gazes locked.

My grip on the rag tightened and I felt my cuts rip open again. The slow, warm drip of blood distracted me enough to look down. When I glanced up again, she was disappearing into Brewed Awakening, the coffee shop below her apartment.

Obviously, she didn't want to talk to me.

I had to make myself turn around and go back into the garage.

Not my problem. Not my girl.

I wrapped the rag tighter around my hand. *Not my problem.*

Maybe if I told myself that enough times it would sink in.

THIRTEEN

"Are you okay, Kelsey?"

I held the door open for Ally and the stroller. "I'm good. I'm fine."
She gave me a narrow-eyed glare. "Well, except for the part about no
coffee. How did you do it?" I knew my voice was too bright, but I
didn't want to talk about Dare. Or the gestating elephant in the room
right then. Or hallway, or whatever.

I just didn't want to go there.

It was too confusing.

Ally blew out a breath. "That whole one cup of coffee a day was the
worst. Not even a real cup of coffee. Like, literally, eight ounces. Who
can live on that?"

"I'm not even a huge coffee drinker and I'm literally dying at my
desk." I pushed my hair out of my face.

"And yet you're bringing us here?" Sage squinted at me. "I still can't
have coffee until I pop out this bowling ball. And even then, not when
I'm nursing. That was not in the fine print."

"You were too worried about putting your ankles up to the sky to
read the fine print, you hussy." Ally parked the stroller and did some
weird snap and twist and the carrier came out with a crazy handle.
"Are you sure we can go in here? Especially with Alex?"

"Yeah, Macy wanted to show off a little. We're going to do a tasting."

Sage perked up. She was always interested in food. "What kind of tasting?"

"Come on in, ladies," Macy yelled. "No, not there. Not every customer is six-foot-three." Macy rushed around the counter to the front of the skeleton of shelves along the longest portion of the cafe.

A tall, bearded man set his drill on the shelf in front of him. "You said you wanted a higher shelf for stock."

"Yes, but not that high." Macy put her hands on her hips. "Then I have to get the ladder out every time someone wants a damn mug. I'm not as tall as you are."

He crouched in front of her and slid out a little step stool that matched the espresso-colored wood. "Care to test it out, Ms. Devereaux? I'd say we could see eye-to-eye give or take an inch or two."

"No, that's fine." Macy cleared her throat. "That's good."

My eyebrows shot up at the blush climbing Macy's neck. I wasn't sure I'd ever seen her be anything but cool and calm with a side of surly since I'd met her.

"Hey, Gideon." Sage settled her substantial self into one of the U-shaped chairs that was actually unwrapped.

"Hey, Sage." Tall, dark and beardy glanced over at us. "I miss you over at the diner. New girl doesn't smile like you." A quick flash of bright white teeth peeked from his bearded face. Pretty green eyes crinkled at the corners before he put yellow safety glasses back on. He nodded to all of us then flicked his drill back on.

"Aw. Such a charmer." Though Sage definitely flushed with pleasure. With the new baby on the way and her hands full with reopening her family's inn and her new staging branch of Hamilton Realtors, she didn't have time to work at the Rusty Spoon anymore.

Sage's life was just like a fairy tale. One day, she was a waitress, and practically the next day, the wife to a millionaire.

Not that I was jealous.

Okay, maybe a little.

I spun around one of the chairs so Ally could tuck the carrier in before sitting across from Sage. Alex was dozing, his bottle tucked into his side, his little mouth slack.

"Milk drunk is my favorite," Ally said and dropped into a chair. "He'll be out for at least forty minutes."

Macy winced. "I didn't know you were bringing the kid."

Ally curled her fingers into her palms. "Was I not supposed to?"

"No, it's cool." She nodded to Gideon. "It's just not exactly quiet in here."

"Oh, that." Ally waved her hand. "He'd sleep if a high-speed train came through the room."

"Well, then, baby away." Macy flicked her dark braid over her shoulder. "Thanks for coming in to test a few things. I don't have a lot of caffeine-free options, but I'll concoct something for you. Sage, right?" Macy swiped the dusty table with a cloth.

Sage patted her belly. "Appreciate it."

I dropped my head onto my stacked arms. "Me too."

"What?" Macy stopped cleaning.

"Me too." I sighed hugely. "No caffeine."

"I thought we went over this already. I'll make you love coffee, Teach. We already have a few taste tests on the books."

"I loved that Orgasm one. I would love to have one every day of my life."

Macy blinked. "Did you mean Chocolate Orgasm?"

"Yes." I frowned. "Oh, well, I like having the other kind too. In fact, it's kinda why I can't have your lovely cup of coffee anymore. Even though it's like heaven created a liquid."

I was babbling. The drill turned off and the hottie carpenter dude slanted a look our way. Yeah, someone needed to stop me.

He let out a strangled cough that sounded suspiciously like a laugh. But he didn't say anything else. The snap of a measuring tape was cut only by Macy's choice of music.

I really wanted one of those coffees though. Maybe it would erase seeing Dare outside. I thunked my forehead on the table. "God."

Ally rubbed my shoulder. "Don't mind her. She just peed on the devil stick and lost."

"Thanks, Al," I said to my lap.

"What now?"

"Knocked up," Sage said sunnily.

"Oh." Macy huffed out a breath. "I'm beginning to wonder if there's an epidemic around here. Do you guys have a special club or something? 'Hey, look at me I want a baby'?"

"Seems like that sometimes, doesn't it?" Ally laughed. "However, I pumped milk for miles today. I want the most gloriously caffeinated beverage you can make."

Macy winced. "Miles?"

"What I eat or drink, pretty much the baby does. So, I pregamed. I chose you over a glass of wine, so it better be awesome."

Macy blinked down at Ally. "Gotcha. I don't have a liquor license yet, but since I'm not selling…" She shrugged. "I can add a little something."

Ally clapped lightly. "Oh, that would be glorious."

"You got it." Macy folded her arms, her spray bottle of cleaner peeking from the crook of her elbow. "So now I have to figure out preggo drinks?"

"Yes." I sighed.

I still wasn't all the way on board with this new reality. Or the stares I got at school. Of course it didn't help that I'd blurted it out to half the town at Sage's baby shower. Nope. I couldn't have waited until later.

Then again, it was all Dare's fault.

"Good thing I only drink my own coffee. I don't want any of what you guys are drinking when you're not in here. Babies," Macy said with a shudder.

Gideon's measuring tape snapped a little more forcefully. Enough to make me lift my gaze from the colorful mosaic tile floor. "Believe me, it wasn't planned."

"Not to be indelicate, but we do live in a state that allows for such concerns."

My hand instantly went to my midriff. "I know, but I couldn't. I mean, it's your decision if you want to do that and all that, but I couldn't." My heart fluttered like crazy at the thought. Even with all the doubts swirling in my head and the less than favorable situation I found myself in at school, I wanted this baby.

I swallowed down a lump in my throat. It was probably the first time I'd actually thought about it as more than just a shocking speck of insanity making my food choices a bit more precarious.

"Then we'll find a way around the baby business. Any allergies? Dislikes?"

We all shook our heads.

Macy swung her spray bottle around her finger then slapped her towel over her shoulder. "I guess I need to learn how to work with the town, huh? I'll be right back." She glanced at the hottie carpenter with a small frown before busying herself behind the counter.

"You sure you're all right?"

"Hmm?"

"Have you talked to Dare yet?" Sage rubbed her hand over the top of her beach ball belly.

"No."

"Don't you think you should?"

"Don't you think I did enough damage?" I tucked my hand under my chin. "I need to get my foot surgically detached from my mouth. I said it in front of *everyone*." I flopped my arm out on the table and sagged. "It's all his fault. If he hadn't been all high-handed and jerk-ish, I could have handled it. But no, he had to spill the beans in public." I hadn't even known for sure and he'd announced it to everyone.

I had a right to my anger.

Just like he had a right not to answer any of my texts.

Then again, his jaw had been pure granite outside. When he'd seen me, the whole world had stopped for a second. I'd tried to recover by talking to Alex. But I'd felt his eyes on me. And God, he'd looked so good.

Dripping wet, for pity's sake. His freckled shoulders dotted with sweat or water or whatever. All around delicious and not even close to touchable.

I groaned and covered my face with my hands. "I don't know what to do."

"You need to go to the doctor. That's what you need to do."

"I know." With a sigh, I dropped my hands to the table. "I meant to call today, but things got crazy."

"Things are always crazy." Sage winced and rubbed circles along her side. "This little girl is determined to kick her way out, I swear."

Ugh. I was being selfish. "Can I get you something?"

Sage placed her hand over mine. "I'm good, honey. This is about you right now."

"I'm fine."

"Far from it, cupcake." Her eyes widened. "Speaking of cupcake."

Macy came back to the table with a plate full of pastries, cupcakes, and a decadent-looking cookie that was mine. I snatched it off the plate before Sage could even lift her hand.

"Wow. And she says she's fine." Sage smiled up at Macy. "You almost lost a finger."

"Hazards of the job." Macy passed out little orange plates with lettering on them. "Especially with Vee in the sweatshop in the back. Hard to resist." She winked. "I'll be back with your drinks in a minute."

I broke apart the fat cookie and moaned when chocolate flowed out of the center. I scooped up a finger full and moaned. "Nutella."

Ally broke off a hunk of the cookie and laughed when I dragged my plate closer to me. She popped it in her mouth with a groan.

"Back off."

"Okay, okay." She lifted a blueberry muffin off the center plate. "Man, I keep trying to get this last ten pounds of baby weight off, but it ain't happening today." She broke off the top and plump blueberries dotted the golden cake. In the center was a jam of some sort. Ally swiped her finger through the rich blue stuff. It had to be some sort of curd. And I only knew that from watching the *Great British Bake Off* for the last three nights. I was officially almost done with season two.

I was pathetic.

The lot of us were moaning through our food when Macy came back. "You're going to give Gideon a hard-on with all the ruckus."

"Worth it," Ally said around a bite.

"Glad to hear it." Macy set a bowl-sized mug in front of Ally. I leaned over to sniff the sumptuous coffee and hint of…mint?

Ally wiped her fingers on the napkin in her lap then wiggled them before cupping them around the cherry red ceramic. "I know it's damn near ninety outside, but there's nothing like a warm mug of coffee." She brought it to her lips and sipped loudly. Her gold eyes widened. "That's a liquid Thin Mint."

"I can't wait to not be pregnant," Sage whined.

Macy hurried back to the counter and returned with two tall, pink glasses. "I have a little something summery for you two. Even if fall is my favorite season, I appreciate a little extension on summer. It doesn't exactly go with chocolate, but I think you'll forgive me."

I sniffed at the glass and the little lemon-shaped ice cubes. "This is the cutest thing I've ever seen."

"Well, taste it."

"Right." I wrapped my lips around the straw and gave Macy a startled look. Not a plastic straw. It was metal and super cold. I took a pull and moaned. "Watermelon and…mint?"

"Figured I'd keep the theme." Macy nibbled on her lower lip. "What do you think? I added some mint and lime juice to the ice cubes. I call it Watermelon Crush."

"I need a case," I said and gulped down half of it. I winced at the brain freeze, but it was worth it. And it just happened to be the first thing I'd had that didn't make my insides flip and try to revolt. I'd been living on room temperature water for days.

"I'm waiting for an order of pressed apples to come in. I'll have a few different kinds of cider, which should be good for you guys too."

"These plates are the cutest thing." Sage licked the tip of her finger and picked up the crumbs off her plate before tucking them into her mouth. "You thought of everything." She tipped it up to show an illustration of a sassy little black kitten chewing on the O in the word *boo*.

Macy tucked her hands into her tight black jeans. "Halloween is my Christmas."

I looked around. Bats and flames were the dominant theme. As well as surprisingly cute black cats tucked into various corners and shelves. "Couldn't tell at all."

Macy ducked her head. For the first time since I met her, she looked a little sheepish. "It's coming together."

"It's going to be really cool."

"Thanks. And I appreciate you guys coming in. Vee just finished a tray of turnovers. I'll pack some up so you can bring them home."

Ally pulled her wallet out of the diaper bag. "Let us pay for something."

Macy shook her head. "We aren't official yet. Besides, you're saving my ass from expanding. Veronica, our baker and all-around artist, has been trying out all her recipes. If I look at another leaf cookie, I'm going to scream."

"I'll take some for my classroom. If there's no peanuts or anything in them."

"You got it." She seemed to straighten her shoulders before walking by Gideon as well. My eyebrow rose when she gave him a dose of side-eye, then my expression turned into a full-on smile when hottie carpenter dude watched her ass as she walked by.

"Who's this Gideon guy?" I asked.

"Local handyman." Sage took a sip of her drink, her eyelashes fluttering in pleasure. She let out a sigh then leaned forward. "John Gideon, but everyone calls him Gideon. Interested?"

"God, no. I think I've had enough of men at the moment. He seems into Macy though."

"Oh." Sage tipped her head as she sucked up more watermelon crack. "Yeah, now that you mention it, he can't keep his eyes off of her. Interesting."

Ally sipped from her mug. "No."

"No what?" Sage asked innocently.

"No, you are not setting them up. I saw that look."

"I didn't do anything." Sage sat back in her chair.

"Macy doesn't seem like the type to need a fix-up." I chopped my straw through the logjam of ice. I'd finished the drink way too fast, but I felt much better.

"She's new in town. I would be doing a public service."

I laughed. Before I could ask for more, Macy came back with a square plate of cookies and a pitcher of gloriousness.

"Here you go, ladies. Vee is boxing up your goodies now. I also made up a thermos of the leftover Watermelon Crush for you, Kelsey. Keeps you hydrated. I'll do some more research on pregnancy drinks and shoot you a text to try another few if that's okay."

"Oh, you don't have to do that."

Macy shrugged. "When in Rome."

"You're spoiling me."

Alex picked then to wake up and wail out his displeasure.

"So much for that forty-minute nap." Ally sighed. "He'll be a bear all afternoon." She swung the baby up on her shoulder with ease and hummed to him absently. He wouldn't be deterred. "Okey doke, looks like that's my cue."

"Aww, really?"

"Yeah, I need to get back home anyway." She smiled up at Macy. "Thanks for letting us come and crash for a bit."

Macy's eyebrows were beetled together at the scowling baby. A minute later, Alex let out an even louder bellow. "Is he okay?"

"Oh, yeah." Ally took another drink from her coffee. "One more, because hello, this is so good. Okay, pal. We're going, we're going." She stood up and settled him back into the carrier.

Sage hefted herself out of the chair. "Thanks, Macy."

"Do you want me to drive you home?" I asked Sage.

"No, I'll go with Ally. You go on up and relax. You look like you're going to drop on the spot."

The two of them swiftly packed up and headed out. Sage was happily picking through the large bag of goodies on her way out the side door.

I was tired, but even more than that, I was restless. I had Sage's doctor's phone number burning a hole in my planner. And an ache in the pit of my stomach I didn't know how to fix.

I wandered over to the counter where Macy was talking to Gideon, but I backed away before I could interrupt. Macy spotted me and patted the bag in front of her. "I've got some stuff for your kids." She screwed up her lips. "You know, the ones in your classroom, not the one you're brewing up in there." She made a little circle in the air.

Gideon's eyebrows went up. "Congrats."

I pasted on a bright smile. I'd come from a pretty small town, but it had nothing on the very involved Crescent Cove. God, I needed to talk to my mom about this too.

I just wanted to hide in my apartment.

"Got anything super chocolatey?" I asked brightly.

"Lava cake?"

"Sold. Or begging, whichever. Just hand it over and no one gets hurt."

Macy gave me her usual sardonic grin. "You got it." Her eyes trailed over Gideon one more time before she disappeared into the back.

"I'm getting the feeling Macy isn't sure what to do with the kid thing."

"I think you'd be correct. I teach them and I'm not sure what to do half the time."

Gideon shoved his hands into his pockets. "Right. Me neither."

Before I could say something else regarding that little nugget of information, Macy came sailing through her swinging door with a little white box. "Fresh from the oven. Hope you like cherries."

My stomach growled. "I do. Let's see if the new intruder does too." I accepted the box with a little wave. "Thanks, Macy. Can't wait to see what else you come up with for drinks. I'm your happy guinea pig."

"Well, we've got two weeks until opening day so I'll be sure to be extra annoying, don't you worry."

Before I was a few steps away, the deep timber of Gideon's voice lowered and I heard a smoky chuckle from Macy in reaction. At least those two were finding their way.

And that made me miss Dare even more. I wasn't supposed to. And if I did miss him a little bit, it was supposed to be the womanly flutters kind of missing. Okay, so they were a little more than flutters. More like my own version of lava cake where he was concerned.

The man could tend my gardens like a master…well, gardener.

Nope, now I had a snake in the garden. Or was he the snake? God, this metaphor was going off the rails. Like my life.

I trudged up the stairs and set the bag for my class on the entry table because something was also wrong with my memory since I'd become a new fledgling member of Babyville. I needed my planner for simple things I'd been doing most of my adult life. Because I could not keep a thought in my stupid brain.

Except one.

The one that was on a loop when I tried to sleep. How much I missed Dare calling me darlin'.

How much I missed Dare, period.

I pulled out my phone and stared at the last text I'd sent to him on Sunday. The one that said it was delivered on my screen, but had not been answered.

Please talk to me.

FOURTEEN

I OVER-CRANKED MY SOCKET WRENCH AND BANGED MY KNUCKLE INTO the radiator I was trying to replace. "Goddammit." I shook my hand with a hiss and made a fist to see the damage.

"You keep busting up those knuckles, you're not going to have a hand left, boy."

"Yeah, yeah." I'd turned into a walking disaster zone in the shop lately. Hell, I hadn't been this messed up when Katherine walked.

Jerome sighed. "Good thing it's nearly five. Get the hell out of here. I'll finish that up. I'm tired of you adding your DNA to every car we service."

I hung my head. "I was hoping for a few extra hours tonight."

Jerome jammed his rag into his back pocket. "Nope. Maybe next week. Go out and have a good time. It's Friday night, for God's sake."

I was a single dad. I didn't have a good time. I accidentally stuck my dick into a kindergarten teacher twice and got her in trouble. Probably. Maybe. Hell, that would be why I looked like I'd been on the wrong end of a Ginsu knife demonstration.

It was the *maybe* part that was killing me more than the baby. What the hell did that say about me? Analyzing shit to death wasn't my thing. The fact that I was still fucked up about this almost a week later was ridiculous.

I dug out my phone, flicking away from Kelsey's text that I still hadn't answered.

I sent a text to my friend who owned the furniture store across the street. I needed a goddamn beer.

Before I finished washing up, I got a *hell yeah* reply. Evidently, August was feeling just as glad for the end of the work week as I was. My mother was already expecting me to work late tonight, so an extra hour wouldn't matter.

It was a quick drive to The Spinning Wheel and a relatively thick crowd for Crescent Cove made for some creative parking. Even after I got inside, it took me nearly five minutes to find him.

He waved at me from one of the pool tables at the back of the bar. There were already two glasses on the shelf behind our usual table. That wasn't a good sign.

I took down a pool cue. If I'd known we were going to play, I would have brought my stick, but it would do to kill some time. Running the table against August was a normal night.

It seemed like it had been ages since normal had been anywhere in my sphere.

We didn't even really talk. Our competitive natures made all the bullshit crowding my brain empty out for twenty minutes—then thirty as we went head to head on a final third tie-breaker game.

A flash of red hair distracted me enough to scratch my last shot.

"What the fuck, Kramer?"

I thumped my head on the bumper and swore. Especially when I looked again and the girl didn't resemble Kelsey at all. I definitely deserved to lose my game.

If that wasn't a direct correlation to my life, I didn't know what was.

August snapped a beer down on the green in front of me. "Obviously, you need that."

I stood up, grabbed my beer, and set my stick back into the rack. August nodded to the next set of guys waiting on a table.

"Nice game, man."

I grunted at the kid who barely qualified as legal. He slung his arm around the redhead who had killed my concentration. She was cute, but too hard-edged to be my girl.

Fuck.

Not my girl.

My hand curled tighter around my pint glass.

August clapped his hand over my shoulder and pushed me toward a table away from the jukebox. "You are wound tighter than Sister Linda over at that school your kid goes to."

I dropped into a chair and caught the waitress's eye. I lifted my beer and flashed two fingers. "Yeah, it's been a shitastic week." I scrubbed my fingers through my freshly shorn hair. "It was picture day at school."

August snorted. "Is that why you're all pretty?" He tapped his own head of wild, spiky hair.

"Well, if I was going to get Wes in a chair, I had to go first. Of course then he decides to see how long he can get his cup to suction cup itself to his mouth."

"Uh oh."

"Yep." I drew a circle around my mouth. "Unfortunately, my kid doesn't have a beard to hide the bruised ring."

"Sucks, but not like you to get wound up over something like that."

"Nah. Just one more thing for my ma to yell at me about. Add in work shit and...other shit. Yeah," I lifted my beer and drained it, "I definitely needed this."

"I hear that. Kinleigh—the new chick upstairs?" At my obviously blank look, August sighed. "The clothing store above my shop?"

"Oh, right. My mom likes that store." I shrugged. Chick clothes kinda went over my head.

"Yeah, well, she's driving me insane. Dude, she plays K-Pop at a decibel that would make a dog shriek." August kicked out his big feet and crossed his ankles, then smiled warmly at the waitress when she brought over our beers.

"Hey, guys. Want anything from the kitchen?"

August glanced at me, then back up at the pretty redhead. Again, not as pretty as my redhead, but since when did we have so many of them in the goddamn Cove? "Two cheeseburgers with everything."

Man, I must look like shit if August was trying to feed me. He definitely wasn't the mothering type.

I nodded at our waitress with a tight smile as I twisted the short stem of my Stella Artois glass on the scarred table. Though my mind was elsewhere, I attempted to click into the diatribe of complaints out of August.

I wasn't sure what K-Pop was, but figured it was close to dance music of some sort. When he mentioned this Kinleigh's skirt, heels, and scent repeatedly, I couldn't help but laugh.

"What's so funny?"

"You like her."

"No, I don't." He lifted his beer and took a long swallow.

"Well, if you don't like her, you at least want to get in her pants. Or skirt—whatever. Because dude, I don't think I've ever heard you mention clothes so much in the entire seven years I've known you."

August tipped his head back. "I sound like a fucking girl."

"Maybe."

"Christ," he muttered. "I do. My man card is going to get stripped away from me."

"Already was," I said as I sipped my beer. "The minute you mentioned K-Pop."

"You haven't heard that shit. It'll make your ears bleed."

I laughed. By the time our burgers arrived, we'd moved onto football as a topic of conversation. It was easy and didn't require concentration. I even texted my mom to check on Wes. He was doing a puzzle with my pop, and wouldn't care if I stayed out another hour.

When we killed another hour arguing about the state of our teams —My Patriots and his shitty Giants—I finally felt like myself for the first time in weeks.

The happy hour crowd had moved on and the bar was full of regulars when I signaled our waitress for the check.

"I got it." August snatched the receipt.

"Since when do you pick up a tab?"

He shrugged. "Since you never text me to get a beer."

"Sure I do."

"No, I text you—not the other way around."

I frowned. "That can't be right."

He waved it off. "Not a big deal. You have a kid. Hanging at the bar isn't exactly your scene anymore."

"Makes me sound shitty."

"Now I know something's up. You and self-analysis don't belong in the same room together."

I couldn't disagree there. I laced my fingers behind my neck and popped each knuckle. "Fuck, man."

"That good?"

"I sorta hooked up with this girl."

"Sorta? What, you trip and your dick fell in?"

I snorted. "Closer to the truth than not. It was a random hookup." I shrugged. "You know how it goes. Sometimes there's that itch."

"Well, we've both had plenty of one-nighters over the years."

"Yeah, but not with women from Crescent Cove."

August winced. "Ahh. Yeah, no."

"Oh, and Wes's teacher."

"Hello. That hot redhead?"

I didn't realize I'd snarled until he held up his hands.

"One-nighter, my ass."

"That's why I don't mess with people from town, man. It gets weird." I stared hard at the table. That was a fucking lie. It would have been fine. Maybe even more than fine if I was still just hooking up with her.

I could handle that.

It was the rest. The army of tests that had sealed my fate.

"I might need another beer."

August leaned back in his chair and waved at our waitress. "Two more, sweetheart."

She nodded.

"Come on, Kramer. Pull the tampon out. What the fuck's the problem?"

"Asshole."

He waggled his eyebrows. "You love it."

"Shithead."

"I love when you talk sweet to me. Makes me all tingly."

"Why am I friends with you again?"

He folded his hands on the table. "Because I saved you in that mosh pit in Albany."

"Pantera," we both said in unison.

"Good times." I leaned back when the waitress put down the beers and a new ticket.

"No rush, but new bill just in case. I'm taking a quick break."

I smiled up at her. "Thanks."

"So…" August frowned. "Is this the chick you got the bed for?"

I stared down at the table, trailing my finger through the condensation on my glass.

"Oh, shit. You've been holding onto that favor for three fucking years. That bed was the best in my stock, you fucker."

I took a long drink of my beer, draining it to almost half.

"Jesus, you're gone for this chick."

"No. Maybe. Fuck, man. She's pregnant."

August slumped back in his chair. "Oh, shit."

"Yeah."

He pushed over his beer. "I'll drive you home."

I laughed and pushed his beer back over to him. "I'm good. It's not even the kid thing. It's worse. Even saying it out loud sounds like it should be on one of my mom's shows, for fuck's sake."

"How about you get off that bush you're beating?"

I flashed him my middle finger. "I don't even know. That's the problem all around. We hooked up twice, a couple of weeks apart. But…" I trailed off.

"Don't say it." August groaned and drained half of his own beer.

Every guy's worst nightmare. His silence was enough

commiseration. "Yeah. What the hell am I going to say? 'Oh, it might be my kid you're having, but maybe not. See ya at the ultrasound'? Fuck me."

"Yeah, that's shitty. I've never met her. I mean, I've seen her around. She's right across from my store. She hangs out with the newly minted Hamilton girls."

"Yeah. Seth's kid is in Wes's class and we got to be friends. And I've helped out with a few house things for Oliver. Sometimes he flips houses instead of just playing realtor." I shrugged. "You know how it goes in this goddamn town. Everyone's in each other's business."

Why I stayed in my own lane most of the time. It was just too fucking weird.

Kelsey was a perfect mistake.

"Does she have a boyfriend?"

"I don't know, man." It didn't feel right though. Kelsey didn't seem like someone who'd have a few guys on the hook. Then again, we weren't much on talking when we were together. We were too busy getting naked.

Or she was getting feisty and then I wanted to get her naked.

"Sounds like you need to talk to her."

The phone burning in my pocket backed up that statement. "Yeah, she blew me off." I took a sip of my beer. "Sort of. We had a fight and we haven't talked since the pregnant thing happened." Except for the texts she'd sent me as a white flag and I'd been ignoring.

It was way too much to go into.

"That's fucked up." August cracked his knuckles. "Is she...you know, keeping it?"

I hadn't even thought about that. I dragged my hands under the table and fisted them on top of my knees. Fuck, I hadn't even...

"I don't know."

"Obviously, you're a little more than messed up about her. Is this where I have to tell you to man up and talk to her? Or you got this?"

I bounced my fist against the wood twice. "No, I got this."

"That's what I thought."

I pulled out my phone and fired off the text before I could stop myself.

Think we should talk. I'll pick you up for dinner tomorrow?

My gut stopped twisting when I saw the bubbles not even a minute later.

Yes, I'd love to talk. Dinner sounds great.

FIFTEEN

I NIBBLED ON MY LOWER LIP AS I STARED AT MY CELL FOR THE nineteenth time today. So like Dare. Right to the point. No fluff.

Funny how I could know him so well, and not know him at all. I slid a hand over my still very flat belly. I seemed to be able to figure him out better than my own self.

Great grammar there, Teach.

But it was true.

If anyone asked me six months ago if I'd have had two different men in my life within the span of a month, I'd have told them they were certifiable. Heck, if it hadn't been for Tommy's grandmother's funeral, I'd never have done…*that* with him.

I didn't want him back.

I was much happier since he'd flaked out of my life.

And now I could be ruining something great. Or not.

I jammed my fingers into my hair. If I thought about this situation any more, I was going to go out of my mind. Add in the whispers and sly glances from the teachers at school—oh, and couldn't forget about the parents.

Yep.

I was ready to pin an S to my sweaters. Or maybe on the soles of my boots? Would that be better, so they could see it coming and going? Who needed Louboutins when you could have that kind of red on your soles?

And now I was being ridiculous.

I sat down to pull on my knee-high boots. I couldn't dress up to run around after first graders, but I could look as good as possible tonight. So I'd pulled out my fawn-colored boots and my favorite corduroy skirt with matching tights.

My usual bird legs had filled out a little, giving me a hint of curves I didn't usually have. And maybe the snap on my skirt was a little tighter than it used to be, but I couldn't think about that. I wasn't due for ages.

I'd even found the nerve to make an appointment with Ally's doctor. Next Friday, I'd know a little bit more about what I was working with. And after tonight, I'd know for sure if I was doing all of this alone or…

I shook my head. I couldn't think about that. We were just going to talk tonight.

As usual, I was getting way ahead of myself.

I jumped at the trill of my buzzer. "Get a hold of yourself, Kelsey." Was my skirt too short? I tugged at the back. Had my ass actually grown too?

When the buzzer went off again, I rushed over to the security panel near my door. "I'll be right down."

"I can come up. And you should ask who it is first, Kel." Dare's gruff voice made my stomach flip. I shut my eyes and sagged against the wall. And him coming upstairs wasn't a good idea anyway. We usually just yelled at each other and then got naked.

We needed to have a grown-up conversation and that required us going out in public. At least that was the game plan I was going with.

"Uh, right. Yeah, I'll remember that. I'll um…be right down."

I grabbed my leather bag and jacket that matched my boots. It felt nice to be an adult and maybe I'd overdone it a little, but my life consisted of a teacher bag in rainbow colors to hide stains and paint. I didn't have a reason to impress much, and I really wanted him to think I was pretty, dammit.

Not that it mattered. We'd done the deed while I was sweaty after moving, for God's sake. He'd even…

I wasn't going to think about what he'd done.

Especially between my thighs. Until I'd been screaming like a lunatic.

I squeezed my legs together and prayed I could tamp down the flood of out of control hormones that were making me increasingly more crazy. I wasn't sure if the usual ones or the pregnancy ones were to blame.

Had it already been happening after Tommy?

I hung my head. Instead of the sweet flip of exhilaration I got from Dare, now I was twisting with unease. I didn't want it to be Tommy's. Not at all.

I huffed out a breath and straightened my shoulders. Nope, I couldn't think like that. I'd know more after my appointment. And after tonight. Maybe.

Hopefully.

I locked up and rushed down the steps. He was standing at the bottom of the stairs, his startling blue eyes focused on me like two lasers.

"Oh, hi."

He rubbed his hand over the top of his head. "Macy let me in."

"That's fine." I glanced down at him and my stomach did a slow roll. He was wearing dark-washed jeans and a blue plaid shirt tucked in with a navy sport coat. He'd dressed up for me. "You cut your hair."

He cleared his throat. "Wes needed a cut, so that means me too."

"It looks good. You look nice." I stopped on the second to last stair, which meant I was a little taller than him with the heels on my boots. I was so damn gangly and tall, it was nice to be with someone who was taller than me so I could wear something other than flats.

Well, except now.

But he didn't move away. He didn't make room for me. He tipped his chin up so we were eye-to-eye. "You're so goddamn beautiful."

I blinked. "I…thanks."

He reached for my hand and pulled me down the last steps. "I thought we'd go to The Cove."

My eyebrows shot up. "That's expensive." I hadn't been in town long, but there were only a few fancy places within the actual Crescent Cove limits.

His eyes narrowed.

"Not that you can't afford it, just wow."

He lifted a shoulder. "You deserve better than a burger at The Spinning Wheel or a blue plate special at the diner."

"I do?"

He crowded closer to me, touching his forehead to mine. "You do." Then he stepped back, but he didn't release my hand.

I trailed behind him, a little drunk on this new side of Dare. If I couldn't have a glass of wine, I'd take this feeling every day. Whew.

Instead of his usual truck, he led me to a matte black car that looked as if it has been modified into something between a sports car and a beast of a car out of the show *Supernatural*. He lunged forward before I could grab the handle and opened the door for me. I murmured a *thank you* and slid inside. It smelled of leather and something else. Dare didn't usually wear cologne, but there was something different about him tonight.

He got in on the driver's side and while it seemed huge from the outside, the inside shrank when he sat next to me. There were two bucket seats, but they were one huge unit inside the car with a monster shifter on the floor.

"I thought you had a truck."

Dare grinned. "Buckle up, Kel."

"So many things I don't know." I thought I'd said it under my breath, but his grin kicked up a notch, making him look younger and sweeter. And somehow more dangerous.

Maybe we needed to turn down the heat.

Were these tights too hot?

He gunned the engine and the vibration of it curled through me and came up out of my chest with a little moan. Well, that was unexpected.

"I used to be a race car driver. We found this old Boss abandoned at one of the tracks we used to use for practice. I hauled it in and rebuilt it over the years." He shifted and eased onto Main Street.

It was dusk and a few people turned their heads to watch us pull away. Suddenly, I felt like I was going out with someone my dad wouldn't exactly approve of. Why that made me inordinately happy, I wasn't going to dissect.

"Race...wow." I turned my body toward him, leaning against the huge door. "Like NASCAR?"

He nodded. "My brother and I chased up from pit crews to drivers. Was a bitch—er, sorry."

I shrugged. "I like adult conversations after listening to six-year-olds all day. Especially the bad words." Especially when *he* said them. There was something about his rumbly voice that made everything come alive inside of me. Like his voice was rusty from disuse.

He turned onto the lake road. "Our reservations aren't for an hour. Okay with a drive and to talk?"

I swallowed. The talking part was the hardest part. I had so much I wanted to tell him, and so much I was afraid to explain. How the hell did I get into this situation? This was more like something my little sister Rylee would do. She was the impetuous wild child. I was the good girl. The boring, responsible one.

Oh, right. My stupid vagina was responsible for all of this. Never having a man who knew what he was doing down there had left me susceptible to Dare's particular brand of excitement. One-night stand with a nine-month side effect.

Hopefully, *his* side effect.

The thought of a baby growing inside of me was already freaking me out, but the mere idea that it could be Tommy's...

Ugh. What a damn mess.

Dare's fingers tightened on the wheel and I realized I hadn't responded to him. "Yes. Talking is good."

He blew out a slow breath. "Okay, good."

"Why did you give up racing?"

"You know that's not what we should be talking about."

I swallowed. "I know. I just…well, I want to get to know you a bit. We kinda skipped that part."

"Does it matter?"

The blunt question made me straighten in my seat. "I want it to. I want this to be more than just…*this*." I covered my middle with my hand. "Unless you don't—"

"I do." His voice was harsh. "Kel, I'm…" He trailed off, his knuckles white on the steering wheel. "I suck at this."

A bubble of a laugh escaped my chest. "Like I'm any better? You get near me and I just want to climb on you. It's so crazy. I never had that problem before. My past boyfriends haven't exactly been like you." I twisted the ring on my forefinger as I took in the streaks of pink and purple along the lake.

"What? Blue collar?"

I whipped my head around. "What? No. I mean, it's not like I dated rich guys, Dare. I'm a regular girl—a teacher, for Pete's sake. I'm not sure why you're always saying things like that." I reached over to grip his upper arm. It was flexed tight, the muscles under his sports coat unforgiving. I swallowed. I remembered every inch of his arms when he leaned over me. "I don't care what you do."

He finally relaxed under my touch. "Not all women feel the same way. Plenty want to have a little fun with a mechanic, but any more than that, not so much." He shrugged.

I let my hand slide away. Evidently, we both came with a bit of baggage. I'm not sure why that relaxed me a little, but it did.

"Let me ask the hard question then."

I clutched my hands in my lap. "Who's the other guy?"

"Yeah."

His voice was low and gruff in that way that made me want to do anything else but talk about this. But it wasn't fair to ignore it. Even if I wanted to do just that. Because Tommy Larson was not the man I wanted to think about right now. Especially with a man as virile and exciting as Dare right next to me. The veritable bad boy complete with a car that made my thighs vibrate.

But that wasn't the important part. That wasn't what would make a good future for my baby. And even without knowing all the meaningless details I could rattle off about Tommy, Dare was still a far better man. The way he took care of his son, took care of everyone —including me. Those were the things that really mattered.

If I didn't have Dare in my life, I'd be okay. Not perfect, but I could do this.

I just didn't want to.

We drove in silence for a few minutes. The sun finally truly disappeared and the night was so clear. I felt like I could reach up and actually touch the stars. I wasn't exactly a city girl, but my hometown seemed so different from Crescent Cove.

I was still staring out the window when I started talking. "Tommy is a good guy at heart. I can't say I hate him or anything. He didn't exactly treat me badly. I just don't think he cared enough to make me a priority in any way."

"Hate to break it to you, but that's a shitty guy."

I turned to him. The dim lights of his dashboard made his face seem even more angular and dangerous. I shivered and he instantly reached for the dials on his heater. "No, I'm good."

He nodded and his hand went back to his shifter.

"It took some time for me to get there, but I agree. We broke up a while ago. Then his Granny Flo died. I actually liked her a lot and when I went to the funeral, one thing led to another. It was stupid. I knew that right after I did it, but we were both sad and there was a bottle of wine." I sighed. "He left the next morning and sent me a text that he had to go find himself."

"What a fucking asshole."

I laughed. Maybe it was part sob, but I blinked away the tears.

"Tell me you're not crying over that dirtbag."

"No. Definitely not." Dare's answer was a grunt which made me laugh even more. "It was just the impetus to me getting up the courage to go out on my own. When the full-time job came up at the Academy,

I wanted to make a fresh start. Last year, I'd just been filling in while one of the teachers was on maternity leave."

So many babies. No more drinking the water in Crescent Cove —check.

"Ah. That makes sense. I knew you were friends with Sage already."

I nodded. "I really loved it here. I was going to keep commuting until I found a place I liked that was a bit closer, but when Tommy up and left after the night we spent together, I impulsively decided to move to Crescent Cove. And you know the rest."

"You moved here without a damn bed."

My cheeks heated. "You didn't seem to mind that first night."

"Of course I didn't. A hot girl gives me a look like that and I'm all in."

"I did not."

"Darlin', you were eating me alive with your eyes."

"I was lusting after the very delicious pizza you brought."

"Right."

I totally hadn't been. Each time we'd been together lived in my head like a technicolor blockbuster movie with all the good sex parts on a loop. Only in my head they didn't cut to black. I got all the dirty parts too.

That's called porn, Kelsey.

Only porn was way less exciting than what Dare had done to me. But was that all we were? Friction and a baby? A baby that might not even be his. What the hell kind of package was I for a guy like him?

Dare pulled back into town, the quiet darkness of the lake replaced by the soft glow from the reconditioned gas lights that lined the streets. He turned up the winding lane that led to The Cove. The restaurant was right on the lake with a breathtaking view of the still water.

He parked and came around to open my door.

The wind had kicked up, reminding us that fall was in full effect. October in upstate New York was a strange mix of hot and cold. The minute the sun went down, the temperature followed suit. He helped me out and closed my door, then caged me against his car.

"Just one more thing before we go inside."

"What?"

He traced the side of his thumb along the couple of curls I'd managed to bend my stick straight hair into. "That day of the baby shower? When we were arguing in the bathroom."

"Where you ordered me to take the tests?"

A muscle jumped in his jaw as he gritted his teeth. "Not my finest hour, but I needed to know, Kel."

"I know," I whispered.

"Did you contact this Tommy guy?"

"No." I frowned up at him. "Why would I?"

He blew out a breath. "I did something that might make you mad."

"Why?" I drew out the word. Where was he going with this? "I'm not with him. I don't want him. I thought you got that."

"Well, while you were in the can—er, the bathroom, he texted you. I was freaking out already and then there's this dude texting you that he wanted to meet up. I believe repeat performance was mentioned."

"Oh." My stomach flipped. "Oh, God. Dare, I wouldn't have. I swear."

"I know. I know that now, but I just reacted. I had no right, but I wanted the right. I was so fucked up about it all and I was standing out there and you might…" He growled. "I deleted the text."

I frowned. "From my phone?"

"Yeah."

"Oh." I blinked. My whole body shouldn't have warmed up as if he'd given me a bundle of roses. But maybe from Dare this was about the same.

Flags probably should've been going up like mad. He'd gone into my phone and deleted a text from my ex. Instead, all I wanted was to understand.

"Why?" I asked.

"Because you're mine, dammit. I wasn't sharing you with some dickhead that put a winky face in a text looking for a damn booty call. Now that I know just how much of a douchebag he is, I'm glad—"

I lifted onto my toes and closed my mouth over his. He slid his arms around me and hauled me close. The kiss was sweeter than his hold. As if he was holding back. I didn't really want gentle.

I wanted all of Dare, but right then, it felt too good to stop.

Finally, he pulled away. "So, you're not mad then?"

"I should be. And if you do anything like that again, I'll...do something."

That little smirk came out again. "Oh, yeah? Like what?"

"I don't know, but it won't be good."

He hooked his arm around my neck and urged me forward with a kiss to my temple. "I'm willing to risk it."

I elbowed him in the gut. "Excuse me?"

"No, I won't go into your phone. But I am kind of curious what your version of vengeance is."

"You shouldn't be."

"I'm a little masochistic it seems." He dropped his arm and twisted our fingers together as he drew me up the stairs to The Cove. "Hungry?"

I smiled. "Starving."

And not just for food.

SIXTEEN

My heart raced as we walked through the restaurant. It was just past the dinner rush and moving into the quiet murmurs of cocktail-fueled pickups. I'd arranged for a table toward the back by the window. I didn't know what the hell I was doing, but Kelsey wasn't just a fling.

Not anymore.

Sitting in the car with her had been far more normal than I'd expected. No shouting and accusations, no epic levels of drama. I'd been braced for them. Nothing had ever been easy with Katherine, or with a lot of the women in my past.

But with Kelsey, everything seemed bigger and quieter at the same time. Part of me wanted to turn around, to run and close off the feelings she was dragging out of me. She didn't demand a damn thing and she could have—*should* have. Even with the unknown paternity floating in the air like smoke, she didn't ask for anything more than my time.

Maybe that was why I wanted to grab onto her. To never let go.

I'd done what was right when I'd gotten Katherine pregnant. But it had never *felt* right. Even standing at the altar of the small church my parents belonged to had been hot and uncomfortable. Seeing her

169

waiting for me at the end of the aisle had reinforced my sense of duty and not much else.

None of the same feelings rolled through me when it came to Kelsey. Being responsible was only a small part of the amalgam of emotions battling for space inside me. Peace, urgent need, and the desire to make her mine were all battling for control.

In the car, she'd stirred that feeling of rightness inside me. But in such a short time, how could she offer me the peace I'd been searching for?

It didn't make sense.

When we sat down, she smiled up at the waiter and ordered water with extra lime. So very Kelsey. Simple with a side of tart. Just like her distractible mouth.

"Whatever you have on tap is fine for me," I murmured. I didn't even care about the beer. I just wanted the guy to scram.

Before I could even think about it, words were tumbling out of my mouth. "Marry me, Kelsey."

"What?" Her golden-brown eyes went huge. "We didn't even order."

I blinked. "That's your answer?"

"No. I mean, of course not."

"No?"

She fumbled across the table for my hand, but the damn waiter was already heading back with our drinks. I growled and pulled my hands under the table to fist them on my legs.

"Can I get you an appetizer or anything? Or do you need a few minutes to look—"

The growl in my chest must have escaped because the waiter suddenly took a step back. "I'll come back."

Kelsey smiled up at him. "That'd be great." She leaned forward as soon as he disappeared. "What did you just ask me?"

"I think you heard me," I said between gritted teeth.

"No, I couldn't have. Because you didn't just sit down and ask me to marry you."

"I did."

She blinked again. Her eyes were more like an owl's now. Stupidly cute. "Why?"

I was so fucking this up. I hadn't even meant to blurt that out. And maybe she didn't want to marry me. Maybe I was good enough to be with and have a baby with, but not be bound to.

Because forever felt huge and impossibly right in my head. Maybe she didn't feel the same way.

"I..." Words wouldn't come. I wasn't a word guy, but I knew I was fumbling this. "I don't care if the kid is mine biologically. In my head, it's mine. In my head, you're already *both* mine. Let me take care of you, Kelsey. I know it's fast, but it's right."

Tears filled her eyes. "You'd do that? For me? You don't have to."

I came around the table and knelt beside her. Suddenly, the conversations around us went quiet. Unnerved, I almost went back to my seat, but I had to get this out. "I know I don't have to. I want to. If you'll have me. I know I come as a package."

She cupped my cheek. "So do I."

"We can figure this out together."

"Are you sure?"

I reached up and slid my fingers through her silky hair to the back of her neck and dragged her down to me. Obviously, I wasn't making myself clear. "Marry me," I said against her lips. Her scent surrounded me and that calm came over me. The quiet sureness that I'd only experienced a few times in my life.

When Weston had been placed in my arms.

When I'd driven a perfect race.

And right now.

Tears fell down her cheeks in earnest now, but she nodded.

"Words, Kel."

"Yes."

"Yes?"

"You don't know what you're getting yourself into."

I buried my face in her neck and breathed in that citrusy scent of hers I loved so much. That was probably very true. "I'll risk it."

"How am I supposed to eat a steak now? I'm blubbering all over you and the table." Her voice went down to a whisper. "Everyone's staring at us."

I leaned back and stood up, twisting her fingers with mine. "She said yes."

Kelsey squeaked behind me. I looked down at her. "No backing out now."

The room clapped and the waiter came back with a huge smile on his face. "Champagne?"

Yeah, that wasn't going to happen. "How about two steaks with the works, two baked potatoes with all the fixings?" I dug out my credit card and turned to her. "Sound good?"

She nodded.

"Oh, and to go."

She dashed away the tears. "Definitely to go."

The waiter nodded and took my card. "We'll put a rush on it."

I tugged her up and even though my skin crawled from all the stares, the delight on her face was worth it. I kissed her in the middle of the restaurant, and the clapping faded as she melted into me.

I drew away and helped her back into her seat. I dropped into mine across from her, but didn't let go of her hand.

"I can't believe you did that. Were you...I wasn't expecting that."

"Neither was I or I would have had a ring."

Her eyes went wide again. "You don't have to do that."

I resisted the urge to growl. I wanted a ring on her damn finger. I wanted everyone to know she was mine, even if she had to get used to the idea.

Surprisingly, I didn't need to. For the first time in days, my shoulders didn't ache and my head didn't pound with anger and unease.

I glanced at the porch through the window beside us. Twinkle lights were still strung up on the pergola stretched across the outdoor dining area. The tables had been stored away for the upcoming winter, but there were large heaters set out on the four-seasons patio. Right now, no one was taking advantage of it. Too many singles were mingling at the bar, not to mention all the late dinners being consumed. But I wanted to be alone with her.

With my fiancée.

After a failed marriage like mine, I should have been quaking in my boots about getting tied to a woman. If you had asked me a few months ago if I wanted to get married again, I would have yelled *hell no*. Until this crazy redhead across from me had blown into my world.

I stood and took her hand. She gave me a quizzical look, but followed me.

I nodded to the bartender to make sure the patio wasn't locked. Jackson Gideon flashed me a wicked grin and waved me off. He was a good guy and I'd fleeced him plenty of times at the Spinning Wheel's pool table.

Sometimes being in a small town had its perks.

I opened the door and tugged her close.

"It's not exactly deck weather," she said, eyes wide.

"I'll keep you warm."

Kelsey flushed. "Of that I have no doubt." Soft music filtered out from the dining room as the hum of conversation faded.

I twirled her once, then back against me. Her breasts grazed my chest as she slid her hands under my sports jacket and around my back. "Still surprises me you dance."

"I don't seem the type?"

She shook her head and giggled quietly. "Sure."

"I seem to remember you have been surprised with my skills a number of times. Maybe I like to keep you on your toes."

"You sure do." Her other hand sneaked up to play with the closely shorn hair along the nape of my neck. I closed my eyes and swayed with her for a minute.

She rested her cheek against my chest and her soft breath teased between the buttons of my flannel shirt. I expected her to be bubbling with questions and wedding talk, but she seemed to need a bit of quiet too.

It wasn't tense, or awkward.

For a moment, we were just us. Not expectant parents with a host of worries coming at us. Not near strangers willing to be tied together because of a little life we hadn't seen coming.

Just Kelsey Ford and Dare Kramer.

"Dare?"

"Hmm?"

"Are you sure?"

I tipped her chin up. "About this? Yeah. I'm sure." I lowered my mouth to hers and forced myself to stay gentle. Emotions ran hot and wild when it came to this woman, but I was determined to show her we weren't just hard, fast orgasms in between busy schedules.

I could be more than that.

"Come home with me. Let me show you."

A soft and sweet, almost shy smile lit up her face. "Yeah."

I drew her back into the restaurant. It seemed even louder now, but there was a bag waiting for us and the check in a folder with my card. I dashed off a good tip, bundled her into her jacket, and passed her the freakishly large bag she always carried. It seemed as if she had purses in every color of the rainbow.

I grabbed the white dinner sack and hustled her through the dining room to the front door. Once the food was loaded along with my precious cargo, I hurried around to the driver's side.

"Half the town is going to know by tomorrow."

"Yeah. Problem with that?" I asked as I buckled in.

"No." Her smile flashed in the darkness as I pulled out of the parking lot. "Do you mind if I tell the girls?"

"Go ahead."

She dug out her phone and her fingers flew over the keys as we made the ten-minute drive to my house. I thought about going to her apartment, but I had a sitter for Wes and didn't want to dash off when our skin cooled for once.

I wanted her with me tonight.

All night.

"Sage sent a gif with Beyoncé."

"Okay."

She laughed. "If you like it, you better put a ring on it."

"Only Sage."

"And now that song is stuck in my head." Her phone buzzed incessantly for five straight minutes between giggles before she tucked it back in her bag. She dashed away tears again and leaned into me. "They're happy for me."

"Good. I wouldn't want to have to outrun a pregnant Sage and her mini-Viking crazy sidekick."

A delighted laugh filled my car. "And that's an accurate picture of them."

She sat up straight as she realized we weren't heading for Main Street. Similar houses lined the maze of my development. They weren't new townhouses anymore. Just old enough to have issues—as I was learning with the house I'd bought after Katherine high-tailed it out of town.

I pulled around to the small garage attached to the house. I didn't take my car out too often. In fact, I usually left it at my parents' house since they had a three-car garage, but I'd wanted to show her I was more than just a grease monkey with a beat-up truck.

"Your house is so nice."

I shrugged. "It's not much, but it's mine. Well, and the bank's."

She touched my arm. "Don't say things like that. I certainly don't have a house. And you did this all on your own to take care of Wes."

I leaned over the console between us and kissed her. It got hotter than I wanted. Showing her I wasn't just a mindless animal when I got around her was far harder than I thought it would be. I forced myself to slow it down, to go easy with her.

When I pulled back, the dazed look in her eyes riled my dick again. That slightly lost, vulnerable softness to her face always did me in and made me want to push for more. To hear the little sounds she made when she was under me, breaking apart for me.

I eased away and tipped my forehead to hers. "Pray for us that Wes actually went to sleep for the babysitter."

"And if he didn't, we'll just get him to bed."

I nodded. "I'd like to tell him tomorrow. Together."

She swallowed. "I'd like that."

175

"Good." I got out and gathered our food. She pushed open her door before I could come around to do it for her. She was taking in the slightly shabby grass of my side yard and scatter of toys Wes never seemed to put away no matter how many times I asked.

Instead of sighing impatiently, she hauled up his bike with training wheels and set it against the stairs. "Looks like Wes has a really nice life here, Dare."

I grunted. "I do what I can for him."

"I know you do. And he's a well-adjusted kid. And I'm not just saying that as his teacher. He's still a handful, but I think he's just one of those kids who has energy to spare."

"Tell me about it. Why I'm crossing my fingers, Michelle, the babysitter, was able to get him to go down."

"It sounds quiet."

We climbed the stairs to my little porch. I eased her along the right side to miss the squeaky part of the third stair. I unlocked the door and gently set the bag inside the door. Michelle popped up off the couch in the living room.

"Oh, Mr. Kramer, I wasn't expecting you for a few more hours."

"We decided we wanted a quiet night in instead." I reached for my wallet and pulled out a few twenties. "Is he asleep?"

"*Animal Planet* and three books later, he finally passed out with his flashlight in hand."

"Gotta power up those glow in the dark stickers," I said ruefully.

"You got it. He was great tonight though. Played kickball with the kids, so he's down for the count."

I breathed a sigh of relief. "Thanks for babysitting tonight. Oh, and this is my…" How much did you tell a babysitter before it was too much info?

"I'm Kelsey." She stepped forward and held out her hand.

Michelle glanced from me to her and then back again with a wide grin. "Huh. Hope you two have a good night."

I slid my palm along the back of my neck. "We will."

Kelsey was grinning when I locked the door and turned back to her. "Afraid she was going to start the gossip chain in your neighborhood?"

I hung my head. The wildfire would be starting soon no matter what I said. Especially since Michelle's mother was the most notorious gossip hound on the street. "I don't bring girls around. It's going to happen regardless. Sorry."

"I'm not ashamed." Kelsey pursed her lips. "Or are *you* ashamed because I'm the knocked up teacher everyone's been talking about?"

SEVENTEEN

Dare crossed to me with a quickness that made me stumble back a step. "No. Absolutely fucking not." He cupped my face and drew me up until I was actually on my toes. My heart was racing and emotions were pinging all over the place. Fight, flight, lust, and love.

God, so much love I couldn't even comprehend it.

I wanted to shout it at him, but we hadn't gone there. In the foggy bit of romance we'd tripped through, we hadn't said that one very specific word. It felt like more than duty. It felt like we were actually a team. Or at least going to try and be a team.

And there was this. The kind of passion I only thought existed in books and movies. Would that burn out and then there would only be a child? Or just friendship. Maybe love that grew over the years?

He traced his thumbs over my cheeks so gently, but his eyes were fierce. "I couldn't give two fucks what others think. All that matters is I'm yours and you're mine. And our family. The one *we* build."

I couldn't stop the tears from falling. Pregnancy hormones, or just too many emotions I couldn't bottle up. I'd never been good at it. "Dare."

Instead of saying anything more, he swung me up into his arms.

I wasn't prepared for that kind of action. Namely because I was too tall for any guy to do that, but he didn't even grunt. He stalked through the arch leading to his dining room, but went right for the stairs.

"I'm too—"

"Kel?"

I blinked at him. "Yes?"

"Shut up. I'm making a grand gesture here. How about you just enjoy it?"

I pressed my lips together and hung on. When we got to the top, he stopped by a cracked open door. My heart melted when he peeked in to make sure Wes was settled.

Maybe settled wasn't exactly the right word. He was sprawled on his back, a league of stuffed dinosaurs lined up around the perimeter of his bed, with the T-Rex tucked under his arm. I brushed my fingers over the softness of Dare's beard. There was love there. A softness around his eyes and mouth, but then his gaze returned to me.

It was different. Maybe not as huge as I felt for him, but it wasn't just lust. Someday, it could be more. I was selfish enough to want it, to reach for it because having this baby was terrifying and exciting and I didn't want to do it alone.

He leaned forward until our noses brushed. Then that purposeful stride was back as he traveled toward the back of the house where the master bedroom was. It was bigger than I expected in a townhouse. Huge and nearly empty save for a bed, dressers, and a chair. A small light was on in the corner of the room. The room was stark white except for one wall.

Normally, I wouldn't have noticed because of the intent firing in Dare's eyes. But the wall was orange. "Wow."

"What?"

"That's very orange."

"Oh." He laughed. It was a rusty sound. I rarely heard him actually laugh. A chuckle sometimes, but more often it was a grunt or a growl. "Wes picked it. Think you can handle it?"

I swung my feet as I peered around his shoulders. "I think I can make it work."

"Is that so?" He placed me gently on the bed and peeled his sport jacket off.

I struggled out of my jacket, pushing it to the floor.

He *tsked* and bent to pick it up and folded it over the back of a rocking chair. "Is this something I need to get to know about you, Kel?"

I propped myself up on my elbows. "That I'm impatient to get you naked? This isn't news."

He slowly unbuttoned the cuffs of his shirt, then proceeded to make his way down the front placket. "No, that you're a slob. I wouldn't have thought so with you being a teacher and all."

I swallowed, trying to follow the conversation. But there was a lot of flesh being shown. The rippling kind that revealed muscles in places that had definitely not been in my purview. I'd caught pieces of him, but I'd never really been able to take in the full effect the couple of times we'd been together. In fact, he'd seen more of me than I had of him.

He left the shirt on, the tails floating around his hips as he dug his wallet out of his pants, setting it on the bedside table with his keys. There was a ritual to each motion. Like this was his nightly occurrence. Why that ratcheted up the tension in my belly, I had no idea.

Then he slowly unbuckled his belt, dragging the leather through the loops before tossing it on the chair with my jacket. He backed up to the door, snicking it shut softly. He dragged a laundry basket full of Legos in front of the door.

I nibbled on my lower lip. Had he done this before? A warning signal if there was a sudden disruption from a certain little boy?

Who was I to say anything about it considering my current situation, but the fact that he worried left me warm and slightly uneasy at the same time. These were things I'd have to get used to now.

My future included a new family, and a pre-existing one at the same time.

He thumbed open the button of his jeans and all thoughts of Wes, other women, and Tommy floated away. This was about us right now. And the bulge behind his zipper told me his focus was on me. That was what mattered.

I hissed out a breath when he lifted my foot to his chest. He dragged his fingers up over the soft leather to behind my knee to the zipper of my boot. His gaze never left mine as he slid one, then the other boot off. Then those strong fingers slipped under my skirt for my tights.

Not exactly the sexiest outfit in the history of man, but I hadn't realized my world would be spinning quite this way tonight. From the proposal to the unerringly slow way he was undressing me.

It didn't feel clinical in any way. But the way he opened me up, divesting me of every piece of clothing, made my skin buzz in reaction. Tights, then shirt, then bra.

All the while, his cock grew harder and more insistent behind his rapidly dropping zipper. As if he was bursting to get to me.

And damn if I wasn't ready for all of it. To touch all of him from chest, to thighs, to that surprisingly luscious butt he hid under baggy jeans. I wanted all of it.

But he was determined to go slow, no matter how I sighed or tried to help speed up the process. He simply pushed my hands out of the way when I tried to help. His heavy-lidded gaze made everything inside of me slow down as if my blood was made from molasses on a cold night.

Finally, he pressed my bare foot against his hot belly and kissed his way up my calf to my knee and then my thigh. He reached for the little snap on my skirt. It wasn't quite as easy to remove as the rest of my clothes.

My body was already changing a little. My belly was still flat, but my narrow waist was widening just enough that my clothes were starting to feel different. He reached behind my waist as I lifted to help him. He slowly dragged the material over my ass and slid it down my thighs to join the rapidly growing pile of clothes on the chair.

I toed open his shirt. "Off."

A slow smirk tugged at his lips. He shrugged it off his shoulders and placed it with the rest of my clothes. A few freckles marched across the center of his smooth chest. A single tattoo bloomed across his shoulder. A checkered flag rippled as if snapping in the wind. The number 44 filled the bigger flag, then a smaller 42 seemed almost hidden in the folds.

So many questions tugged at me, but he dragged me down the bed, opening my legs enough for him to resume his path.

I reached over my head for the headboard and he smiled from in between my legs. "Think you need to hold onto something, darlin'?"

"I think so."

He slowly licked my slit. "Good plan."

The Dare I'd been with before tonight had always been thorough, but in the past, there had seemed to be a timer in the back of his brain. As if he was rushing to be in too many places at once.

Not tonight.

Not now.

He was unhurried as he knelt on the bed and widened me with his shoulders. He slid his arms under me and laced his fingers over my belly, holding me down on the bed.

"Oh, God."

The smirk was back. The one I remembered from our first night. But then a serious look came over him and he bent to me. I arched off the bed as he slowly, methodically learned every inch of me.

I didn't have time to be embarrassed by the fact that he seemed to be mapping out every square corner of my lady garden. I was too busy trying to breathe through the slow building pleasure.

I could actually see the word *recalculating* flicker in his eyes as he watched me and listened for every reaction. And gosh, did he learn everything. I was a panting mess when he finally stopped teasing and went in for the kill shot. Fingers, tongue, and a sucking bite tossed me over the tumultuous ledge that only Dare seemed capable of throwing me over so easily.

When he finally covered me, I was writhing on the bed. His jeans hit the floor and his mouth crashed onto mine. Probably to try to quiet me down, but I couldn't seem to work my brain around stopping the sounds. Instead, he silenced me with his lips, his tongue, and his wonderfully solid body.

He rolled his hips against me and slid inside.

Dear God.

I hissed out a breath as he stretched me wide. His hips pressed me deeper into the mattress as he slowly glided in and out of me. He gripped my hair, turning my head where he wanted me as he kissed me with his usual intensity. The kind I was used to from the rest of him. Hungry and quieting at the same time.

I grabbed onto his amazing butt, trying to get him to go faster. To pump into me like he'd done before. Harder and rougher. The tempo had been just exactly what I'd needed that afternoon when he put my bed together.

But no, he was determined to go slow. To drill into me until his body literally seemed to be becoming part of me. I raked my nails down his back as I lifted my hips up for more.

He pinned me and stared down at me with such naked intensity I could do nothing but take what he was giving. A gentleness trapped under coiled aggression.

"Dare," I whispered.

He buried his mouth against my neck and sucked, then did this thing with his hips that gave me the friction I needed. I curled around him as the slow rolling orgasm finally unfurled like the flag on his arm.

Soft and lovely.

So different than any other time we'd been together. He shuddered in my embrace and dragged in a harsh breath before warmth filled me. I'd never been with anyone without a condom.

Hard to believe since I was currently pregnant, but it was the truth. It felt intimate and overwhelming in a way I couldn't describe. Like a piece of him was finally inside me and couldn't be taken back.

Even if, God forbid, the baby wasn't his—this was. Right now, us together was as all-encompassing as anything had ever been in my life.

He drew out of me, but instead of flopping onto the bed next to me like I was used to with any other man I'd ever slept with, he curled behind me. His strong, ropey arms held me close and he buried his beardy chin into my neck.

The low, slow groan reverberated through his chest and into my back and I folded my arms over his to hold it inside me. I felt cherished for the first time in my life and I never wanted to let that sensation go.

We must have fallen asleep because suddenly a crash and a bang jerked me into consciousness.

"Shit."

"Dad?" A pair of eyes peeked in from a crack in the door.

"Just a second, buddy."

"Why are the Legos in front of your door?" Wes put his shoulder into the door to get it to open.

I squeaked and dragged the sheet up to hide my absolute nakedness.

Dare jerked the blankets up and over my shoulder. "Hey, buddy. You're supposed to knock when you come in."

"You never close your door."

I buried my face in the covers and couldn't stop the smile. Maybe he didn't bring women home after all.

"Why don't you go back to your room and get dressed? We're, uh, going to make pancakes today."

"Pancakes?" Wes's voice was still timid, but there was an uptick. "Can we have bacon?"

"Is there any other way to have breakfast?"

"Do you have someone in there with you?" Wes's voice got closer. "Did you have a sleepover?"

I winced. Was I supposed to hide? I mean, we were going to get married, but how did that go with talking to Wes?

Oh, hey there, I'm your teacher and your new stepmom! Won't that be cool?

Good God, I was going to be a stepmom and a brand new mom all at once.

I flipped the sheet over my head. Why did I think this was a good idea? I couldn't cook brownies without burning them more than half the time.

Dare cleared his throat. "Yeah. We're going to talk about that at breakfast, okay?"

"You don't let *me* have sleepovers."

I snorted and Dare pinched my butt.

"You're too young for sleepovers."

"Who is it? Is it Uncle Auggie?"

I burst out laughing when Dare choked. "No, you know Aug sleeps on the couch when he stays over."

"Yeah, like after the Supahbowls."

"Right. Go on. If you get a move on, I'll make trucks."

"Yes!"

When I heard feet stomping down the hall, I flipped the covers back. "Should I sneak out?"

"What? No. We're going to go down and talk to him like adults. Besides, you'll be moving in here soon, right?"

"Who says? I have my own place."

"We're getting married."

"Yes. Not like tomorrow or anything."

"Maybe we should."

My heart stuttered to a halt. "What?"

"Should do it as soon as possible. Like right after we get a license."

I blinked at him. Mostly because that was all I could seem to do.

He rolled onto his side and loomed over me. "I mean, you were worried about school stuff, right? And getting you settled here would make things easier for everyone."

"Easier. Right." *Easier* was the most logical step.

I cupped his face, my thumbs stroking down his tightly groomed beard. He'd even done that for me last night. The last time I'd seen him, he was definitely more on the woolly side.

"The longer we have with Wes, the more he can get comfortable with the changes before…" His hand drifted down my breast to my middle. "Until there's questions about here." He lowered his mouth to mine then coasted down to my middle. "So I can make sure both of you are taken care of. The whole family." He glanced up at me as his mouth brushed over my belly button. "*My* whole family."

He was being smart and sweet. And that was what I needed to be doing. Not just hiding my head about this whole thing. It didn't matter that I'd always wanted a winter wonderland of a wedding. Right now, I had to think about the little girl or guy growing inside me. It wasn't about me anymore.

"We'll start moving you in today if you want."

Even though I hadn't been thrilled with my new apartment, a pang of sadness moved through me at the thought of leaving so soon. So much for my fresh start.

Well, I was getting one, all right, just not like I'd anticipated.

I cleared my throat. "I have to talk to my landlord."

"I'm sure Forrester will understand under the circumstances."

Because everyone knew I was the knocked up teacher of Main Street. "You're moving things really fast."

"I know, but the sooner we're married, the sooner we can get everyone settled."

Settled. Settling? Again, I couldn't stop focusing on the duty part of this whole thing. I should be happy he was stepping up, being the best man in every possible way.

He rolled off me and quickly pulled on sweatpants and a T-shirt. "You can take a shower before you come down if you want. I can't guarantee bacon will still be available."

I flipped the covers back. Nope, I could do this. "Do you have something I could borrow?"

He opened his drawer again. "They'll be big on you, but here you go." His eyes went dark as I stood up.

I took the shirt from him. "What?"

"Damn, I wish I had time to appreciate all of that more." His eyes trailed over me. I wanted to cover up, especially since I seemed to be losing my waist with the whole pregnancy thing already. And yet his eyes were as hot as they were that first night. As any time we'd been together. "Last night wasn't enough."

I blushed and quickly tugged the T-shirt over my head.

He dragged me against him before I even got my arms through the huge holes. "But now I can have you whenever I want you."

"Is that so?" The little niggle of doubt started to fade. This part worked. He wanted me. I didn't have to wonder about that. Even if he was a little less intense about it last night.

Except the look on his face when he was right on the edge of orgasm. Then I'd seen the Dare who had come into my life like a tornado those two times. Destructive and fast, leaving me disoriented and wrecked.

But then again, he'd also treated me with such softness. So much more than anyone ever had before.

After he helped me get the shirt all the way on, he curled his fingers under the T-shirt and gripped my ass. But then his face gentled again and he touched his forehead to mine. The crumpled sweats were crushed between us, our fingers touching. "We'll make this work, Kel. I swear it."

I swallowed. "I know." I didn't know, but I had to believe it. *Fake it 'til you make it* was definitely my motto lately.

He smacked my ass. "Now put some pants on before my kid comes in here and gets an anatomy lesson I'm not ready to give."

Another thing I'd have to get used to. Dare's rare humor and having a child around. As a teacher I had to be hands on with the kids, but there was definitely a line I didn't cross. I wiped dirty faces and gave an occasional hug, but having one right down the hall while I was naked or doing all manner of things with Dare—yeah, that was new.

Wes Kramer was far more likely to come zooming in demanding food or to play outdoors. He didn't really have a lot of boundaries in my classroom, and considering the way he came tearing into Dare's —*our*—bedroom, all of this would definitely take some getting used to.

I backed out of Dare's arms and tugged the sweatpants out of his grip. They were too big for me, but the elastic kept them from sliding right back down my hips.

I glanced up to see him watching me with those serious blue eyes again. "What?"

"For the first time, I wish my kid slept in for reasons other than my personal shut-eye."

My hair slid forward and I couldn't stop the shriek of laughter when he grabbed me by the waist and lugged me out into the hallway.

"Miss Ford?"

"Uh oh," I whispered.

Dare set me down and I cleared my throat. "Hi, Weston." I shook my head. Nope, that was my teacher voice and that would totally confuse him. I crouched low to his height. "Wes, I know this might be a little strange."

The little boy, a carbon copy of Dare down to the little cowlick sticking up, looked from me to his father and back again, then put his hands on his hips. "Are you boyfriend-girlfriend?"

I shot a look up at Dare.

Dare knelt down next to me. "Actually, that was what we wanted to talk to you about. How would you feel about having Kelsey here more often? Like *a lot* more often."

Wes tipped his head to the side, his hands still on his hips. "Can I call her Kelsey?"

I chuckled. "I'd love it if you called me Kelsey. Except maybe not at school, if that's okay."

He shrugged and dropped his hands to his sides. "Sure."

Dare curled his big hand around Wes's back and gave him an absent rub. "What about having Kel here most days? Even every day?"

Wes frowned. "Live here?"

Dare pressed his lips together. "Yeah, buddy. Living here. I asked Kelsey to marry me."

Wes's eyes rounded. "Whoa. Do I hafta call her mommy?" His voice was almost timid.

My breath stalled. What the hell was I supposed to say to that one?

Dare coughed. "How about we start with Kelsey first?"

Wes threw himself into his dad's arms. Dare grunted, but caught him close. Wes's eyes, so much like his father's, met mine as he monkeyed himself around Dare's neck. "Do you like pancakes, Miss— I mean, Kelsey?"

"Only if they look like trucks."

Wes's eyes got bigger. "Me too!"

"I do, however, demand to share the bacon," I said as Dare and I rose.

"Well, bacon is pretty awesome." Wes wiggled down out of his father's hold.

"Hey, why don't you go take the syrup out of the fridge, so it can warm up?" Dare mussed his son's hair.

Wes raced down the hall to the stairs. "I'll get the milk and eggs out too," he shouted.

"Be careful," Dare called after him before he shook his head. "He's totally going to break the eggs."

I laughed as I twined my fingers with his. "I could go for scrambled eggs."

Dare blew out a breath. "Let's hope they are salvageable and not on the floor by the time we get down there." He dropped his arm around my shoulders. "That didn't go too badly."

"I'm not sure he totally gets what marrying me will entail. Are you sure we shouldn't slow it down a little? Give him time to adjust. We have a few months before—"

"Nope. I want you here where I know you'll be safe."

"It's not like we live in a rough area, Dare."

He turned me to face him, then smoothed my hair away from my face. "The coffee shop is opening at the end of the month, and then there will be tons of people coming and going. No way you'll get enough rest." He clenched his jaw. "And I'm fucking selfish. I want you here where I can make sure you're being looked after. And it will give you more time to get to know Wes as someone other than a child in your class."

Part of me wanted to shriek, "hold it!" and there was another part of me that wanted just that. To have someone to talk to about the baby, along with all the things that could go wrong. Maybe he'd be able to calm me down.

To not be alone.

To be connected to someone.

I ached to tell him all that, but there was a crash downstairs, which had Dare taking the stairs two at a time. I trailed him into the room by a few seconds and couldn't stop the laugh when I saw the island counter scattered in flour and a half-spilled carton of milk. The eggs had miraculously made it without incident, but the mixing bowl had not.

It was spinning on the tiled floor, flour pouring out.

Wes stood on a chair with a mixing spoon in his hand. The other half of the flour that hadn't been sprinkled all over the butcher block counter was dotted on his shirt, face, and in his hair. "I dropped it."

Dare had shoved his hands into his own hair in frustration, so I took over.

This I knew how to handle.

I rushed forward and took the half-ripped flour package from its precarious position on the edge of the counter and scooped up most of the flour into the bowl. "Started without us, huh?"

Wes's chin was down, his shoulders scrunched up as if he was bracing himself for a scolding.

"It's okay. We can make this work." I scraped the excess flour into the bowl and dumped it into the trash. "How about we measure it out this time? Where are your measuring cups?"

"I can get them." Wes scrambled down off the chair and across the kitchen to a drawer. He came back with bright green nested measuring cups. "Here, Kelsey."

"Do you have a recipe?"

"No, Dad just knows how to do it."

I looked up at Dare. "Well, come on, Dad, show us how it's done."

Dare glanced between us with a rueful grin. "Amateurs." He grabbed an orange apron off the hook near the fridge. "I guess I could use two helpers today."

"I'm a very good helper," Wes said with a big smile.

"Yeah, you are, buddy." Dare looked over his head at me and mouthed, "Thank you."

Just maybe this would work.

First, we'd handle pancakes, and then we'd tackle marriage and having a baby.

No sweat.

EIGHTEEN

I PACED THE HALLWAY OUTSIDE THE SMALL ROOM THE COURTHOUSE USED as a dressing room. The door opened and I whirled around.

"What are you doing here?" Sage whispered in an exasperated tone. She maneuvered herself through the door and kept bobbing and weaving to block me. "You can't see her."

I feigned left and almost got around her. "I just need to talk to her for a second."

She pushed me back, leading with her belly. I jumped back with a growl. "Um, that's a no can do. You can't talk to her or see her until the wedding."

"Who said?"

Sage blinked at me. "Stuff and people. And wedding things. I don't know, but it's bad luck and that's all you need to know, buddy."

I wiped my palm down the leg of my suit pants. "Do you want a chair or something?" Sage was about a second away from popping, for God's sake. Should she be walking around so much?

"Stop looking so nervous. Besides, this is your future, pal." She patted her belly. "It's natural, I swear. Minus an extra pint of Ben and Jerry's or two."

I rolled my eyes. "I know." I held up my hands. "Not about the ice cream part."

"Another thing you better get used to. Maybe not ice cream, but something will strike her fancy and require a midnight trip to the all-night supermarket in Laurel."

I could barely remember what Katherine had craved other than beer. She told me that one every day. Also that me and the baby stopped her from living. That being with me was about as fun as watching paint dry. I had to drive three states away the week before she was due to haul her back home.

We'd been fighting the whole pregnancy and she'd taken to disappearing so she wouldn't have to listen to me ask about sonograms and doctor's appointments. In fact, I'd actually had to beg her to marry me. The minute I'd asked, I'd known it was a mistake.

A week after we got married, I'd spun out and hit the wall. Not only was she pissed about carrying my kid, but now she was married to a race car driver with no car and no team. Luckily, I hadn't been hurt, but the car was beyond repair. I'd just started making a name for myself in the circuit, but not enough for a major endorsement yet.

My career had been over before I'd been more than an up and comer.

Another strike against me.

Another reason for Katherine to hate me. From almost famous to a mechanic in the time it took to get through half of her pregnancy. Part of me wished she hadn't taken me up on the offer, then I wouldn't be so damn anxious about it a second time around.

Then it would be Kelsey who took my name the one and only time.

I fisted my hands.

I hadn't seen Kelsey in two days and I was going fucking crazy.

She wouldn't change her mind. She couldn't.

"It's bad enough you rushed her into doing this in less than a week. I had no time to prepare or even throw her a shower. I barely got her parents here. Who you're supposed to be entertaining." Sage straightened her dress over the beach ball she was carting around. The color was something between a fall leaf and a sunset.

I cleared my throat. "You look nice."

Her eyebrows shot up. "Man, you really are nervous."

I frowned. "Why? Because I said you look nice?"

"Yes, you're being polite. You men only start with charm and politeness when you're all nervous."

"We do not," Oliver said as he came up behind me.

"Not you. Your default is polite. You make paper animals."

"Oh, like this?" Oliver held his hand out, palm up where a little frog rested.

Sage sighed. "Yeah, like that." She took it and tucked it in the little bouquet of flowers she was holding. "What do you have to be nervous about? You already married me. Your life is perfect."

"Of course it is, love." Oliver slid his arm around her waist. "Maybe you should be off your feet?"

Sage waved him off. "I'm fine. Just a little lower back pain. I'm not used to carrying so much in the front. Don't give me that look." She turned to me. "You need to get back in that little office and make sure the music is cued up. We've got a wedding to pull off." Sage rubbed her belly. "Okay, kiddo, give mama a break."

Oliver hovered. "What?"

"She's just kicking up a storm." Sage patted Oliver's chest. "Relax, Dad. We've got some time still."

The clomp of heels made the three of us turn.

"I found it. Coming through." Cindy Ford was walk-running down the hallway. Kelsey's mother was a shorter, rounder, slightly grayer version of her daughter.

The door opened again and a woman with dark hair ducked her head out. "What took you so long? Kels is walking grooves in this ugly carpet. Hurry up."

"Coming. Make way."

Mrs. Ford frowned at me. "You should be in the other room, Charles."

My shoulders tightened and lifted up to my damn ears. "Yes, ma'am."

"Charles?" Oliver and Sage parroted.

"Even my mother doesn't call me Charles," I muttered.

"I can't call you a word that means trouble."

I felt my cheeks flush. "Yes, Mrs. Ford."

"And stop calling me that. It's Cindy." She stopped in front of me and smoothed my collar, inching my tie up tighter until I could barely breathe. "This may not be the way I wanted my daughter's wedding day to go, but you're about to be family." She blinked rapidly and sniffed. "Now go back into that room with the judge and wait for my daughter. I have to give her something borrowed and blue." She disappeared behind the door with Kelsey's sister, Rylee.

I shook my head. None of them understood why I wanted to rush through the wedding. But between the school's morality code that seemed to only count with the female teachers, and the constant murmurings in town, I just wanted everything to stop.

It wasn't 1952 anymore, but I was pretty sure none of the matrons in this freaking town got the memo. While I didn't give a damn about those conventions, I wanted to protect Kelsey from them. She didn't deserve anyone's judgment.

This wedding was just a formality, and a legally binding one. She was already mine—as was the baby, same DNA or not. All I could think about was making sure they were with me.

And safe.

I fingered the ring I'd managed to buy last night. Which I wanted to give her before the ceremony, but evidently, that would have to wait. August had the simple white gold bands I'd gotten for the ceremony, but something had niggled at me.

Enough that I'd driven like I was on a track to get to Laurel before the jewelry store closed. And had spent money I didn't have, and now I was nervous to give it to her.

Christ, I was an asshole.

I nodded to Oliver. "Come on. Before the girls kill us."

"Yes, go. We'll be down in ten minutes." Sage paused at the door. "Go. I'm fine."

Oliver followed, but kept glancing over his shoulder at the closed door.

"She's in good hands. If nothing else, Kelsey's mother is a drill sergeant. She'll have her sitting down with her feet up."

Oliver gave me a tight smile. "I was beginning to think you were the Terminator, but you're as nervous as the rest of us poor bastards on our wedding day."

"I'm not having second thoughts."

No, I was too worried that Kelsey was. I knew what I wanted, what I needed and it was her in my house and in my life. Period.

"Impressive. Even with a divorce in your rearview."

I glanced up at him. "Good pep talk."

"Sorry. I mean, this isn't a shotgun wedding or anything, right? We don't have to save you?"

"No. My idea."

"Or is it the teacher we're watching the back door for?"

"Shut up."

Oliver grinned and clapped a hand on my shoulder. "If it makes you feel better, I think she's into you. Kinda into you."

The sing-song quality of his voice had me narrowing my eyes. "What are you, twelve?"

"More like Sage is going through a Harry Styles phase. I requested Beethoven for the IQ improvement component for the baby. She rejected my request. For the last month, that's all I've heard."

"So glad I have a boy. None of that boy band crap in my house."

"Just you wait. Kelsey has been hanging out with Sage for the last two days."

I shook my head as we turned into the doorway labeled Ford-Kramer wedding. My mother was sitting on one of the benches with Wes on her lap. Considering he never sat on anyone's lap anymore, another layer of guilt threatened to put me on my ass.

Was I making a mistake rushing this along?

Wes had been unnaturally quiet for the last week as Kelsey's boxes started arriving.

My mom looked up when I walked in and Wes wiggled down to run to me. "Daddy."

I crouched and fixed his tie. "Being good for Gram?"

"I'm bored."

"I know, buddy. The ceremony is going to start in a few minutes then we'll go get some dinner."

We'd made reservations at The Cove. The least I could do was make sure she had a nice dinner, even if we couldn't pull off a full reception right now.

There hadn't been time to save for a reception, or to pull anything together. Another mark in my bad bet column. But I'd make it up to her. I'd make it up to everyone.

August crossed the room to me. He was opening and snapping shut a small ring box over and over.

Wes pulled out of my hold and rushed to August. "Can I see the rings again?"

Aug flipped open the box.

"Can I hold them?"

"Gotta be careful with them. Leave them in the box, okay?" I smoothed down his little tie. The suit was a Kohl's special. It would be in the donation pile in three months, but maybe we'd get Christmas out of it at least.

My mom was big on Christmas mass. Giving her a daughter-in-law who taught at a Catholic school wasn't the worst thing I'd done in my life. Or another grandchild. My pop wasn't so sure on the marrying Kelsey thing, but my mom was definitely from the do-the-right-thing camp.

So here I was again.

A non-traditional traditionalist. A little fun turned into a lifetime attachment one more time. Only this time, I wanted the girl as much as the baby. I still didn't know how to handle that part, but I had time.

After today, all the time in the world.

Rylee came around the corner. She was the dark to Kelsey's light.

Lush to her lean, and abrasive to Kelsey's sweet babbling. "Okay, she'll be on her way down in five minutes. Do we have the judge?" She scanned the room and her lips slid into a bombshell smile when Asher Hamilton stood up.

Our newest judge for the courthouse was definitely on the young side compared to the one who had been busting all our balls for as long as I could remember. Since Asher—who had some blue blood in him thanks to some distant relation to Seth and Oliver—had run unopposed, he'd been the youngest judge in the county to take over Crescent Cove's post.

Rylee crossed the room and hooked her arm into Asher's and led him to the front. "Thank you for making time for this crazy little shit-show."

"Rylee Jane," came a commanding voice.

"It's not church." She scrunched up her shoulders and shot a look over at her father.

"It's a courthouse. Show some respect."

Rylee glanced up at Asher. "Did you feel disrespected?"

"We don't generally like cuss words in court, Miss Ford."

Rylee gave an exaggerated shiver, patted his arm, and murmured something under her breath.

I rolled my eyes. She was definitely not like her sister. Then again, Kel had said plenty of off-color things to me over the last few months.

And yet somehow they sounded sweeter and more growl-inducing. Hell, it was pretty much how I ended up in this predicament. I hadn't been looking for laughter and sex and a future, but I had damn well found it.

I moved to the front of the room where the judge stood. August followed me and we both pulled at our collars.

Wes raced over to stand between us, the ring box clutched in his hand.

Now I just had to hold onto what I'd found.

NINETEEN

I worried my grandmother's locket between my fingers as I paced the small dressing room.

"Would you stop, you're making me nauseous." Sage sighed from the couch we'd set her up on.

"Is it time yet?"

"Are you sure you don't want me to go out there and tell him you changed your mind?"

"No, Mom. I want to marry Dare."

"Then why are you so anxious?"

"I just thought I'd have a little more time to get used to the idea, that's all."

I hadn't even gotten to buy a wedding insert for my planner. The entire process had taken up one list page.

God, I was such a sap.

Then again, Principal Gentry had been practically delirious when I told her I couldn't do the fall pageant this weekend because I was getting married. She tried not to ask questions about my pregnancy. Heck, no one would have known about it yet if Dare hadn't blurted it out at Sage's baby shower.

Then again, me screaming the baby might not be his didn't help that one either.

All in all, the small town mentality had definitely been at work in moving the timeline for this marriage up from quick to warp speed. We'd picked out the rings at Kohl's with Wes's suit. So matter of fact and simple. Like we'd been picking out earrings, for God's sake.

No jewelry store with gleaming glass cases full of sparkly jewels. Nope, just picking a band that came in both our sizes. Column C in the main case right under the religious crosses.

How was this my life?

"Honey, that school is good, but it is definitely behind the times. You could find another job."

I stopped pacing. "I love my job."

How could I tell my mom I wasn't sure if my possible baby daddy was marrying me only for social propriety? As it was, there was a hint of disappointment living her eyes because I was pregnant. Oh, and the father might be one of two men.

I was officially a statistic.

I was supposed to be the good Ford sister. Considering my sister had skipped out of the room as if I'd given her a lottery ticket, I was pretty sure there had been a few conversations between my family I hadn't been privy to.

So far, this was definitely not shaping up to be the wedding of my dreams.

But he is the man of your dreams.

That didn't seem wholly logical either, but he was. I mean, he was a little—a lot—pushy and he was a bit of a steamroller personality-wise. I was learning more about that aspect of him since we'd agreed to do this crazy thing.

He and August had me packed up and moved into his house while I was working. I'd gone from independent for the first time in my life to a near wife and mother in under two months. Part of me wanted to push back and tell him to hold up, but a tiny piece of me was glad I had one less thing to stress about.

The fact that he'd replaced his own bed with the one he bought me was one of those little things that made up for the pushy barbarian he turned into. And why I was so conflicted.

Dare was all action and limited words.

All the things he had been doing were to make my life easier. So what if it wasn't the most romantic thing in the world? A lot of women dealt with men who were far more careless and apt to trample on their feelings.

I listened to fellow teachers talk about their husbands every day.

I glanced over at Ally as she tucked a blanket around her little boy. Okay, so Ally and Sage weren't the women I should be looking at for non-romantic men. Seth and Oliver were the kind of guys who believed in grand gestures. They were very much the "I love you so much, I'll shout it from the rooftops" sort of men.

But they weren't the norm.

So what if Dare was quieter about it? Actions were the important part. The way he stepped up to help without asking questions. The way he held me like I was the most precious thing in the world at night. And no, he didn't flip me over and fuck the crap out of me like he couldn't stand not to be inside me anymore.

It wasn't the end of the world.

He was a caretaker. A gruff one, but a caretaker nonetheless.

I smoothed my hand down the skirt of my white dress. Kinleigh's Attic had been a treasure trove of amazing clothes. And I'd found my makeshift wedding dress in the back of the store with the help of her, Ally, and Sage. Kinleigh had even altered it for me on the spot.

The silk and lace was perfect. The one bit of romance I'd allowed myself in this whole shindig. I might've been walking down an aisle in a courthouse, but I was going to look spectacular, dammit.

And maybe, just maybe, I'd catch a glimpse of that fiery Dare one more time.

My mother handed me the small bouquet I'd ordered. The happy faces of the sunflowers and scattered baby roses made everything feel just a little bit more real.

"Are you sure, baby?" My mother's eyes matched mine. There were a few more tears in hers. I didn't even feel the prick of tears in mine.

As if this was happening to someone else and I was just a stand-in. Bride on page thirty-seven of a play. "If this isn't what you want, we'll move you home and help you take care of the baby. I don't want you to feel like you're trapped."

Sage got herself up off the couch. "Girl, you gotta stop being so morose about this. You have a super hot guy who wants to play house with you. And he wants to put a ring on it. And the way he looks at you? It's not just because he is feeling altruistic. All right?" She blew out a breath and rubbed the side of her belly. "Man, this little girl is trying out for soccer practice for sure."

Ally hopped up. "You should be sitting down."

"I'm tired of sitting. I'm also tired of everyone making excuses for Kelsey to leave."

"Easy for you to say. Oliver made sure you had a crazy amazing wedding. He even flew everyone to Vegas." I was a jerk for even saying it, but it was true.

"Yes, but he was an idiot before then. Oliver wouldn't have known a romantic gesture if you whacked him upside the head with it, until I let him know he needed to step up. And Ally? Seth sat on the fact he was in love with her for years. Men are dumb, okay? You know what's not dumb? This great guy rushing you to get married."

"But why is he rushing?"

"So you don't get away, you idiot. Guys who don't want to get married will make any excuse to avoid it. Dare? Nope, he wants you forever. So stop looking at the bad side of this, okay?" Sage held up a finger. "Okay, maybe I need to sit down now."

Ally flew forward, holding one of the chairs that had lined the wall. My mom ran for a cup of water and rushed back to Sage's side.

For the first time, tears actually filled my eyes. "You think so?"

"I know so." Sage took a swig from the water. "I also know so because I saw him freaking out in the hallway. The boy is toast. Put him out of his misery, woman. Time to put a ring on it."

I tipped my head back so the tears wouldn't fall and ruin my makeup. "I didn't think of it that way."

"Of course you didn't. Because you're our sweet Kelsey with a big romantic heart." She made gimme hands at me and I went over to crouch in front of her. "You just have to alter your thinking about romance a little. Dare's a little rougher around the edges. He's more likely to do maintenance on your car and take it to get vacuumed as a sweet gesture. He'll learn how to be a bit more romantic with some subtle training."

"You're good," Ally said with a laugh. "And she's right. Seth is a big smushball now, but he sure wasn't when we were first together. I have the contract to prove it."

I frowned. "What?"

Ally waved her fingers. "Never mind. Just know that the boy definitely took a lot of wrong turns before he got it right." She held her hand out to me to help me up. "Now, we have a wedding to go to, right?"

I nodded and straightened my dress. "We do." I hugged Ally, then Sage. "I'm so ready to do this."

"Good, now help me up," Sage said with a laugh. "Getting out of chairs is the suck."

We both grabbed an arm and they lined up to go out ahead of me. I squeezed my mom's hand. "He's a really good man."

"I know it. But if he wasn't right, I'd take you home right now."

"Thanks, Mom." I brushed a kiss over her cheek. The familiar scent of White Diamonds settled my nerves.

On the other side of the doorway was my dad. My eyes overflowed again. Evidently, the tears had just been trapped and now I couldn't control them.

He held out his arm for me to take and my mother flanked me on the other side. We all walked down the hallway with the late day sun streaking over the worn vanilla-colored tiles. As we reached the room, I saw more sunflowers tied to the benches and two more swags of them on the bench behind the town judge.

We'd gotten our wedding license on our lunch break the day before. Again, so clinical and quick. Thirty minutes out of our day to sign for permission to do this. The paperwork had been rushed through thanks to our friendship with the Hamiltons, who might as well have owned Crescent Cove.

Sage and Ally were blocking my line of sight as they walked down to stand on my side of the aisle. Then it was just me and my parents on the threshold of the room. Dare was there with Wes holding onto his pinkie, our ring box clutched in his little hand.

The strings version of one of my favorite songs filled the room. The words weren't right yet. And Dare might not know how fast I'd fallen for him. I didn't even know how to put the feelings into words. But they were bursting inside me and suddenly, I knew that this was right for us.

For our little family.

It didn't matter that we were doing it in a courthouse. We were doing this because we believed that being a family meant more than a ceremony. It was the safety of his arms and his home that we'd make ours. And this little life growing inside me who I loved already. He or she wasn't a mistake, just a new start.

Exactly what I'd been looking for.

Dare cleared his throat as my dad kissed my cheek and took my hand and put it in Dare's. My mom moved up to cover both our hands and then pulled Dare down for a quick kiss on his cheek before she did the same to me. While I sniffled, they walked to the bench behind us to join my sister Rylee.

Dare wasn't sure what to do with Wes, so I just held my other hand out to him until we made a little triangle in front of Judge Hamilton. Dare gave me that fierce look again and I didn't care if the tears flowed. This rough, intense, frustrating man was going to marry me today.

Both of these Kramer men were going to be part of my family from today on out.

Dare stepped closer to me. His hand never left his son's, but he was definitely intent on saying something. He dipped his hand in his pocket for a moment, fisting his hand before withdrawing it and taking mine once more.

"All that matters to me is that you want this."

I smiled at him. "I want this." I swung my hand with Wes's and tightened mine around Dare's. "I want all of this."

"That's all that matters to me. I hope you know that."

I swallowed down the stupid tears that wanted to flow. "I do."

"Good. Get used to saying those words. You have to say them again in a few minutes."

I laughed. "You too, pal."

"I'm ready." Dare stepped back a little and nodded to Judge Hamilton. "We're ready."

The judge read off the vows, and I echoed them to Dare and to Wes. It was a simple ceremony with no fanfare. Even the American flag floated gently behind the judge's bench thanks to the fan slowly circulating the air in the stuffy room.

None of that seemed to matter when it came right down to it. Wes handed me Dare's ring, his face beaming with pride. We exchanged "I dos" as his son practically vibrated between us.

This man and this little boy were now mine.

"You may now kiss the bride."

Dare leaned in and the kiss was sweet and almost chaste.

"Gross!" Wes made a gagging sound and I laughed against Dare's mouth.

We turned toward our clapping friends and family. As I scanned the faces of the people I loved, my laughter stopped. "Sage?"

"Oh, crap." She put her hands on her hips. "My kid is not keeping to the schedule."

Oliver practically jumped over the bench between him and Sage. "Did your—"

"Water break? Sure did." She scrunched up her nose. "I was really looking forward to that steak at The Cove, dammit."

I glanced at Dare. "Happy wedding day to us," I mouthed.

TWENTY

DARE

I scooped up Wes and handed him to my mom. "Things just got crazy, I think."

She sighed. "Kelsey has been worried about Sage since this afternoon. Probably best to go with them. We'll take care of Wes."

Wes's face scrunched up and I knew waterworks were imminent. "Hey, buddy. Our friend is going to have a baby. That lady right there?" I pointed to a now seated Sage. Oliver and Seth had disappeared to get the car, if I had to guess.

Wes sniffed. "Yeah."

"Kelsey's really good friends with her."

"Do you have to go too?"

I hated when he gave me that look. I was gone a lot with working so much, but I was hoping with Kelsey in our lives now, maybe we could alleviate some of that. That one of us would be home with him. "I don't think I should leave her alone, do you?"

"No." His voice was tentative.

"We'll be back home as soon as we can. And tomorrow, we'll do breakfast, okay?" I'd planned on taking Kel to the Sherman Inn as a surprise for an overnight. We didn't have a honeymoon planned. Life, kids, money—it wasn't something we could pull off right now. Especially since she had school too.

Obviously, all the festivities were over for the evening.

When Kelsey gave me a helpless look, I quickly dug my beard into Wes's neck until he giggled. "I'll check in with you later, Ma."

"We'll be fine. How about we head over to Sugar Rush for some ice cream?"

"Yes!"

I gave my mom a quick kiss on the cheek. They'd be fine. It was Kelsey I needed to worry about now. This was a close-knit group I'd married into. There was no way she was going to let them go off without being a part of it.

I strode over to her. She and Ally were flanking Sage, who was taking long, slow breaths.

"I just thought it was my usual back pain." Sage's voice was close to a whine. "I didn't mean to ruin the wedding." Her eyes welled.

Oh, hell. Didn't need that. "Nah, you waited until we kissed and everything. After that, it's all fluff, right?" I winked at Kelsey.

She blinked at me with her big, gorgeous golden eyes. Would our baby have those eyes, or my blue? Or a third option? I shook that thought away.

"Right. Everything was perfect and now I might share a perfect date with your baby. How cool would that be?"

Sage gave her a watery laugh. "Wouldn't forget your anniversary that way."

"Definitely not."

"Oh, shit." Sage's breath whooshed out. "Guess those contractions are real now. No more Braxton Hicks for this girl. Where's Oliver?"

"I'll go check." I stood up and went into the hall. Oliver came running back, his eyes darting everywhere. I met him near the door. "Hold up."

He tried to go around me. "I have to get back in there."

"She's scared. She's trying really hard not to be, but she is. So take a breath."

Oliver fisted his hands, but followed my directions.

"She's doing great. Way better than my first wife. She'd already thrown a toaster and phone at me by the first contraction."

Oliver's eyebrows shot up. "Wow."

"Yeah. You're in the winner's circle. At least until you get in the labor room."

"Gee, thanks."

"Just keepin' it real."

Oliver slugged me in the arm. "You're all heart."

"I do what I can. Now, let's go get your girl." I let him go ahead of me. He rushed to Sage's side.

Kelsey stood back to give him room. Oliver was murmuring to Sage and through her tears, there were a few giggles. Just what she needed. I took Kelsey's hand and pulled her back to me.

"I want to go with them. Is that okay?"

I nodded. "I figured as much. My mom is going to handle all the dinner stuff and Wes."

"I'm sorry." Her voice was little more than a whisper.

"For what? She's your friend. We'll go be with her."

She watched Oliver slowly lead Sage out of the room and into the hallway. Ally had the baby in his carrier. Kelsey looked a little lost as to what to do. To follow or to get out of the way.

I pressed my hand along Kelsey's lower back as her parents and Rylee came forward.

"Is there anything we can do?"

"I'm so sorry, Mom. I feel like I should be with her. I know you guys came out and are all dressed up."

Her mom shook her head. "Don't worry about us. We'll just take us and our fancy duds out to dinner with Rylee."

"We will?" Rylee frowned. "I figured I'd get to take me and my cute dress out tonight instead."

"You will. With us."

I pressed my lips together at Rylee's deep sigh.

"I mean, I knew I wouldn't have a hot guy to hook up with here, but I figured The Cove would have something. Thanks a lot, sis."

Kelsey's eyes filled.

"Good grief, I'm joking." Rylee came forward and hugged her sister. "Pregnancy hormones are doing you wrong, girl."

"I feel bad enough as it is."

I rubbed Kelsey's back. "Don't feel bad, darlin'. We're going to follow the caravan to the hospital and grab a few snacks for everyone. How's that sound?"

"Oh, that's a great idea. The hospital food is awful."

"We'll pick up some sandwiches." I pulled out my phone and opened up the food app. Even as small as our town was, it was set up for takeout like a damn boss.

"Okay." Kelsey nodded. A plan was always better than no plan when it came to my wife. I hadn't known her long, but I knew that much. Her checklist in her planner centered her.

She hugged her parents and looked around the room. "The flowers. I don't want to just throw them away."

"Don't you worry. Me and Dare's mom are going to collect everything and bring it to your house."

"My house," Kelsey repeated. "Right. Our house. Yes, thank you so much. I'm so sorry—"

"Stop with the sorries, kiddo. Just go take care of your friend." Kelsey's father was no nonsense, which I appreciated. Right now, that kind of personality was very much needed.

I helped Kelsey gather her wrap and her bag. We both said goodbye to everyone who was left. Asher was waiting for us at the door.

"I hope your friend is all right."

"Baby is a little early, but not that much." Kelsey smiled as she clutched my hand. "Thank you so much for such a lovely ceremony."

"Of course." Asher shook my hand and patted Kelsey's arm gently. "I'll take care of the rest of the paperwork and give it to your parents."

"Thanks again." I hustled Kelsey out before someone else could stop us. I had my car, but wished I'd taken the truck. It had seemed wrong to drive my new bride in my truck after our damn wedding ceremony.

"Which hospital?"

"Laurel."

I nodded and helped her in. She swung the skirt of her dress in and looked up at me with a tremulous smile. I leaned in and gave her a soft kiss. "You're beautiful, Kel. And so much more than I deserve." Before she could reply, I closed the door on her and rounded the car to my side.

It was a warm day, but she was still shivering in reaction to today, my words, or the situation—I didn't know. I just flicked on the heat and peeled out onto Main.

I took a detour into Jersey Angel's deli for a bunch of sandwiches that would hold us through the long night. My buddy worked in the shop and brought out a case of water for me to put in the car. I wasn't much use to anyone in these situations, but I could at least feed them.

I pulled a water free and handed it to Kelsey when I got back in the car. "How are you feeling?"

She frowned. "I'm fine."

"You sure? It's been a long day already."

She gave me a soft smile, then leaned in and gave me a sweet kiss. "I'm fine. I'm just worried about Sage. So take my mind off of it. We've got a little drive."

"Okay. What do you want to talk about?"

"Your ex-wife."

My stomach plummeted. "Not exactly what we should be discussing on our wedding day."

"You seem to be awfully calm about this baby stuff. Is it because of Katherine?"

Evidently, she would not be deterred. "Definitely not. Katherine was the worst patient in the history of man." I tightened my fingers on the steering wheel. "You don't want to hear this."

"I do."

"Why?"

"Because she gave you Wes. She couldn't be all bad."

Yes, she could. But it was true, she had given me an amazing kid. "We met on the circuit."

"Racing circuit?"

I nodded as I navigated the town limits and got on the highway. "She got off on race car drivers. I wasn't fresh on the scene. I'd been around long enough to know what I was getting into with her." I shrugged. "A few good races and I was hitting the top of the leaderboards for a good part of the season. She was fun and I was invincible."

Kelsey tugged at the little bit of lace on her dress. "Sounds like a different life."

"It was. And I loved it. Me and my brother had been working pit crews at the derbies as soon as we hit sixteen. He's a few years younger than me and snuck in before he got his license. I swear, the only reason I pulled ahead and landed a team was luck."

"I doubt it."

I untwisted her fingers from her dress and wound them with mine. "It's the truth. I was a good driver, but there are a lot of them out there. If Jeff—the driver of the team I took over—hadn't fucked up and failed a drug test, my life might be a lot different."

I might still be living my life one race at a time. I might never have had my kid. I might never have met Kelsey. It was unsettling to think about. There were some nights when I wondered what life would be like if I'd made a different decision. Now, it seemed even more terrifying.

"That's how you ended up racing?" Her voice was filled with wonder.

"Yep. Crazy, right? Right place, right time. Hell, if I hadn't raced the track three tenths of a second faster than my brother, he might have been right where I was."

"And with Katherine?"

My laugh was harsh enough that she flinched. "No, probably not with Katherine. Racing was his sole focus. Still is. He knew how to party, but he always had his eye on the winner's circle."

"And you didn't?"

I shrugged. "I loved it. But the moment Katherine told me we'd gotten pregnant, my life changed. I wasn't just thinking about the leaderboard anymore. Maybe that's why I fucked up in the end. Your head has to be completely in the car and the race."

I hadn't thought about that before. I wasn't big on self-analysis. Never had been.

Walking away from racing should have been harder. But Wes had meant more to me than leaving him alone all the time. Or using a nanny while I raced and trained.

"And Katherine isn't in Wes's life at all."

I shook my head. "I'm actually shocked she lasted a few years. I get a text on his birthday every year, but otherwise, she left both of us behind." The exit for the hospital came up and I let Kelsey's hand go as I downshifted to turn off.

"God, I couldn't imagine. I was only his teacher and he was definitely one of my more memorable students. And now he's mine...well, if you are okay with it."

We came to a light and I cupped the back of her head to drag her mouth to mine. Just the idea that this woman could want to take both of us on—that she wanted my kid even in the midst of all these huge changes—made my kiss a little wild.

She turned in her seat to me and cupped my face, her fingers scraping through my short hair as she held on and kissed me back with the same intensity.

When a horn blared behind us, I pulled away. "Sorry."

She collapsed back in her seat. "Don't be sorry."

"Yes. I love that you want both of us."

"Of course I do."

We rode in silence, then parked and gathered up the food for the waiting room. I loaded half a dozen bottles of water in with the sandwiches to keep them cold and handed her a bag with six more. Laurel wasn't a terribly huge hospital, but it had a good-sized maternity ward. Evidently, with a few towns surrounding the hospital, there was a lot of babymaking going on.

I knew it definitely included me.

"You have a doctor's appointment coming up?"

She nodded. "Friday."

"Is it all right if I come?"

Her smile was sweet, and her cheeks pinked up. "I'd like that."

I tried not to ground my molars because she didn't immediately demand for me to go with her. She wasn't alone, and I was determined to make her aware of that every moment of the damn day.

She rushed forward with her bag to hug Ally when we made it into the room. There were a few people in there, but it was mostly the Sage contingency.

I lifted a bag. "Brought rations."

"Oh, thank God. I was just looking at the vending machines with tears in my eyes." Seth dug into the bag. "You must like us or something. Jersey Angel's roast beef on rye? I'd kiss you if I was into beards."

"Pass."

"I do have a talented tongue. You're missing out." Seth grinned and ripped open the deli paper. "So good. Thanks."

I dug out two waters for Ally and Kelsey and handed them out. "Drink."

Kelsey wrinkled her nose at me. "Yes, sir."

The *sir* thing didn't do it for me, but her looking up at me like that sure fucking did.

I just grunted at her and went back to the bag for my own water and a sandwich. There was a lot of sitting involved and the girls all took turns going back to see Sage. Kelsey seemed edgy and distracted and she disappeared once or twice. I hoped she wasn't dealing with nausea again.

Finally, Sage was settled into a room. By then, my ass was asleep and my noose of a tie had landed in a pile with the rest of the guys' ties and jackets. The food had been demolished in the waiting room, since Sage couldn't eat anything now that she was in active labor. Even though she had threatened bodily harm to all of us for daring to eat when she could not.

She was a scary chick.

Oliver came down the hallway. "Hey, guys. She's finally settled in a room." He ran a shaky hand over his hair. His tie was long gone and his dress shirt sleeves were rolled up, tails out of his pants. I didn't think I'd ever seen Oliver quite so disheveled.

Kelsey popped up from her place next to Ally. They'd been FaceTiming with Sage's parents. They were heading back to Crescent Cove, but they were still a few hours away. They'd taken an impromptu trip, thinking they had a bit of time until the baby was born.

I crossed to my wife and took her shaking hand. "Sage is doing great. It just takes time."

"Why is it taking so long though?"

"Babies come on their own timetable."

"God, knowing me and my luck, ours will come out sideways."

My gut clenched and unfurled when she said *ours* so easily, but I could see the bloom of panic on her face. That and how very tired she was.

"How's Wes?"

"Having the time of his life. He and Pop got a new puzzle." I was forever shocked that he would never sit down for anything—my boy was always running and active—unless there was a puzzle in front of him. But it gave him some much needed quiet time.

"Oh, that's good. He loves them. We picked out some when we took a Target trip earlier this week." She hugged herself and rubbed her arms. "Why do they keep it so cold in here?"

Personally, I was dying and was running out of things to take off, but I knew she was beyond overtired. I pulled her into me. "How about we go see Sage and then you lay down for a little bit?"

"I'm fine."

"I know, but you've been up since dawn, I bet."

She shrugged, then settled her cheek against my chest. "She threw a jug of water at Oliver last time I went in."

"Planning to do the same?"

She pulled back. "I don't know. I don't deal with pain well. Might be more like the bed itself."

"Well, then." Her giggle made me smile down at her. "Good to know." I uncurled her hand from between us and tugged her down the hallway after Oliver. She gripped my hand with both of hers when shouts reached the hallway.

"Drugs! Give me the goddamn epidural!"

I pushed open the door slowly. Kelsey's mouth dropped open as Sage dragged the nurse down by her stethoscope.

"Mrs. Hamilton, you're past the point of having one." The nurse's voice was calm as she peeled Sage's fingers off her stethoscope. "The doctor will be in soon." She gave us a tight smile and rushed out.

"Because you left me in the damn emergency room for hours," Sage yelled after her. "Ice chips. Where are my damn ice chips? Sweet bloody fuck, this baby is ripping me apart."

Kelsey rushed over to the table for her cup of ice. "Here you go. Can I do anything?"

Sage crunched on two cubes, her eyes like hellfire. "Yes. Can you reach in there and rip this thing out? That would be great." She threw her head back on the pillow and growled. "I'm having a demon. That's the only explanation for this." She slapped the railing.

"Honey, just breathe." Oliver brushed Sage's hair back. "You have to calm down."

"Are you having this baby?" She sat up until they were nose to nose. "I think not. If you had something trying to rip its way out of your parts, you would *not* be so calm."

Oliver paled, but he didn't move. In fact, it was impressive how he eased her back against the bed as he glanced at one of the monitors. He took her hand and kissed their clenched fingers. "Here we go."

"Fuck!" Sage's voice was like nails down a chalkboard with a lightning strike chaser.

"Breathe," Oliver said in a stern voice.

"Breathing." Sage's voice was little more than a snarl as she slowly calmed and collapsed against the pillow. "I'm sorry. I'm so sorry. I didn't mean to yell. I love you."

Just like that, she turned into a blubbering mess as the contractions eased off.

I curled my arm around Kelsey and pulled her to the side as the door opened again. A woman in a white coat bustled in. "Hello, Sage. Evidently, your little one decided to come early."

"Doctor, could you please tell your staff that I'm so not too late for the drugs thing. I really need them."

The doctor lifted Sage's gown and I turned my head away. I had no need to see all the things when it came to Sage. There was friendship and then there was *hell no.* The doctor reached around in there and I winced as I turned Kelsey to face me.

From the color of my wife's cheeks, she was well on her way to freaking out.

"Nope. You are about ready to go, young lady. In fact," the doctor turned to us, "out you go, guys. Unless you're a birthing coach or the father."

"Birthing coach!" Ally yelled as she came in. "I'm here."

"Where have you been?" Sage's voice was accusing.

Ally held up a stuffed unicorn. Or was that a pony? I was eternally grateful that my son didn't go for anything in the girl realm of toys. Not that I wouldn't let him play with anything he wanted to, but I sure as fuck didn't need to buy him anything else since I currently owned every damn dinosaur I could find on Amazon.

"I have Sparkles." Ally waved the stuffed toy.

"Oh." Sage made grabby hands. "I need Sparkles. Thank you. I love you. You're the best."

Kelsey buried her face in my chest. "Sparkles is what she focuses on to breathe through the pain."

"Oh." Considering I hadn't been able to get Katherine to show up to a birthing class, we definitely hadn't known about anything like that.

Yeah, it was time to hustle my girl out of the room.

We got down the hall, but instead of turning into the waiting room, she went out through the front doors of the hospital. "Kelsey!"

She shook her head. "Nope. I'm good. We don't need to do any of that." She waved her hand up in the air. "I changed my mind. Having a baby isn't what I want after all."

My belly twisted for a second before I chased after her. She didn't mean it, but God, hearing that was fucking sobering. "Kel, come on."

"No way. There is no way I can do that. Nope. I take care of kids after they come out and grow like five years or whatever. That part? Nope." She shook her head. The curls from the ceremony were long gone and it was back to her long, perfect red hair. "I can't do that."

"Yes, you can. You're the strongest woman I know."

"You are sorely mistaken, sir. I am a wimp. I cry when I have cramps. You think I can do that?"

"Yes." I curled my fingers around her upper arms and forced her to face me. "You are going to be awesome at that. And you've told me that Sage is a bit of a...what do you call it?"

"Drama llama," she muttered.

"Right. And you can do anything you set your mind to. You wrangle twenty-four six-year-olds and seven-year-olds. Having a baby is nothing compared to what you do every day."

"Yes, but there's no blood—well, usually no blood."

"See?" I tipped her head up and kissed her. "You're already ahead of the game."

"You're just trying to placate me."

Fuck yes, I was. I truly didn't know how any woman gave birth, but I wasn't telling her that. "Yes, how am I doing?"

She stuck out her lower lip and crowded into me. "Okay."

"Yeah?"

Her lips twitched.

"I see that smile trying to come out. Come on, let me see it."

"Stop. You are being ridiculous."

"Oh, and flying out of the hospital saying you changed your mind isn't?"

She punched me in the belly. "Get used to it, buddy. I haven't even begun to be an irrational pregnant woman yet. I reserve the right to get way worse."

"Looking forward to it." I curled my arm around her shoulders. "Now let's get back in there before you freeze."

"Too late." She shivered and huddled in close.

An ocean-liner-sized vacation home on wheels pulled up and a woman scrambled down the stairs.

"Mrs. Evans?" Kelsey took a step toward the woman.

"Oh, goodness. Did I make it in time, dear?"

Kelsey laughed. "I think you did. Hurry up, let's get you inside." She turned to me and I waved her ahead.

My wife needed to have a plan of action. Nerves fell by the wayside when she had something to do.

I stuffed my hands into my pockets and took a deep breath of the cool night air. The canned air inside the hospital was killing me slowly. I checked my phone and gave my mom an update. She sent me a sleeping picture of my kid.

The scrape of sneakers and a lanky guy shuffling around the side of the building, then back toward the emergency entrance made me look up. I glanced back down as he disappeared. Twenty seconds later, he returned.

"You lost, man?"

"What? Oh, yeah. Not sure." He pushed a mop of curls out of his face. "I, uh, am looking for my girlfriend—well, ex-girlfriend." He huffed out a strained laugh. "So fucked up."

My gut tightened. I straightened and stuffed my phone back in my pocket. "I've been here all night. I can at least point you in the right direction."

"Maternity. Shit. I can't even believe I said that word. She said she was here."

I swallowed hard. "You found it." I nodded to the doors behind me. "Who are you looking for?"

"You probably wouldn't know her."

"I've been in the maternity waiting room all night." My hand fisted in my pocket. The bad vibes got louder in my head.

"Oh. Well, then yeah, maybe." He speared his fingers into his hair, pushing it back from his pale, emo fucking face. "Kelsey. She's a cute ginger girl. Sweet, a little goofy."

The door opened behind me, but the growl that came out of me made the kid take a step back. "Whoa, dude. If you don't know her, that's cool." He tried to go around me and stopped. "Kelsey, babe. I got here as soon as I could."

"Tommy."

I didn't know that blood truly could run cold until that moment.

Now, I knew that it was a sterling fact.

TWENTY-ONE

My heart stopped.

Literally.

There was no way this should happen in my life. Today of all days. "Oh, God. What are you doing here, Tommy?"

"You texted me."

I glanced at Dare. His face was red and the tendons in his neck were bulging. He was still wearing half of his suit. His dress shirt was half open, showing a V-neck undershirt with the tails untucked. Instead of seeming unkempt, all I could notice were the ropey muscles of his arms on display, making my ex-boyfriend look even younger and more slight.

Tommy bounced on his heels, his Converse sneakers untied as always. He was wearing skinny jeans and a plaid shirt two sizes too big for his lanky frame.

Seeing them side-by-side was sobering.

My husband versus the boy I once knew. That I'd even had a moment's sadness about Tommy breaking up with me seemed so stupid. I'd leveled up by miles.

I rushed forward and curled my hand around Dare's arm. He pulled back and stepped away from me.

"Dare."

"What is he doing here, Kel?"

I swallowed. "I texted him."

"Why?" Dare shook his head. "Today of all days? Are you kidding me right now?"

I stepped toward him, but again, he sidestepped my touch, folding his arms. "I had to. Seeing all this happen today with the baby and then with us and our conversation in the car. I had to. It wasn't fair that I hadn't told him yet."

I glanced at Tommy.

Tommy's gaze pingponged between me and Dare. "I'm not sure what I'm walking into here. All you said was we had to talk and then you said you were at the hospital. Are you okay?" He looked me up and down. "Are you wearing a…" Tommy tipped his head. "Is that a wedding dress?"

"Yes, it's a fucking wedding dress. She's my goddamn wife."

"Wife?" Tommy's shocked eyes were almost comical.

Almost.

Because my husband was about to rip someone's head off and I was pretty sure it might be mine. Okay, no, he wouldn't. I didn't know Dare as well as I wanted to, but there was one thing I knew. He'd never hurt me, no matter how mad he was.

And holy crap, was he mad. I didn't think I'd ever seen him so angry. Even the day at Macy's, he'd been annoyed and possibly ready to throw a punch, but not like this.

Not pop-a-blood-vessel angry.

I straightened my shoulders and stalked up to my husband, ignoring Tommy's wide open mouth. "Yes, I texted him. But I didn't think he was coming here." I lifted my hands to cup Dare's face and he flinched.

Part of me wanted to back up and flee. God, I hated any sort of conflict. Things between us were still so tenuous. So very unsure. But he deserved more. And knowing a little about his past, I knew I owed it to him to never ever lie. And for him to know he was the one who mattered most.

Even if I was spilling the beans about my—no, *our*—baby. I'd been saying *our* baby for days now because it was true. It was ours regardless of the actual DNA strands doing their thing inside my body.

"Dare, I had to tell him about the baby."

"Baby?" Tommy took two giant steps back.

Dare frowned at me, his beautiful blue eyes hard and flat. I smoothed my fingers through his beard. "It was right to tell him. But it doesn't matter. You said that to me. It doesn't matter because it's our baby. We're going to raise it and make a family. And maybe even have more babies."

Just a few minutes ago, I was so scared to have this child. Truly and utterly terrified to endure that kind of pain, but I was positive I'd do it again for him. It didn't matter to me if this was Dare's baby by blood, it was his in love. But if he wanted another one, I'd certainly give it to him.

The knowledge of it should have put me on my knees.

It was too fast.

Everything about me and Dare was too fast, but God, I loved him. And even now I knew it was only going to get stronger.

"I'm sorry I didn't say anything. I didn't think he'd show up here. I just thought we'd go and talk about it. That we could go together even."

Maybe I hadn't really thought that far, but saying it didn't make it any less true. I'd impulsively texted Tommy that I had to talk to him about something, but I hadn't done it maliciously. "I'd never go behind your back." I touched my forehead to Dare's chin. I didn't quite reach him in the flats I'd changed into.

The anger seemed to drain out of him slowly. His arms came around me until he was crushing me against his chest.

"Dammit, Kel."

"I know. I'm sorry. I swear it. I was just overwhelmed with the baby stuff in there and then us getting married."

"I thought you wanted to marry me."

"I do, but not like this. Not like it was a checklist. And I know I should have said something, but you're being so supportive and wonderful. I don't want you to feel like you're trapped—"

"I'm not feeling trapped. I just don't want you to leave."

"What?" I pulled back.

He gripped the folds of my dress at my hips. "I couldn't bear it if you left. I wanted to marry you fast so you'd be mine."

The tears came faster than I could blink them away. "Why would you…" I closed my eyes. God, I was so stupid. The conversation in the car came back to me. Both of them. "I'm never going anywhere," I whispered.

"Guys? I mean this is all very interesting. And actually, wow, Kelsey. You hooked up with him really fast."

I dashed away my tears, but I couldn't help but smile. "I did. Crazy how it happened."

Tommy jammed his hands into his pockets. Well, as much as he could into his skinny jeans. More like just his fingertips. It was a rare man who could pull off the skinny jeans look, and Tommy just looked like he was trying too hard to be young and carefree. "Now, what's this about a baby?"

I blew out a breath. "I'm pregnant."

Tommy paled. "And you think it's mine?"

"I honestly don't know. We had that night after Granny Flo's funeral."

"Oh." He scratched his head. "Yeah, wow. I mean, we used a condom and stuff. I thought you were on the pill?"

I shook my head. "I hadn't gotten my full time job yet, so I didn't have insurance. And we'd broken up way before that."

"Shit. I mean…you know. Just I don't know what to say."

"You don't have to say shit." Dare's voice was more rumbly than usual.

Actually, it was about as close to a growl as I'd ever heard. I patted his chest. "What Dare means is we don't expect anything from you. I just didn't want to keep it from you."

"Yeah. I get that. And thanks, I guess. I mean, if it's mine I'll step up if you want. I didn't really ever want kids, but if it's mine, I'll do what's right."

I peered up at Dare and stroked his beard with the back of my hand before stepping out of his hold. I turned to Tommy. "I appreciate it. And if the baby is yours, I'd be more than happy to let you be part of his or her life. If that's what you want."

"I wouldn't want to get between you guys if you're doing the family thing. Maybe if I thought about it more or something, but…" He shrugged. "It would be okay with me if you wanted to take care of everything. I'm not trying to get out of taking care of it or anything, but you know…"

I reached back for Dare's hand. "I found a place that will do a blood test. It's a paternity test. Takes a while to get the results." I cleared my throat. "Regardless of the test, I want Dare to help me raise the baby."

Tommy gave me a tight smile. "It's probably best. I'm not really dad material."

No, he really wasn't. Dare was the perfect guy for me and for our baby. In so many ways. "I'm sorry."

"Don't be. Looks like you've got yourself a great guy. Wow—married, huh?"

I took a step back to Dare. "Yeah." I laced our fingers more tightly together. "Crazy, but amazing."

Tommy nodded toward the parking lot. "I'm gonna go." He cleared his throat. "So, just text me the info for the blood test or whatever."

"I will."

With an awkward little wave, he took off at a near run.

Shaking my head, I smiled faintly. Amazing how a few months could change your perspective so much. I definitely didn't regret my breakup with Tommy now. It was probably the best thing that had ever happened to me.

No, that was falling in love with Dare and making a family with him.

I glanced at my husband. "I don't think I've ever seen Tommy move so fast in my life."

"Like his ass is on fire," Dare muttered. He hauled me into his arms and his mouth came down hard on mine. "Not me. You're fucking stuck with me, Mrs. Kramer. Can we get out of here yet?"

"I was coming out to tell you Sage had the baby."

"Thank fuck."

"Dare."

"Sorry. We've been here a long damn time. Not exactly the place I was looking to spend my honeymoon."

"No, I don't suppose it was. I really am sorry about this whole thing—" He kissed me again, with more than a bit of pent-up frustration.

"I don't want to talk about that emo kid. I want you under me so I can show you how excited I am to be your husband."

I swallowed. "Is that right?" I stared at his neck, not quite able to look him in the eyes. "I was wondering if you still wanted me like that."

"What? Of course I do. I can't keep my damn hands off you."

I nodded. "It's not like we don't have sex or anything, but you know. Not like we did at first."

"What?" He sighed. "What are you talking about? Every time I look at you, I want to get you naked."

"It's good you still want to have sex with me, but it's different."

"Of course it's different. I'm not banging some girl I don't know anymore."

"Well, maybe I want to be banged."

"What?"

I didn't know how to explain it. Was I really so wrong about everything about us? "I want all that passion. I was so afraid you didn't see me as a woman anymore. Just someone you had to deal with out of duty."

"Oh, for fuck's sake, Kel. I can't stop thinking about you. Please tell me I can take you home and show you. I'm way better at that than words. Because believe me, after tonight, you'll have no doubts."

I swallowed hard, darting a glance back at the hospital. All of a sudden, I was having trouble speaking without fidgeting. Laying it all on the line was so hard. "It's a girl. Sage had a girl. I think her name is going to be Star. Not sure how that got by Oliver, but it did. I'm sure there's one hell of a story behind her name."

"Great." Dare took my hand and headed into the hospital. This time, Dare's ass was the one on fire and so was mine. Or maybe it was my panties. "Can't wait to hear the story another day. Right now, we're getting our stuff and I'm taking my wife home for a proper honeymoon fuck."

God, that sounded amazing.

Saying goodbye to everyone took much longer than I could stand. We both tried to get out of conversations, our gaze drifting to each other with way more steam than should be happening in a baby ward. And just when I thought we were finally in the home stretch—I even had my purse and jacket in hand—the nurse came out to tell us we could see the baby.

I couldn't *not* go look.

I could feel the matching frustration in Dare as we walked hand-in-hand to the viewing room. There were only a handful of babies. All little bundles swaddled tight in pink and blue blankets. A few were fussing, but most were sleeping.

And right in the middle was baby Hamilton.

"She's perfect."

Dare moved behind me, his arms around my middle, the flat of his hand over my still flat stomach. "Soon, that'll be us with a little one getting toasty warm."

I giggled as I pressed my hand to the glass. "Do you want a boy or a girl?"

"The right answer is whichever is healthy. But if I end up with a girl who looks like you, I may end up in jail. There's no way I'll survive it."

I turned in his arms and linked my fingers at the back of his neck. "I probably shouldn't love that answer so much, but I do. Take me home."

"About time."

We practically raced down the hallway. We caught sight of Ally in a small alcove and we both froze, but we didn't have to worry. She was too busy with Seth to bother with us.

Evidently, seeing a baby revved them up too.

Dare and I grabbed our bags and finally made it out the door. It was nearly two in the morning. A few nurses were standing along the edge of the parking lot, smoking cigarettes. I was too wrapped up in thoughts of Dare to care who saw us.

I pushed him up against the car door and went on my toes to meet his mouth.

He seemed to have the same problem as I did because there was no reining in the lava-level kisses between us. He pressed his cock into my belly. "I only slowed myself down because I want you too much, Kel. It's not duty between us. I promise you."

I wanted to climb him. To mount him and rub against him until the ache went away. Until I could feel every part of him around me and inside of me. Until there was nothing safe about us.

I'd had safe before. I wanted the wild that I could only find with Dare.

He reached behind his back for the latch of the door and maneuvered me into the car with his hot breath on my neck and my skirt and slip riding up around my ass. He pressed himself against the lacy white panties and garter I'd worn under my dress.

I'd been hoping to show him I was still sexy—not just a mom-to-be.

Dare gripped my hips. "You've been wearing this under your dress all day?"

I nodded. "I wanted you to want me." I hated how tremulous my voice was, but I wasn't going to hide how I felt anymore.

He pushed my hair aside and dropped his mouth to my neck. He nipped at the skin there. "I do. So goddamn much." He put me in the seat and instead of pulling my dress down he hiked it higher. "Fuck. So beautiful. So much mine." He lowered his head between my thighs for a quick second. He dragged my panties aside and swiped his tongue along my slit. "I'll start you off and you'll finish before we get home."

The hint of a growl made my thighs shudder. Actually, it made everything shudder.

He slipped two fingers inside of me and I arched up on the seat, his name more moan than words. He covered my mouth with his as he flicked his thumb over my clit and pumped into me. I could taste myself on his tongue and it made it even hotter as he pushed me up and held me right on the edge of release.

"Shh," he said against my mouth. "Don't want the nurses to know I'm finger-fucking my wife, do you?"

"Maybe I do."

His lips tilted into that smirk I remembered from the day he delivered a pizza to my door. From the bar, the first time we flirted, and finally, a new one to add to my memories.

My husband making out with me in the car because he was so hot for me.

"I'll remember that." He drew his fingers out of me, then pulled my hand down between my legs. "Now you." He guided my middle finger inside slowly then pulled it free and sucked it clean with a hard pull ending in a bite. "Again." Then he stood up and closed the door.

I collapsed against the seat, my legs splayed open. God, he was going to kill me.

He got in the driver side and leaned over. "Don't forget to buckle up." He drew it tight across my hips until I was strapped into the seat. He slid the shoulder strap between my breasts then flicked a fingertip over my rigid nipple. "For safety."

Yep. I was a dead woman.

He gunned the engine, checked his mirrors, and pulled his own seatbelt on. "You have about thirteen minutes to come twice."

"Twice?"

He threw a look at me. "Twice, Mrs. Kramer."

I shivered. Okay, maybe I'd like this game. Maybe two of us could play. I couldn't move much thanks to the seatbelt, but the dash lights would give him a good show. And it was exciting enough that I wanted to give him a show too.

It didn't have to be only about how much he showed me he wanted me. I had to do the same.

I hissed out a breath as I rubbed the pad of my first two fingers over my clit. It was already hard and I was beyond wet. The lace of my panties was damp from just a little teasing from my husband. I winced at the sounds my fingers made.

"So fucking wet I can hear it." His fingers tightened on the steering wheel as he turned out of the parking lot.

"I am. Because of you."

His jaw tensed and the little muscle there ticked. It made me bolder. I slipped two fingers inside my pussy. "I ache, Dare. My fingers aren't enough."

"Jesus."

I smiled in the darkness. "I want it to be your fingers. They're thicker than mine." I lifted my hips restlessly. "Too bad you have to use them to shift. Go faster."

"You are so getting fucked."

"Promises, promises."

He glanced over at me then back to the road with a hiss.

"I'm really wet. It's almost embarrassing."

"Fuck no. I want to smell you on my seats tomorrow."

I dragged in a breath. That was way naughtier than what I could come up with and it drove me closer to the edge. I was a master at getting myself off fast. It was usually just to kill the need on a lonely night or the perfect insomnia cure. But I'd never had to touch myself after I'd been with Dare.

Doing it for him felt decadent and thrilling. Not wrong—no, nothing about it was wrong. It was exactly what I'd wanted. To feel wanted, to feel sexy. There was a power to it and desire was all tangled up in my emotions for him. Add in a few pregnancy hormones and I was up and over the first orgasm before I knew it.

I blew out a harsh breath as I sagged in the seat. "God, I don't think I've ever come so fast."

He shifted and the gunning of the engine kept the hum inside me alive. His knuckles were white on the wheel. "Again," he said in a low voice.

"I might need your help."

"Fuck."

I reached over to his thigh and gripped the rigid muscle. I inched higher, curling my fingers over his shaft. "I need this. We're almost home, right?"

"Not close enough," he muttered on a groan.

"Can I take care of that for you?" I leaned closer to him. "If I loosened my belt a little..."

"No." He covered my hand, squeezing him harder. Harder than I would have ever dreamed to do. He moaned. "Not safe." He kissed my fingers then put them on my breast. "Show me these while you come again."

I dragged in a breath. "Okay." I loosened the little snap behind my neck until the dress slipped forward. "They're so sensitive now. Never used to be until I got pregnant." I cupped one, tugging at the nipple with a little moan.

"You're so fucking hot."

I smiled in the dark and tugged a little harder as I circled my clit. The exit for Crescent Cove came up and my fingers worked harder.

"Yeah, you better work that sweet pussy because we're almost home. And if you don't come again..."

"What? What will you do?"

"I'll make you wait hours to come."

"What?" I couldn't have heard him correctly.

"Hours. I can make you almost come all night. Until you're swearing at me in made-up languages."

"You wouldn't."

"Oh, I would." He downshifted as we came to a stop sign just outside of our development.

I circled faster, using whatever tricks I'd learned about my own body up to that night. I was so close, but I couldn't quite get there. Tension was firing through me and my skin was alive with need. Frustration made me arch my back and then Dare was there. His big hand over mine as he followed my fingers inside and the fullness was just what I needed.

"God, yeah. Like that. Come for me, darlin'."

He leaned over to catch the screams coming out of my mouth. His car couldn't muffle them all that was for sure. When I came back to myself, I saw the stop sign on our corner.

I flicked off the seatbelt and threw myself at him.

The kiss was wild and full of laughter, then he buried his chin into the space between my neck and shoulder. "Some other time, we'll play this game again. And we'll see if there's a night of punishment in store. Tonight? Tonight, I just want you screaming my name."

I smiled. "I'm definitely up for that game."

"We have plenty of time." He slowly pulled up the driveway to our house and turned off the engine. "Now, you better run."

I flung open my door and headed for the house. My dress was half falling forward and I hoped to hell everyone was sleeping in the neighborhood or they would be getting a show.

A second before I dashed over the threshold, I remembered he should have carried me over it.

I would only have this opportunity for that, new bride and all. But the intent in his eyes when I turned around made me keep moving.

I ran up the stairs and his pounding feet made my heart race. I got to the top and almost through the bedroom door when he scooped me up and over his shoulder. He set me on the bed gently.

When I frowned at him, he shook his head. "I'm not tossing my pregnant bride on the bed." He stripped off his shirt and undershirt. Next came his belt. "I *am* going to fuck the hell out of her though."

I scrambled up to get out of my dress. He was right. There was rough and then there was safe. And I loved that he wanted me to be safe. For our baby to be safe. But the heat in his eyes made my toes curl.

"Stop."

I stopped at the strap of my bra. "What?"

"That's my job."

"Oh." I knelt in the middle of the bed in my white demi-cup bra, garter, and panties. He stepped forward and drew the strap down slowly. My breasts weren't overly large, but they filled the cup and held it up. He lowered his mouth and nudged it down. He bit down on the tip and tugged, sucking on it strongly until my head fell back.

I scraped my fingers through the close-cropped hair along his nape. When he looked up at me with my nipple between his teeth, I shuddered. How could I ever think he was anything but the wild man of every fantasy I'd ever had?

I'd been so worried about second-guessing every move that I hadn't let myself enjoy every part of him.

That was changing right now.

He pushed me back on the bed and rolled me onto my stomach. "Now, we're going to just get rid of these." He pulled down my panties slowly, his nose brushing lightly over my swollen folds as he inched it down past my thighs and knees until finally, I was free of them. He drew his tongue down my slit and spread me wide. I reached for the headboard and he laughed.

"You better hang onto that, darlin'."

I cried out as he left not one inch of me untasted. Even parts of me I never thought I'd want him to search out. I couldn't even wiggle away from him. He eased me onto my side and ducked his head under my leg so I was open to him in every way. He looked up at me as he lapped at me, teased me, and toyed with me.

When I couldn't breathe around my frustration anymore, he gripped my garter and snapped it. The little sting of pain shocked me into the first wave of an orgasm. He ducked back under my leg and settled behind me. I backed up against him and sighed when he slid his cock into me with a slowness that made my eyes cross.

"Dare."

"Kelsey. My Kelsey." He eased out and back in until every square inch of me was filled. I melted into him as he slowly rocked into me again and again. He tucked his arm under my knee until I was splayed open and so full of him I couldn't think.

I could only feel.

He tugged my earlobe with a harsh growl. "Hold onto that headboard, darlin'."

I reached up, wrapping my fingers around the lip at the edge of the mattress. He snapped his hips forward and my teeth vibrated from the force of his thrust. "Yes."

"Fuck yes," he growled as he let go.

The thing I'd wanted most was mine.

Dare's frenzied strokes hurled me head first into another release. Before I could recover from that one, his fingers were plucking at me, demanding another. My skin was flushed and sweat coated my back where our bodies met.

Still, he didn't stop.

My breath came in pants and I reached behind me with my other hand to drag him closer.

"Fuck yes," I echoed him. I was already riled up from the car ride and now, my husband was unleashing all the passion I'd worried he didn't have for me until there was nothing left but the truth.

I arched and sobbed my release. And still, he held on and demanded more. Filled me until all that remained between us was sweat and the love I'd been so afraid to give. I held onto him, curling into a tight ball as his hips pummeled into me again and again before finally jerking tight into me. The strangled groan he let out allowed me to finally relax against him as we sagged against one another.

He slid his hand down between my legs and flicked over where we were joined. "See why I held back?"

"Never again," I said against my arm. I lifted my head to try and catch his mouth over my shoulder. The angle was wrong, but I needed the connection. Needed him.

Always.

"Never hold back," I whispered. "Even if you almost kill me." I flexed my inner walls against him, not wanting him to slip away from me.

He groaned. "We'll end up having eight kids."

I laughed and turned in his arms. "No, we won't. But three is a nice number."

He laughed against my mouth. "Or two."

I shrugged. "Or two."

TWENTY-TWO

<small>AFTER THE SECOND ROUND, I PLANTED FACE-FIRST ON OUR BED.</small> "I <small>LOVE</small> you, babe, but I think you killed me."

"What did you just say?"

I winced as she gripped the slightly longer hairs on top of my head and tugged me closer until our eyes met. "Kel."

She knelt beside me. Obviously, I hadn't done my job since she'd been as dead to the world as I was not even five minutes ago. I still couldn't breathe, for fuck's sake. I hadn't realized I needed to start training to keep up with my wife.

Damn. *Wife*. Never thought I'd say that with a smile on my face.

"I asked you a question, sir."

I rolled onto my side and traced my finger down the slope of her breast, tweaking her nipple lightly. "Which part? That you killed me?"

"No." She launched herself at me, shifting me on my back and straddling my stomach.

"Darlin', you keep that up and we won't be talking again."

She balanced herself and brushed her very fine ass against my rapidly hardening cock. "We'll get back to that. Impressive by the way. I don't think my boyfriend in college had that short of a recovery time and he was nineteen."

I growled and swung her onto her back, caging her in with my arms and knees. "Don't talk about other men being inside you, wife."

Her eyes widened and her nipples went to bullets against my chest. I angled myself between her thighs and slid inside of her. "Evidently, I need to remind you there's only one man and one cock you should be thinking about."

Her beautiful golden eyes fluttered shut as I slowly canted my hips to grind against her. She arched under me with a long, delicious groan. I lowered my mouth to hers. "I love you, Kel. Call it too fast, call it insane, call me out as a liar if you want." I shifted my hips so I could pull her leg up to take her deeper.

She lifted her hands to my shoulders as her eyes filled.

I reached up for one arm, then the other, dragging them over her head until there was no air between us and she couldn't move. I wanted to make sure there was no way she could misunderstand me. Not again. Not ever. I grasped her wrists together and slowly punctuated each word with my hips, joining with her again and again. "I. Love. You. Always."

The tears rolled and she took each word with a nod. And I watched as the orgasm stole her breath, and her speech. Then she broke free and wrapped her arms and legs around me as she trembled, the words finally tumbling from her mouth. "I love you too. So much. Too much."

I lost it. I didn't think there was anything left in my damn tank, but as it always was with her, I had more. Always more to give her. I pressed my forehead to her shoulder and shook over her as I came inside her one more time. I dragged my lips over her neck. "Never too much." I coasted over her jawline to her mouth. "Never too much between us. I'm just sorry you didn't know that until tonight."

She shook her head. "It doesn't matter. I know now." She played with her wedding ring and her soft smile broke apart the last of the doubts rattling around in my brain. "And I'm Mrs. Kramer today. It's a good day." Then her stomach gurgled—loudly. Her eyes widened. "Sorry about that. I didn't really eat much of my sandwich."

"Then let's get you fed." I slipped out of her with a groan, nibbling on her neck before I rolled off of her.

She let her legs and arms drop open. "Am I hungry enough to move?"

I picked up my dress pants off the floor. No way I was putting them back on. Nope, definitely time for sweats and maybe some cold pizza from the fridge. I automatically checked the pockets of my dress pants for change or receipts. Doing laundry and losing my debit card or credit card was a constant battle.

Then I felt the ring.

My gut clenched and I slipped it down the first knuckle of my pinkie. "Kel?"

"I'm getting up." She groaned and rolled up to a seated position. God, she was freaking beautiful. Even with her hair a hot mess from rolling around with me for the last few hours and her face smeared with leftover makeup from the ceremony and the tears from the day and night, she was miles more amazing and gorgeous than I deserved. "What? Don't look at me like that."

I grinned. "Like what?"

"Like you have a dirty secret."

I dragged her up to a standing position and slid her arms into my dress shirt, twirling her around to face me as I did up a few of the buttons. Not all of them, because I still wanted access to her. Especially her epic legs that made me hard just by walking behind her.

She shook her hair back. "Do you have a dirty secret?"

"Maybe a few."

"Oh, yeah? I thought we were through with secrets and lies." She swept her hair over one shoulder as she always did, twisting it into a loose braid to keep it out of her way.

"I wouldn't exactly call them secrets. More like surprises I feel you need."

"Yeah? I like surprises." She wrapped her hands around my wrist. "Tell me."

I curled my fingers into my palm to hide the ring.

"What do you have there?"

I smiled down at her. "What?"

"There." She tapped my hand. "Come on. Is it chocolate?"

I laughed. "No. Not chocolate."

Her lower lip pushed out adorably.

"But obviously, you're hungry. It can wait."

"No, I can wait to eat." Her stomach roared. She pressed her hand over her middle. "Okay, maybe me and the baby need a little food. But I want to know."

I grabbed a pair of sweats out of the dresser behind me, then pointed to the door before I tugged them on. "Go on."

"But—"

"Get. I'm making you pancakes."

She frowned. "We have cold pizza."

Damn this woman. She kept me on my toes. Only part of why I loved her so much. "Yeah, well, you deserve pancakes on our damn wedding night."

She crossed to me and wrapped her arms around my neck. "Okay. I can deal with that."

I slipped my hand under the tails of my shirt and cupped her bare ass. "Don't distract me or we'll end up naked again."

"Naked brinner—you know, breakfast for dinner—isn't a bad idea. We can make it our anniversary thing."

I groaned and turned her toward the door. "You are dangerous."

She threw a smile over her shoulder. "Really? I kinda like being dangerous."

I rolled my eyes. She had no idea just how appealing she was on every level. I pinched her ass and she yelped and ran down the hall. She got to the banister just before I caught up with her. I hauled her back against me, my arm tight around her waist. "Careful on the stairs." I nipped the skin between her shoulder and neck. "Precious cargo—both of you."

She laced her fingers over mine. "You kill me when you say stuff like that."

"It's the truth." I followed her down the stairs and we immediately fell into a familiar rhythm. We didn't bother with bacon, and I cracked her up with the goofy animals I drew on the griddle with the squirt bottle I used to make shapes for Wes.

She fed me a star for the newest addition to the crazy circle of people I called friends. Then I made a silly heart with our initials. She blushed and dipped the corner of the D into our little joint saucer of syrup.

I lifted the bottle again and she giggled, then covered her stomach. "I'm stuffed."

"You will be."

Her eyes heated and she drew closer to play with the strings of my sweatpants. "Is it like swimming? I have to wait twenty minutes after I eat?"

"I don't think that's a rule." But I carefully drew a few words on the griddle. The batter bubbled lightly as she glanced away from me and to my question.

"Marry me, again?" Her words were soft and questioning. "We're already married. Shouldn't you be asking that after we're celebrating ten years or something?"

I held up my pinkie. The simple band with four small diamonds winked in the kitchen light. "I bought this a little bit ago, but I couldn't figure out how to give it to you. I guess it was just because we had to wait for the right time. Patience isn't my virtue."

She covered her mouth with her left hand, her eyes brimming with tears. That gold band already made her mine. This part was for her.

"I don't always get shit right. And sometimes you'll probably want to strangle me, but I'll do everything in my power to make you happy, Kel. And I know our little wedding wasn't what you need."

She shook her head and the tears spilled down her cheeks. "I have everything I need. I swear I do." She crashed into me, her arms sliding around my neck. "I have you and Wes and this baby. I have everything."

She meant it. I knew she did, but I also knew she deserved the fairytale. To be the center of attention for one day.

I eased her back and slipped the ring down next to her wedding band. "We'll do it up right with all our family and friends. Might even be able to get my brother Gage into town for it. I want it too. I'll even wear a monkey suit for you."

She wiggled her finger, making the diamonds flash. "One for each of us. You, me, Wes, and whomever is still cooking." She pressed her hand to her belly and I covered it with my own.

"A little bit of perfect."

"No, a lot perfect." She rose onto her toes and kissed me. "Perfectly perfect."

EPILOGUE

KELSEY

"I can't believe I'm doing this again," I whispered into the mirror, touching the sparkly crown that sat atop my hair.

Okay, it wasn't a crown. Not exactly. More like a tiara-ish thing with a filmy veil on the back. It still shimmered like a crown. Like the thin layer of diamond-like snow that I knew covered everything outside.

Everything was glimmering tonight, even me.

Especially me.

"That pregnancy glow is really working for you, sis."

I smiled and gripped my tiara as I turned toward my ridiculously beautiful little sister. Rylee was wearing a dark blue crushed velvet wrap dress and her dark hair was piled high with those little tendrils hanging down. Effortlessly beautiful, like she always was.

Except now she was staring at me as if *I* was the beautiful one.

The happy one.

Better yet, the one who deserved to be happy and wasn't going to miss a minute of this night and all the ones that came after.

"Thanks. But I think it's a Dare glow too. And a Wes glow." I swallowed hard and glanced back at the mirror, afraid to see the joy on my face had vanished like smoke. But no, it was still there. "And maybe a me glow too. Just a little bit."

"Or a lot. You're coming into your own. Own it, sister." Rylee moved up beside me and bumped her hip into mine. "It's about time."

I touched the tiara again though that sucker wasn't going anywhere with all the pins and gunk Ally and Sage had used to attach it to my surprisingly wavy hair. Even my stick-straight strands had cooperated with Sage's curling iron.

Everything was going my way tonight.

"Yeah, I guess it is. What about you? You look...smug," I decided after a minute. Rylee had the most expressive face and she wasn't shy about sharing her emotions. Right now, she was practically flushed with pleasure. "What's that all about?"

Rylee fiddled with the bodice of her dress, not meeting my gaze. "Let's just say someone had a very good night last night. And this morning."

"Oh, jealous." Then I remembered my own very good night and morning and bit my lip to hold back a grin. "Well, okay, not jealous, but curious. Do tell. With who?"

Rylee shrugged and my eyes popped wide.

"Is that shrug because you won't tell me or because you don't know his name? And just FYI, you might want to be careful with the unexpected hookups, because—"

"Because I might end up pregnant by a super sexy dad who is good with his hands and blissfully happy with a brand-new family like you are?" Rylee rolled her eyes. "Yeah, such a downside. Hold me back."

Hmm. She kinda had a point. But still. Wasn't I some sort of fertility cautionary tale?

Besides, there were no guarantees that the guy she'd done the nasty with was a decent dude like mine. In fact, it was probably likely he wasn't. What were the odds that both Ford sisters would bag themselves a wonderful man within one calendar year?

Slim to go fish.

"Okay, I won't press. But this very good night, does it come with repeats?"

My sister shrugged again. "That's the best part. It was just a hot night. No strings. Sometimes you can let loose the most with someone you know you'll never see again." She waggled her brows. "You know, let out your inner freak."

"My inner freak is much more comfortable coming out to play in a committed relationship." I had a feeling our car action the night of our first wedding had opened a door I hadn't even realized I had inside me.

"Why doesn't that surprise me?" Rylee shook her head and grabbed my arm as the church bell for six o'clock tolled outside. "Eeek, you're late. C'mon."

"Oh my God, I can't be late to my own wedding." I hurried out with her and turned to wave a final goodbye to the apartment where I had started my new life. Gavin hadn't rented it out to someone new yet, and its location was the perfect place to get ready for the ceremony taking place across the street.

Plus, sentimentality. Tonight really was goodbye to this apartment and the new life I'd briefly had here.

The new life that had started and ended with Dare.

And a damn fine pepperoni pizza in both cases, depending on how things went tonight after the ceremony. I really had my heart set on a double stuffed pie—

"Come on, slowpoke." Rylee tugged on my arm. "Everyone's already waiting at the gazebo. Minus your ladies-in-waiting, of course," she added as we rushed down the stairs to where Ally and Sage—and the princess in pink attached to Sage's left boob—waited expectantly.

Baby Star pulled her mouth away from Sage's breast, took one look at me, and started to wail. Loudly.

"There's an auspicious sign."

"Shh, shh. She just thinks you're going to take her milk away. She's very possessive. There now," Sage soothed, returning Star's petulant mouth to where it belonged. It took her a moment to latch on, but soon enough, she was self-soothing with her mother's milk. "Not entirely unlike her daddy," Sage said almost to herself, making Rylee snort with laughter.

"I do hope you don't mean the milk part." Ally shuddered and pulled open the door to the building, letting in a gust of frosty air.

"No, not the milk. Jeez, your mind is in the gutter. Or the pasture. Like out on the farm. I'll have you know we haven't even had sex since the blessed event." Sage sailed out with baby in tow past Ally, who was shaking her head and trying not to laugh.

Rylee glanced back at me. "Your friends are kind of weird."

I grinned. *My friends.* I truly had friends now, ones I hadn't made just because of proximity or work events. They were like my sisters, quirks and all. "I know, and I love them."

"Hey, hey, hey," Ally said. "Though we love you too. Now get a move on before Dare pulls off his bowtie and chucks it into the lake."

"Aww, he's wearing a bowtie? How sweet is that? He must be dying." I blinked at Sage, hoping that I really hadn't just seen as much of her ample cleavage as I was pretty sure I had. "Speaking of dying, it's cold out here. Too cold for exposed…bosoms."

"No kidding." Sage flipped the bodice of her dress into place and tucked her now slumbering baby back against her chest like an old pro. "Tap's off for now, babycakes. Mama needs to protect the supply."

I touched my own barely-there belly. Would I be so natural with my child after giving birth? So ready to expose my breasts and feed him at a moment's notice, no matter where we were?

A few months ago, I would've said no. Now? Who the heck knew what I'd do or who I was becoming?

It would be fun finding out.

The soft strains of the traditional wedding march drifted over to us and I gasped, reaching out for Sage on one side and my sister on the other. "Do you hear that?"

"Yes, seeing as we're right across the street."

Rylee's dry tone and Sage's giggle barely dented my consciousness. "That's my wedding march. For me. Traditional all the way this time." Well, minus the pizza joint reception after, but even that suited us right down to the ground.

Dare's parents' pizza place was now a family business. *Family.* I had one that I'd made, not just been given.

"Minus the bun in the oven. Though gotta say, in Crescent Cove, it pretty much is becoming traditional to get married while knocked up." Ally grinned at my sister. "Better get out of town while you can."

"I don't live here." Rylee sniffed. "I live in Turnbull."

"Ah, yes, but have you had sex in Crescent Cove?" Sage pointed at my sister and nodded, well, sagely as Rylee visibly flushed. "That is the true test. Beware, little sister."

"You didn't get knocked up in Crescent Cove," Ally reminded her. "Hello, Vegas."

"Yes, but it was with a homegrown Crescent Cove penis. Same difference."

"Homegrown?" I frowned. "Are you implying there's a better success rate for local dicks? Because Dare isn't from Crescent Cove and he inseminated me just fine."

"Yoohoo, hello, ladies, wedding happening over here," Seth called across the street. "You planning on joining us anytime soon?"

"We were waiting for traffic," Ally called back, making a show of looking up and down the street. Her gaze stopped on the line of cars waiting for us to cross at the crosswalk.

Whoops.

My sister grabbed my arm and we hauled ass. The snow was still swirling and between that and the blur of my tears as I stared at the brightly lit gazebo, I couldn't see much clearly. The Christmas tree in the gazebo shone with a rainbow of colors, and thick red velvet bows hung from the eaves, their long tails blowing in the breeze. But as beautiful as the scene was before me, that wasn't why I was nearly blind from crying.

It was because there was a handsome man waiting for me on that gazebo, holding his little boy in his arms. A little boy who was waving to me as if he couldn't wait for me to join them.

Just like a regular mom with a regular family.

I waved back and hurried up the walkway, belatedly forgetting that Ally and Sage were supposed to go first. And where were my flowers? Rylee was supposed to be holding them for me, but unless she'd stashed them in the bodice of her dress, they were MIA.

So much for traditional. I was just going to have to wing it.

"Ahem," Ally said pointedly, raising her brows as she and Sage moved ahead of me up the walkway.

I waited for Rylee to do the same, since she was now part of the wedding party, an oversight I was making up for from my first wedding. Truthfully, I hadn't thought she would be interested. We were close, but maybe not close enough, and she wasn't exactly responsible, though I'd figured she could hang on to my flowers since she worked for a freaking florist.

But not only did she not remember to produce my flowers, she'd clearly also forgotten how to walk.

"Psst," I said none too softly, causing some of the guests seated on the lawn surrounding the gazebo to laugh softly. Including my beaming parents and Macy, who toasted me with a warm mug of something that probably wasn't entirely java.

"Do you have my bouquet?" I asked my sister.

Rylee was staring straight ahead, transfixed. Her mouth moved, but I wasn't entirely sure her brain had engaged. "Yes. It's sitting on the dashboard in my car."

"Oh, *that's* helpful. I'll just go get it right quick." I dashed away from the walkway, one hand on my now precarious tiara and the other holding my belly.

Gasps sounded behind me, and all too swiftly, I realized the crowd thought they had a runaway bride situation on their hands.

"Sorry, no, I'm not running away, promise." I stopped dead and gave my stricken groom a sheepish smile.

Dare looked absolutely crestfallen, as if the idea of me escaping was the worst possible thing that could happen. And wasn't that sweet?

Lord, I was crying again.

So, this ceremony wasn't altogether different from the first one after all.

Thanks, baby boy. I'm blaming this sobfest on you.

"I'll get the flowers." Rylee dragged me back onto the walkway leading to the gazebo, casting one more glance over her shoulder at the waiting men. "And then I may not come back."

"Um, okay, thanks?" She was already sprinting up the sidewalk to the long line of cars parked along the curb as if she wasn't wearing six-inch spiked heels and there wasn't a fine layer of snow on the ground.

I debated if I should wait for her or just keep moving, since the wedding march was winding down and I still had not made it to the gazebo. Maybe she really didn't intend to come back? Something had spooked her for sure. Possibly just the idea of the wedding itself, though Dare and I were already married. And she hadn't seemed out of sorts at our first wedding.

"Kelsey!" Wes called, falling silent as his father set him down and clamped a hand on his shoulder. "I mean, Miss Kelsey." He shrugged as if he didn't know what his father was correcting him for.

Everyone laughed. Not me. I was too busy sniffling as I made my choice.

No flowers were worth missing another second of this ceremony.

Holding up my lacy white dress—I'd worn the one from our first ceremony with an added white cloak due to the weather—I ascended the stairs in a hurry, unable to drag my attention from Dare's face. He was smiling down at me, but his brows were furrowed and his gorgeous eyes still held worry from my momentary flight.

He extended a hand to me, pulling me up that last step, and I totally broke protocol by reaching up to pull his face down to mine for a quick kiss. *Oohs* and *aahs* registered around us as I spoke against his lips. "I'm not going anywhere. Ever."

"Damn straight you aren't." He squeezed my hand and I reached for Wes's, making that same triangle we had the first time around.

With the Christmas lights twinkling and the snow softly coming down over the lake, we made our vows to each other in front of our friends and family and all of Crescent Cove who wandered by. I caught a glimpse of some of the townsfolk out of the corner of my eye, standing on the sidewalk in their winter best, watching us with glowing smiles. It felt like everyone in town wanted us to be happy.

"I pronounce you husband and wife—again," Judge Hamilton said with a grin and a wink. "You may kiss the bride."

And this time around, Dare didn't keep things quite as chaste. He dipped his head to mine, taking my mouth with that hint of aggression I'd never stop loving.

My gruff, rough, sweet-as-heck husband, kissing me for the whole world to see.

Including his son. *Our* son now.

"Eww, my eyes," Wes wailed, yanking on the hand I still gripped so he could cover his face.

Laughter broke out around us and with that, the ceremony was over. Sage rushed forward to hug me hard, followed by Ally and my parents and Dare's parents. His brother, Gage, stepped forward, his handsome face creased in a smile, but he came to a halt as heels pounded up the steps.

"Really? Isn't this overkill?"

I turned at the sound of my sister's voice. She was staring hard at Gage, and frozen petals from my bouquet of winter white roses were fluttering around her feet.

"Um, can I have that, please?" I asked. "I'd like to dry the flowers," what remained of them anyway, "and press them into my planner."

Rylee stuck the bouquet out at me and propped her other hand on her hip. "I thought we agreed on no repeats. So you, what, stalk me here? Seriously, dude, not cool."

I glanced at Dare, who was giving my sister a rather intimidating look. It was kinda hot, to be honest. Not that I wanted him to be staring down my sister, but hi, this was our wedding. And yes, we'd had more than the usual allotment, but jeez.

"Stalk you here?" Gage's smooth, deep voice rumbled out and answered a number of my questions. Well, sort of. "You think very highly of yourself. As well you should, but not that high." With a smirk, he adjusted the cuff links on his crisp white cuffs.

"Um, Ry, don't suppose you could—"

"That isn't what you said last night!"

The audible gasp that went through the crowd had me closing my eyes.

See, now this wedding fit right into my life story perfectly. Just as I'd been dumped via text after pity sex post funeral, which had led to me moving to Crescent Cove so impetuously, now my sister was decimating my lovely second wedding with her booty call antics.

My eyes sprung open as the full realization of what had transpired descended on me. "You slept with my husband's brother?" I asked, earning another round of gasps.

None the least of which came from our parents. And Dare's parents.

Yay.

"Kel," Dare said, his tone indicating he was not amused.

Neither was I. I was stunned and disturbed and feeling a little like a camera would soon extend from the nearest set of bushes, but not amused.

Gage lifted a hand and ticked off on his fingers. "One, two, three times." He smiled, revealing blinding white teeth. "Welcome to the family, sister-in-law."

"Sister-in-law, because you don't know my name. Now, do you?" Rylee whirled around and fled down the steps.

I turned to follow when Dare gripped my upper arm. "Not our circus, not our monkeys, darlin'," he said against my ear, making me laugh despite everything.

I'd said that to him last week when talking about something that had happened at school, and he'd needed an explanation as to what I meant. Tonight, he was using the phrase like an old pro.

"You're right." I turned toward Dare and snuggled against his chest as he tugged my cloak tighter around me. "Besides, we need to have a very important chat."

"Already?"

I smiled up at him and shifted my bouquet so it didn't get any more ruined than it had already been. "Yes."

"Thanks for coming, everyone," he called out. "We'll meet all of you over at the pizza shop in a few minutes. Pop?" He motioned to his dad. "You mind taking this guy with you?" He ruffled Wes's hair.

Wes pouted. "I don't wanna miss the chat."

I bit my lip and glanced toward Ally and Seth for help. "Laurie will be there. Right?" I asked more than a little desperately.

I didn't like excluding Wes from anything family-related, but this conversation really wasn't appropriate for little ears.

Bad enough he'd just had to hear my sister and his uncle re-enact an episode from the *Jerry Springer* show.

Seth and Ally exchanged glances. "Well, she's with Alex at my dad's," Seth began, jumping back when Ally slipped her hand in his pocket. Probably to pinch him. "Okay, okay, fine. We'll bring them to the pizza parlor. The night will probably end a little late for the kids to be out, but hey, it's the holidays and a celebration. Besides, this one's out and about." He nodded at Sage and Oliver, who were fawning over Star as if she were the Christ child herself.

Neither of them paid him any mind.

"Thank you so much." I smiled at them and rushed down to hug everyone one more time before our friends and families dispersed.

Gage had already taken off, right after Rylee. I hoped he wasn't chasing her down to argue with her. Or have more sex. That probably wouldn't end well. Rylee always insisted on winning arguments, and she was pretty pissed at Gage.

I didn't think she'd harm any vital parts of his anatomy while he was sleeping, but you could never be sure with my sister.

"Whew." I feigned wiping my brow as the last car full of guests peeled away from the curb. "It was touch and go there for a minute or two, huh? Imagine if—"

Dare drew me into his arms and fisted a hand in my hair, dislodging my tiara and whatever words I'd planned to say. His mouth was warm and soft against mine, but he added a bite of teeth just to remind me of the honeymoon night we would have as soon as we'd stuffed ourselves full of pizza and good cheer.

I couldn't wait.

"I've never seen you look so beautiful," he said roughly, his gaze dropping to my belly before lifting again to my face. "And that's saying a lot, because you're the prettiest damn woman in the world."

My eyes filled and I tipped my forehead to his. "Do you know how long I waited to have someone look at me the way you do? To see me and want what he sees, just the way I am?"

"It had to be a long time, because I damn sure have waited a helluva long time for you." He tucked a strand of hair behind my ear. "You've made me the happiest man in Crescent Cove, do you know that?"

I let out a watery laugh. "You have some stiff competition for that title. And speaking of stiff…" I swayed against him, giving the hard column in his tuxedo pants a quick rub. "I can't wait for our honeymoon."

"Even though we aren't jetting off to some fabulous island like the rest of the fancy pants couples in this town would?"

"Um, yes, because our island doesn't include clothing. Thank you very much." I gave him a swift kiss, then swallowed hard. "Dare, our son is yours. For real. The tests came in, and I'm sorry they told me when you weren't there, but he's yours. There's no doubt left."

Dare tipped back his head and his Adam's apple bobbed before he met my gaze again. "Our son? It's a boy?"

And *that* was why I loved this man so fiercely. He wasn't focused on the fact the baby had the same DNA as him, but that he was a sweet, already so beloved little boy. "Yes." I knuckled away a tear. "Wes is going to be the best big brother to this little guy."

"Yes, he is." Dare shut his eyes and when he opened them, I would've sworn there was a sheen of wetness there before he blinked and it was gone. "And I'm gonna be the best damn dad to him."

"Just like you are to your little boy." I took a deep breath. "To *our* little boy. We have two of them."

"We damn sure do." He flashed me a blinding grin and then he swept me up into his arms. I shrieked and tried to hold onto my tiara and veil as he carted me down the steps.

"Oh my God, put me down. Where are you going?"

"We have a reception to attend, don't we?"

"Well, yes, but it's a few blocks away—Dare!"

He bent his head and gave me a hard, quieting kiss. "I didn't get to carry you over the threshold the first time, so I'm gonna do tonight right."

"Does that mean we're going to christen the back of your parents' pizza shop?" I asked breathlessly as he strode down the sidewalk as if he was toting a loaf of bread. He wasn't even winded. "Since you're carrying me over that threshold and all…"

He winked. "Never know, Nuts Lady. Might just close down the shop in our own way."

I laughed and tossed back my head so that the gently falling snowflakes could cool down my suddenly warm cheeks. "Happy honeymoon to us."

WHAT'S NEXT?!
Gage and Rylee of course!

Thanks for reading WHO's THE DADDY!
We appreciate our readers so much!
If you loved the book please let your friends know.
If you're so inclined, we'd love a review on your favorite book site.

Want more Gage and Rylee?

Turn the page for a special sneak peek of
PIT STOP: BABY - Crescent Cove Book 4.

PIT STOP: BABY

December (The night before my sister's wedding)

THE CHEERS AROUND ME THREATENED MY STEADY HAND. THAT AND maybe the hundred proof whiskey I'd been drinking all night like it was Diet Coke. I was here for a good time and that was what I was having.

Mostly.

Mopping up the floor with the third team of dart players didn't hurt. Or the extra seventy bucks in my ass pocket from the idiots betting against me.

When you lived in a small town like Turnbull, there wasn't much else to do but play darts and pool with the guys. Especially since I wasn't the type of girl to join a flock of women and preen at the bar. I liked to be in the middle of the action and knew I pissed off more women than I became friends with. I was the girl who excelled at darts, but could run a table when needed.

"Come on, sweetheart, we don't have all night."

I ignored the guy with the two-pack-a-day voice. Justin? Jerry? I couldn't remember and didn't particularly care. He was just pissed because I'd trounced him first tonight. I'd taken twenty off of him before he even realized I'd won the round.

Judd, right. That was his name. Like the hot dude from *The Breakfast Club*. He even looked like him a little. Only it was the version of him on the wrong side of forty and didn't turn my crank. Not that I had a problem with guys heading for forty and beyond. I'd played trophy girlfriend a few times when I was in my early twenties.

The bling was alluring. Guys in their twenties couldn't afford sparklers like men with careers. The only problem there was I actually liked having a conversation with a guy. When you were from a different generation, it made things a little difficult. And I didn't have it in me to be shallow enough to just enjoy the rich guy ride.

"Come on, Ryan, I just want a chance to win back my money."

"My name is Rylee." I flicked my dark hair over my shoulder and lifted my lucky purple dart.

No do-overs. One and done only for this girl. Getting fired three weeks before Christmas made a girl grab some perspective.

It was time to finish this damn game. I'd been stringing it out with the guys around me calling out their own numbers in the game of 301. Each time I aced the shot, I picked up another five bucks.

But if I had to listen to Billy Joel's "Piano Man" come belting out of that jukebox one more time tonight, I would eject the ancient record with my boot.

I blew out a slow breath and hit the center of the triple ring. Six guys groaned. "I believe that's the final sixty points I needed?" I turned, downed my shot. I made gimme fingers and they each dropped a twenty on the table. I swiped up the pile. "Pleasure playing with you guys."

"Bet you can't hit a double bullseye in three rapid shots."

The voice was deep. It carried from the back of the pack of men. The fact that my nipples instantly hardened and tried to bust through my glittery babydoll shirt made me swallow my acidic reply.

Maybe not so bored anymore.

"Another round for the table, darlin'." The voice was smooth caramel over chocolate lava cake.

"You got it."

Our waitress's voice went breathy. At least that was a good sign that Mr. Caramel's voice might in fact have a matching face.

Not that I cared. Much. My current jobless status meant I'd take his money regardless.

I twirled my dart through my fingers. "What's the bet?" I had a cool two hundred in my pocket. Enough to cover groceries for a month. If I could double that, it would be even better.

The guy came out of the shadows and my nipples weren't the only thing at attention. My clit and heart did a double-tap like I was at the top of a rollercoaster one click past the drop.

Hello, Caramel.

He matched the word in every way. Dark blond hair cut close, along with a scruffy face that was just beyond sandpaper to that perfect buzz that could make the very best friction when used correctly.

His smirk told me he was aware of his appeal. It remained to be seen if the smirk came with a boatload of asshole or charm.

But it was the eyes that had me sunk. Barrel-aged whiskey—my favorite. Even in the dim bar, they glowed hot and interested.

Did I mention my clit was doing a salsa beat? No? It sure was.

Unfortunately, I had just enough of said barrel-aged whiskey in my system to drown out self-preservation.

"What do you have in that perfect ass pocket?"

I grinned up at him. "Three hundred."

Lies. But if I could take him for a little more…

He glanced around at the men who were suddenly finding their boots very interesting. "Is that right? Then obviously you are needing a bit of a trouncing."

I turned back to the board. "So, that's a bet then?"

"Don't want to shake on it?" His voice came from right behind me. Far too close.

But remember that little mention about too much whiskey? Yeah, tequila had nothing on whiskey when it came to me.

I turned until we were almost lined up. I nibbled on my lower lip as I stared at his full, mack-worthy mouth. There was something about a man who had full lips. No teeth mashing would be a part of our future.

Because I was going to taste that mouth if it was the last thing I did tonight.

I locked my gaze with his. "Sure, we can seal the deal." I rested my hand on his chest and went up on my toes.

His eyes went wide with surprise as I gripped the deceptively gorgeous cashmere of his sweater. Not exactly the kind of guy who belonged in a dive bar. I yanked him down and covered his mouth in a quick, hot kiss.

I was expecting a little buzz, but not *this*. Not the urge to drag him down closer. Usually, I was more talk than action when it came to men. I enjoyed flirting and could spin it out for ages without it ever coming to anything.

This fried my plans and my circuits like a...

Now Available
For more information go to www.tarynquinn.com

CRESCENT COVE CHARACTER CHART

BEWARE...SPOILERS APLENTY IN THIS CHARACTER CHART. READ AT YOUR OWN RISK!

Ally Lawrence:
Married to Seth Hamilton, mother to Alexander, stepmother to Laurie, best friends with Sage Evans

Andrea Maria Fortuna Dixon Newman:
Mother to Veronica 'Vee' Dixon

Asher Wainwright: CEO Wainwright Publishing
Involved with Hannah Jacobs, father to Lily and Rose

August Beck: Owns Beck Furniture
Brother to Caleb and Ivy, involved with Kinleigh Scott

Beckett Manning: Owns Happy Acres Orchard
Brother to Zoe, Hayes, and Justin

Bess Wainwright:
Grandmother to Asher Wainwright

Caleb Beck: Teaches second grade

Brother to August and Ivy

(Charles) Dare Kramer: Mechanic, owns J & T Body Shop
Married to Kelsey Ford, son Weston (mother is Katherine), son Sean, brother Gage

Christian Masterson: Sheriff's Deputy
Brother to Murphy, Travis, and Penn, sister Madison 'Maddie'

Cindy Ford:
Married to Doug Ford, mother of Kelsey and Rylee
Damien Ramos:
Sisters Erica, Francesca, Gabriela, Regina

Doug Ford:
Married to Cindy Ford, father of Kelsey and Rylee Ford

Gavin Forrester: Real estate owner

Gabriela 'Gabby' Ramos:
Brother Damien, sisters Erica, Francesca, Regina, best friend Hannah Jacobs

Greta: Manager of the Rusty Spoon

Hank Masterson:
Married to JoAnn Masterson, sons Murphy, Christian, Travis, Penn, and daughter Madison

Hannah Jacobs:
Involved with Asher Wainwright, mother to Lily and Rose, best friend Gabriela Ramos

Hayes Manning: Owns Happy Acres Orchard
Brother to Zoe, Beckett, and Justin

Ian Kagan: Solo artist
Brother to Simon, engaged to Zoe Manning, son Elvis, best friend Rory Ferguson, friends with Flynn Sheppard and Kellan McGuire

Ivy Beck: Waitress at the Rusty Spoon and owns Rolling Cones ice cream truck
Sister to Caleb and August, engaged to Rory Ferguson, best friend Kinleigh Scott, friends with Maggie Kelly and Zoe Manning

James Hamilton: Owns Hamilton Realty
Father to Seth and Oliver Hamilton

Jared Brooks: Sheriff
Brother to Mason Brooks, best friend Gina Ramos

Jessica Gideon: Famous actress
Ex-wife to John Gideon, mother to Dani

JoAnn Masterson:
Married to Hank Masterson, sons Murphy, Christian, Travis, Penn, and daughter Madison

John Gideon: Owns Gideon Gets it Done Handyman Service
Daughter Dani, ex-wife Jessica Gideon

Justin Manning: Owns Happy Acres Orchard
Brother to Zoe, Beckett, and Hayes

Kellan McGuire: Lead singer Wilder Mind, solo artist
Brother to Bethany, married to Maggie Kelly, son Wolf, friends with Rory Ferguson, Ian Kagan, and Myles Vaughn

Kelsey Ford: Elementary school teacher
Married to Dare Kramer, son Sean, stepson Weston, sister Rylee Ford

Kinleigh Scott: Owns Kinleigh's
Cousin Vincent Scott, best friend Ivy Beck, involved with August Beck

(Lucas) Gage Kramer: Owns J & T Body Shop, former race car driver
Married to Rylee Ford, daughter Hayley Kramer, brother Dare Kramer

Lucky Roberts: Works for Gideon Gets it Done Handyman Service

Macy Devereaux: Owns Brewed Awakening and The Haunt
Best friend Rylee Ford

Madison 'Maddie' Masterson:
Sister to Murphy, Christian, Travis, and Penn

Marjorie Hamilton:
Ex-wife of Seth Hamilton, birth mother of Laurie Hamilton

Mason Brooks: Owns Mason Jar restaurant
Brother Jared Brooks

Maggie Kelly:
Married to Kellan McGuire, son Wolf, best friend Kendra Russo, friends with Ivy Beck and Zoe Manning

Melissa Kramer: Owns Robbie's Pizza
Married to Robert Kramer, mother of Dare and Gage Kramer

Mike London: High school teacher

Mitch Cooper: Owns the Rusty Spoon

Murphy 'Moose' Masterson: Game Designer/Construction Contractor and Owns Baby Daddy Wanted
Married to Vee Dixon, son Brayden, brother to Christian, Travis, Penn, and Maddie

Oliver Hamilton: Owns Hamilton Realty and the Hummingbird's Nest
Married to Sage Evans, daughter Star, twin brother Seth Hamilton

Penn Masterson: Graphic novelist
Brother to Murphy, Travis, Christian, and Maddie

Regina 'Gina' Ramos: Waitress at the Rusty Spoon
Brother Damien, sisters Erica, Francesca, Gabriela, best friend Sheriff Brooks

Robert Kramer: Owns Robbie's Pizza
Married to Melissa Kramer, father of Dare and Gage Kramer

Rory Ferguson: Record Producer/Rhythm Guitarist
Brother to Thomas and Maureen, engaged to Ivy Beck, best friend Ian Kagan, friends with Flynn Sheppard and Kellan McGuire

Rylee Ford: Barista at Brewed Awakening
Married to Gage Kramer, daughter Hayley, sister Kelsey Ford Kramer, best friend Macy Devereaux

Sage Evans: Owns the Hummingbird's Nest
Married to Oliver Hamilton, daughter Star, best friend Ally Lawrence

Seth Hamilton: Owns Hamilton Realty
Married to Ally Lawrence, daughter Laurie, son Alexander, twin brother to Oliver Hamilton, ex-wife Marjorie

Tish Burns: Owns J & T Body Shop, custom fabricator
Friends with Gage Kramer

Travis Masterson:
Brothers Christian, Penn and Murphy, and Maddie, daughter Carrington

CRESCENT COVE CHARACTER CHART

Veronica 'Vee' Dixon: Pastry Baker, owns Baby Daddy Wanted
Married to Murphy Masterson, son Brayden

Vincent Scott: partner in Wainwright Publishing Industries
Cousin Kinleigh Scott

Zoe Manning: Artist/photographer
*Sister to Beckett, Hayes, and Justin, engaged to Ian Kagan, son Elvis, cousin
Lila Ronson Shawcross Crandall, friends with Ivy Beck and Maggie Kelly*

GET HOOKED!

Have My Baby

Claim My Baby

Who's The Daddy

Pit Stop: Baby

Baby Daddy Wanted

Rockstar Baby

Daddy in Disguise

Crescent Cove Standalones

CEO Daddy

ALSO BY TARYN QUINN

For more information about our books visit

www.tarynquinn.com

ABOUT TARYN QUINN

USA Today bestselling author, T*ARYN* Q*UINN,* is the redheaded stepchild of bestselling authors Taryn Elliott & Cari Quinn. We've been writing together for a lifetime—wait, no it's really been only a handful of years, but we have a lot of fun. Sometimes we write stories that don't quite fit into our regular catalog.

* Ultra sexy—check.
* Quirky characters—check.
* Sweet–usually mixed in with the sexy...so, yeah—check.
* RomCom—check.
* Dark and twisted—check.

A little something for everyone.

So, c'mon in. Light some candles, pour a glass of wine...maybe even put on some sexy music.

For more information about us...
tarynquinn.com
tq@tarynquinn.com

QUINN AND ELLIOTT

We also write more serious, longer, and sexier books as Cari Quinn & Taryn Elliott. Our topics include mostly rockstars, but mobsters, MMA, and a little suspense gets tossed in there too.

Rockers' Series Reading Order

Lost in Oblivion

Winchester Falls

Found in Oblivion

Hammered

Rock Revenge

Brooklyn Dawn

OTHER SERIES

The Boss

Tapped Out

Love Required

Boys of Fall

If you'd like more information about us please visit

www.quinnandelliott.com

Made in the USA
Coppell, TX
31 October 2022